I0645685

Logan County Love

SCORCHED

ROXANNE BLACKHALL

Scorched
ISBN # 978-1-80250-706-5
©Copyright Roxanne Blackhall 2024
Cover Art by Kelly Martin ©Copyright November 2024
Interior text design by Claire Siemaszkiewicz
Totally Bound Publishing

SCORCHED

Dedication

To all the amazing and hardworking emergency
services personnel — thank you!

Chapter One

Katie
September 8, Friday

Twenty screaming five-year-olds broke from their orderly line and ran across the playground.

"Walk, please!" Katie Tilman laughed at herself. Getting her students to comply was a lost cause, but she had to try. She couldn't blame them for being excited. The big red firetruck had all its lights flashing and several crew all geared up. Still, she had to try.

"Oh, come on. What kid can resist? Public Safety Day is always a fun event." Cinda Gable pointed to her first-grade class, gathered around the police car.

Katie pushed a lock of hair behind her ear and smiled. She knew she should remember Cinda—they were only a year apart in school—but Katie had left Orchard Creek just before she turned fourteen. Eleven years had passed.

She dutifully laughed at Cinda's comment and hurried to catch up with her kindergartners. Half of her students joined the line waiting to play with the truck's sirens. The other half stood behind a firefighter who was training a hose on a target that looked like flames painted on a piece of plywood with a hole in the middle.

She did a quick head count—hard to do with everyone moving around—but she managed. One of the playground monitors caught Katie's eye, then pointed her finger at the group waiting to play with the sirens. Katie shot the woman a relieved smile and refocused on the guy with the hose.

He'd shut off the flow of water and was squatting, telling the kids how the truck could hook up to a fire hydrant so they could pump water on a fire.

"That's why you should never park in front of a hydrant," he said.

"Because 'mergency trucks are big!" A little boy with blond curls stood with his arms crossed over his chest and a wide smile on his face. Katie was pretty sure he was from the first-grade class.

The firefighter tipped his head back and laughed. He turned to face her and Katie caught her breath. Even in the shadows cast by his helmet and visor, she couldn't miss those bright blue eyes, or the wink he dropped.

"I'm sure they'll all remember that in ten plus years when they start driving." Well, if that didn't make her sound like a complete stick in the mud. "Please tell me you're showing off and not letting them play with the hose. I'm not sure they all have changes of clothes here, and…"

She stopped as the man rose to his feet. From across the playground, he'd seemed big, and now she had to keep looking up and up to see his face. Or attempt to. Between his height, the angle of the sun and his helmet, his features were cast in shadow, but she couldn't miss those eyes.

His hands were still wrapped around the hose nozzle in a way that at any other time might have sent Katie's head into not entirely polite places. Now, she was at work, and instead of sexy thoughts, her brain imagined a bunch of soaked children and the inevitable angry parents.

"Awww, bet me they all do." Another wink. A scruff of a beard covered his chin and framed a full mouth, but the rest of him was a mystery. "Everybody knows kids are gonna get wet and messy today. We usually let them have a go—with help, of course. Don't want anyone knocked on their...ahhh...bottom. What d'ya say? You go first?"

He held out the hose nozzle to her and Katie backed away. "Oh... Umm... No... I couldn't. I'd get all wet."

His lips curled up in a smile and heat rose in her face. He gave a shrill whistle and shouted something to another firefighter who sat on top of the truck. An instant later, something hurtled toward them. He caught it one handed and held it out to her.

"We have smaller ones for the kids. This one will be too large for you, but it'll keep you from getting doused. C'mon, teach, give it a try. That's what today's all about."

Her students were staring at her. She couldn't very well refuse—how would it look to them? She hefted the beat-up yellow coat, then shrugged into it, sure she was putting it on wrong.

"Okay. How do we do this?"

He cracked another grin as he helped fasten the coat, giving her a glimpse of his face. Good grief, the man was handsome under that helmet. Then he straightened up and faced the students.

"All right y'all, pay attention. Your teacher and I are gonna show you how this works. Then you're going to line up and see Cadet Stewart right there who will get you into a coat. You ready?"

A chorus of squeals and giggles and shouts of "yes" filled the air. He had the students' full attention, and the crowd was growing as some of the other children finished with the sirens and joined them at the fire target.

"When it's your turn, you'll stand right here." He pointed to a spot about a foot from where Katie stood. She took a step forward. "Good job. I want you to put your feet a little wide — not too wide, just about shoulder distance."

He looked back at Katie until she moved her feet apart. "Perfect. Now, the water comes out of the hose really hard. There is a lot of pressure there. It takes a lot of strength and practice to handle it. So I'm gonna be your buddy. That means I'll stand behind you, like this."

He stepped behind Katie and she held her breath. He leaned in so close his visor brushed against her hair, then spoke softly near her ear. "I'm going to have to put my arms around you for this. Are you okay with that?"

Her brain whirled in so many directions she couldn't find words. All she could do was nod. This man had asked consent to touch her instead of assuming. He was remarkably good with children. She missed the next thing he said to them, but caught something about how he would show them where to grip the nozzle.

"This is a one-inch hose," he continued. "It's the smallest we have, but it can still be hard to handle. The nozzle is a straight tip — which is what we use to hit specific spots, like the hole in our target over there."

He shifted the hose to one hand and stepped a little closer. "Here we go."

His other arm came around her and Katie was surrounded by the smell of smoke and a clean, crisp scent that had to be his cologne. He pointed to the nozzle and guided her hands. This guy could make a mint doing this at a bar or someplace like that. On her school's playground, with her students watching, Katie was struggling to keep her mind out of the gutter.

Then his hands tightened over hers and the hose jumped as he opened the nozzle. The stream soared over the target and the children laughed.

The man's chest rumbled with his own laughter and he leaned down to her, bringing the scent of his cologne even closer. "It's stronger than you think, isn't it? Use your core, it'll make it easier to control."

In a complete fog, Katie tightened up and found he was right. Instead of feeling like the hose was trying to lift her arms away from her body, she was able to bring it down and get the stream right into the target.

"That's it!" His breath was hot on her ear, but that had to be her imagination. "Just like that. Hold it steady. Now count backwards from ten."

Everything in Katie was at war as she mentally started a countdown. This felt like flirting. Serious flirting. If she were anywhere but at work, she'd be flirting right back.

She got to one and his hands twisted, the flow of water stopped, but the hose still felt like a live thing in her hands. "There's always tension in the hose," he said. "Great job. Thanks for being such a good sport."

Her class cheered as she stepped away. One of her students, nearly swimming in even the children's size coat, rushed forward for his turn. Cadet Stewart helped Katie out of her borrowed coat.

"We've got three kid-size coats," Stewart said. "If you help, we can get the next two students ready while this one takes his turn. Then we'll just kind of assembly line it from there."

Katie watched as Cadet Stewart demonstrated how to fasten the coats. Everything went quickly after that. The firefighter kept up a steady stream of encouragement that was always cheerful. The playground monitor brought the rest of her class over and took the ones who had already had their turn up to the front of the truck.

"I'm next!" The boy with the blond curls took his place in front of Katie and held his arms out for the coat. Cadet Stewart took over and thanked Katie with a smile. She did a quick check — all her students were in the care of a playground monitor. She could relax for a minute and process whatever the hell had happened between her and the firefighter.

"You look like you're in a daze." Cinda gestured to the picnic tables under the trees and the two sat. "You okay?"

Katie forced a smile. "Yeah, that was just..." She didn't have words for whatever that was. Even if she did, she didn't want to be sharing them with the first-grade teacher.

"Amos is a bit like a big kid himself," Cinda replied. Katie's stomach did a flip flop and she swallowed hard.

"Amos? As in...Kimmel?" She looked back at the tall man now squatting next to the little blond boy. "That is Amos Kimmel?"

Oh no. No. No. No.

Amos had been best friends with her older brother, Miles. She'd had the most crushable crush on the boy with intense blue eyes and a laugh that had rung in her dreams for years after she'd left. She'd kept those feelings to herself, mostly, but it wouldn't have taken a genius to see it.

How did Amos of all people become a firefighter? Miles had been staunchly anti-establishment — police, fire, it didn't matter. Just like their father. If they wore a uniform and worked for the "gov'ment", he didn't like them. And neither did his friends.

The Amos she'd known had been thin and a little awkward. His firefighting gear might make him appear larger than life, but the arms around her earlier, and the wall of chest she'd felt behind her, said he was not skinny now.

"Didja see me, Miss Cinda? Didja see?" The blond boy jumped up and down in front of them, talking rapid fire about Mister Amos and how he was going to grow up to be a firefighter someday. Or maybe police, like Miss Drea. Or maybe he'd become a vet like Papa Brian. Or a ranch manager like his mama.

"Yes, Kyle," Cinda replied. Katie recognized the patient teacher voice and took the opportunity to make some polite comments before going to gather her class. Unsurprisingly, none of the students were interested in the police cars or the road equipment after the excitement they'd already had. They were thirty minutes from the half-day pickup time and many of them were getting tired.

She herded everyone back to class and encouraged them to take turns talking about their favorite part of the day while they gathered their things and got ready to go home.

After her last student had gone, Katie went back to the playground, now filled with the older children. She looked toward the fire truck and tried to tell herself it had nothing to do with catching another glimpse of Amos.

It took her a minute to spot him. He'd taken off his coat and removed his helmet and now sat perched on top of the engine. Katie's mouth went dry. His blue uniform T-shirt pulled tight across his shoulders and heavy lines of tattoos coursed down both arms. His dark hair was cropped close—she remembered him with longer hair that flopped into his eyes, he'd always been flicking it back.

She'd spent enough afternoons doing her homework at one end of the kitchen table while Miles and Amos had hunkered together at the other end, supposedly working. She pushed those thoughts away. Miles was the last person she wanted to think about. Well, the second last. Their father took first place in that category.

She hadn't chosen to move away. She had just graduated eighth grade and Miles had barely passed tenth. That summer, without any warning, their mother had packed Katie's and her brother's things and the three of them had left Orchard Creek. For the next several years, they'd moved around wherever their mother could find work and cheap housing.

Jan Tilman's intentions may have been good, but the reality was, nothing changed with Miles. No matter where they moved, he found the same crowd and fell into the same habits. Miles' behavior had gotten worse, not better, and Katie needed to stop this little trip down memory lane. She hadn't talked to her brother in years, and didn't want to. After college, she'd never imagined she'd move back here, but in all the time away, she'd never found a place that felt like home. She'd missed the mountains and the woods.

When she'd seen that Orchard Creek had an opening for a kindergarten teacher, she'd jumped at the chance. In the four weeks she'd been back, she'd found a few familiar faces and a lot of familiar names. She never imagined that Amos would still be here. Or that he would have grown up so fine.

* * * *

Amos

It was nearing five by the time the crew got the rig packed back up and ready to return to station. Amos Kimmel stretched, trying to ease the cramp in his back from spending so much time bent over talking to the kids. Public Safety Day was always a fun time, even if it was draining.

He glanced back at the school. She'd have left by now. Most of the teachers had. He'd heard there was a new teacher. He had not expected a tiny woman who looked like a goth fairy with an edge.

From the streak of blue in her hair to the chunky pink Doc Martens on her feet, she tripped every happy button he had. Which went a long way to explaining why he'd gotten a little flirtatious when he'd shown her how to handle the hose. He didn't think he'd crossed a line, but he'd had his toe on it for sure. The way her cheeks had turned red when he'd talked about controlling the hose had him wishing they were someplace he could flirt for real.

He shook his head of those thoughts and turned his attention to his crew. They were still a bunch of volunteers, but he and Drea had put forward a proposal for a paid department. She remained confident the town council would approve the plan for next year. If he was proud of anything in his life, it was this.

He'd been a major fuck up in high school and he'd gotten lucky that Chief Lawson had seen something good in him and turned him around. The fire department had done the rest.

If the proposal went through, and he could get paid for the work, it would mean he could finally leave his old man's garage. Speaking of which... *Shit.* He'd promised he'd come straight over to help with a transmission job.

"Hey, Shawn! You mind getting everything situated? We're a little later than expected."

His second in command shot him a thumbs-up. "Surprised you didn't bug out earlier. Just figured you were hoping to catch that Miss Katie on her way out."

Amos flipped him a middle finger, but he didn't miss the woman's name. He'd been so busy with the garage, the fire department, and the whole proposal to the town council that he'd not paid any attention to local talk. Not that he ever really did. He could ask his sisters. One of them always seemed to know the latest. Small-town gossip spread like wildfire.

He grabbed his gear from the truck and took off at a brisk walk. The garage was only a few blocks away. He was starving, but it was a safe bet his big sister Leah would have a pot of soup or something going, just like their mother had whenever the shop got busy.

He bypassed the garage and went around the corner to the house. A page from a yellow legal pad sat stuck in the screen door at his eye level. Leah's tidy printing filled only a couple of lines.

There's soup in the microwave. Your coverall's in the mudroom. If you wanna get on Pop's good side, grab the six pack that's in the fridge before you come out and tell him to take a load off.

Amos hit the button to heat his food then kicked off his uniform boots. It took less than ten minutes to gulp down a meal and change clothes. A lifetime of experience told him what his sister's words did not.

Their dad was only in his sixties, but wasn't in the greatest health and should have retired years ago. He figured Amos would take over the garage and Leah and their kid sister Grace would do the part their mother always had—keep the books, keep the place clean, and handle customer service.

Trouble was, Leah was the better mechanic. Amos had no real interest in the garage, and once the department started paying for his time, he'd barely be around. And Grace? Well, Grace wanted to leave their small town behind. The kid had dreams.

Amos fished around in the fridge to find the six pack. In the shop, Leah was elbows deep in an old Ford—probably the Tanners' by the looks of it—and their dad was hovering so much he was getting in her way.

"'Bout time you showed." Roy Kimmel had lost whatever softness he may have had when his wife died seven years ago. He looked older than his sixty years, thanks to a lifetime of smoking, a terrible diet and, Amos was convinced, just being a general pain-in-the-ass grouch. He dropped the beer on a tool cart and pulled up a rolling stool.

"We got this, Pop. Siddown."

Maybe not quite Leah's words. She was usually nicer than Amos was. But Pops expected girls to be soft and boys to be tough. Surprisingly, the old man didn't complain. Amos rolled up his sleeves and turned to Leah.

"All right, boss. Let's finish this thing."

For the next few hours, he and Leah worked side by side as they had most of their lives — the only words exchanged were short requests and comments related to the job at hand. Amos looked up once when their dad rose from his stool, grabbed the half-finished six pack and headed into the house.

By nine, they had the old truck humming along just fine. They cleaned up in the shop sink, silently following their mother's longstanding rule — don't track garage dirt into the house. Inside, faint sounds from down the hall said Pops was watching TV in his room.

"The second you show up, he can relax." Leah sank into a kitchen chair, then made a face at the full ashtray sitting in the middle of the table. Amos emptied it before she could get up and do it herself. It was Leah who'd held the family together after their mom passed. Grace had been in her senior year of high school, hellbent on going to university. A dream she still hadn't realized. Amos spent more and more time at the fire department because it got him out of the house.

Leah had stepped into their mother's shoes as if she'd been doing the work all her life. She'd also started picking up the slack at the garage — first because Amos was rarely around, then because their dad's work had started slipping.

Roy Kimmel didn't see any of that. He never truly saw any of his children. Grace's brilliance and thirst for knowledge. Amos' passion for helping people. Leah's skills as a top-notch mechanic. All were things their father couldn't — or wouldn't — see.

"Grace's been making noises about moving again," Leah said. "End of this semester, she'll have finished all the classes she can take locally."

Amos wiped a hand over his face. Grace had passed on going to university because of their mother's death. That had cost her the scholarship that would have made college affordable. She'd had a couple of rough years but pulled herself together. Last year, when she'd turned twenty-four and no longer needed a parent's signature on the FAFSA forms, she'd started talking about university again. Pops had talked her into continuing part-time classes at the community college in Logan.

"If you think I'm gonna try talking her out of it..." Amos stopped when Leah's mouth dropped open, then snapped shut.

"More like I figured you'd tell her to get her ass in gear and submit her application and start picking up extra photography work so she can save up and make this happen next fall. Maybe even take a class or two in spring, if she can get in at Charleston."

A flood of relief surged through him. As much as he loved Orchard Creek, Grace was never going to be truly happy here.

"That, I can do," he replied. "And gladly. What about Pops?"

He didn't want to lie to the man, but if he found out Grace was thinking of leaving, he'd start in with the guilt trips.

"That's my department," Leah said. "I'll deal with him. How was the school thing?"

Typical Leah. Address a problem head on and as soon as you make a decision, you move on.

"You know I love those days. It's fun letting the kids see all the emergency services when there isn't something bad going on. Makes their parents happy, too. And since parents are voters..."

Leah threw her head back and laughed. "I never thought I'd see the day when my brother was thinking about politics."

He scoffed at her. "Robert Moore kinda cured me of keeping my head in the sand. That man nearly ruined the department."

Leah cursed under her breath. "He did a lot worse than that, but I understand your take."

"Did you know there's a new kindergarten teacher? Like new, new—not from here." *Why the hell did I say that?*

Leah's expression shifted to something he couldn't read. One eyebrow arched up and she crossed her arms over her chest and smiled.

"Kinda surprised you hadn't heard." Grace leaned in the kitchen doorway.

Her tone set Amos on edge. There was a hint of something he was missing. It wouldn't do any good to ask directly. Grace would never spill until she wanted to. The kid had learned long ago to keep her thoughts to herself.

"Like a new kindergarten teacher is news." Amos rolled his eyes and looked away, hoping the old trick of blowing it all off might get her talking.

"Nope." Grace crossed to the fridge, pulled out three bottles of pop, then stuck two on the table in front of Amos and Leah.

"I'm friends with Lily, and her son is in first grade. Of course I knew."

Amos didn't see what that had to do with anything. He cracked open a bottle and took a sip. Leah's eyebrows furrowed, then she turned to their kid sister.

"I think your head is fried from working too hard. You're not making sense."

It was Grace's turn to roll her eyes.

"Also, she's not new. Not like that." She pointed at Leah. "You were too busy being the big sister, already working full time in the garage. Then dealing with Mom and Dad when Amos got in trouble."

Grace turned to him and smiled. "Who were you hanging with back then? Doesn't surprise me that you somehow missed that your best friend's little sister had a major school girl crush on you. Or that you didn't recognize her today."

Amos nearly choked on a mouthful of soda. *Miss Katie. Katie Tilman. Fuck me.*

"Have a good night!" Grace threw a wave over her shoulder as she flounced toward the stairs.

Leah's laughter rang in the small kitchen. "The look on your face is priceless. If I didn't know you better, I'd think you did something like try to put the moves on her."

There was no point in lying to his big sister. She'd spot it a mile away. "Uhh...well..." He rose and tossed his empty bottle into the recycling bin. "I flirted a little. Okay, maybe more than a little. I'm goin' home. 'Night."

He hurried out the door before Leah could say something else.

Miles Tilman. He hadn't thought of him in years. His best friend since childhood and the reason he'd gotten in trouble back then. His little sister Katie had always been around — sitting at the table while they did their homework or hanging on at the edge of their crowd. She'd worn her hair in pigtails and had braces. He'd never thought much about her. She was his buddy's bratty kid sister.

He pulled in a breath of the cool night air. The stars seemed extra bright tonight and the walk home might help clear his head. It was only a few hundred yards to the group of tiny cottages that used to house coal miners.

For the first few years after he'd come back, after graduation, Amos had lived in an apartment above the extra garage bays. Then their mom had passed and Leah had returned home. He'd moved out to give her the apartment.

He liked his cottage better. It wasn't fancy, but having his own space was a good thing. Right now, he needed it. He sure as shit didn't want to be talking to his older sister about how right Katie had felt in his arms.

Chapter Two

Katie
September 16, Saturday

A small basket of gorgeous golden apples caught Katie's eye. She leaned down and inhaled their scent. She'd been to farmer's markets in the city, but this was different. All the vendors were local and everything looked amazing.

"Got some good tomatoes, too." The young woman working the stand held out another basket filled with plump red fruits still on the vine. It would be a crime to pass them up.

"I'll take both," Katie replied. "And some of that zucchini, please."

Another week done and she still wasn't feeling settled in. She'd hoped the farmer's market would - scratch the home-town itch.

She paid for her purchase then got distracted by the aroma of fresh-made apple fritters. It was only a couple of weeks into September and she was still wearing a T-shirt, but she couldn't resist the sweet and spicy treat. She grabbed an iced coffee and found a spot to sit and people watch. This was what she'd missed, and why she'd come home. Folks here seemed to care and ask about each other.

"Miss Katie!"

The blond boy from school smiled and waved. *Kyle. His name is Kyle Elkins.* He tugged at the woman next to him and for once, Katie immediately recognized someone.

"Lily Elkins!" Katie slid over on the bench to make room. "And Kyle. How are you?"

The little boy climbed up and sat next to Katie. "We got Brussels sprouts." He made a face to show just how he felt about that. "But we also got pears. I like pears."

"Hey, Katie." Lily sat and handed Kyle a phone. "You can play a few minutes of the word game."

"Yes, ma'am!" The boy already had the phone unlocked and was focused on the screen.

Lily glanced back to Katie. "How are you settling in?"

"It's early still," she replied. "I wasn't able to move until just before start of term, so I feel like I haven't even acclimated yet. I'm a little embarrassed by how many folks I don't remember."

As a teen, Katie had occasionally babysat Lily's younger siblings when the older Elkins children weren't available. That and the fact that Lily had been Grace Kimmel's best friend went a long way to sticking her in Katie's memory.

"It'll come back to you," Lily replied. "You going to the Fall Festival? That'd be a great place to get reacquainted. Everybody comes out for the bonfire."

Katie hadn't decided yet. Her weekends had been filled with unpacking. This was the first chance she'd gotten to really explore the town.

"It's next week?"

Lily leaned over to help Kyle with something on the phone. "Yep. Whatever Saturday is closest to the equinox," she said without looking back at Katie. Parents and teachers — chronic multitaskers.

"I can do it." The plaintive note in Kyle's voice had Katie resisting a fit of giggles as Lily held up her hands in surrender. She turned back to Katie.

"This year is great since the equinox happens to be on a weekend."

"I can't wait for the weather to shift," Katie replied. As far as she was concerned, back to school was supposed to mean cooler days. She still kept her windows open for sleeping, but she had thrown an extra blanket on last night.

"At the safety day, Kyle said something about becoming a ranch manager, like his mama. Is that what you're doing?" She'd feel incredibly silly if Lily wasn't the boy's mother, but was instead his aunt or something. Kyle looked like Lily, so she crossed her fingers.

"Yep. Working at Parsons Acres. Been there for a while now and took over managing once Brian graduated vet school."

A pang of sadness twisted in Katie's gut. She'd lost all her childhood friends when her mother had moved them away. While she'd grown to understand the reasons, it didn't stop her from feeling like she'd missed something special here. Instead of knowing everyone in town, and having fun memories and stories, she was a stranger. Like she had been every time they had moved—again—because her mother lost her job, or the rent got too high, or Miles got in too much trouble.

Then again, it was probably a blessing they hadn't stayed. Her older brother was a troublemaker and her father was neither liked nor respected. She'd always been on the outside—not cool enough or outdoorsy enough for the horse crowd and too bookish for Miles and his group. Moving had given Katie the opportunity to grow up very differently than she would have here.

"You know, I think I will go to the festival," Katie said. "I came back because I missed the feeling of home, but…"

She stopped. She had no idea why she was telling Lily all of this. Maybe she just needed a friendly ear. Katie looked up when Lily laid a hand on her arm.

"Best thing you can do is get involved," she said. "And volunteer for all the school stuff. The Parent Teacher Association is always in need of help. It was good seeing you."

Kyle waved as they walked away and Katie picked at her fritter. Lily was right. She needed to do something. She needed to get involved. She'd come back expecting to find Orchard Creek waiting for her, as if everyone had been on pause while she was away. Like Sleeping Beauty or something. It had been eleven years—people had lives. And she'd been a nobody at best, a dreaded Tilman at worst. If Katie wanted to call this town home, she had to fit into their world.

If she was going to do that, she'd have to get busy. The PTA sounded like a solid place to start. She sighed and leaned back on the bench. The leaves still bore the deep green of late summer, but soon the colors would start to change and the days would get cooler and shorter.

She could start by getting her butt up off the bench and finishing her grocery shopping. Then going home and unpacking the last couple of boxes cluttering up her tiny living space.

Chapter Three

Amos
September 23, Saturday

"At least it's finally cool enough to warrant a fire later." Amos sat a box of extinguishers down near the makeshift fire pit. "We far enough from the orchard?"

Eliza Perry waved a hand at the nearest plot of trees. "Oh yeah. Those are well established, planted last year and it's a calm night with only a light breeze. Get yourself a cider and enjoy the afternoon. We've got a couple hours before the bonfire and Micah Stewart said he'd come by and help."

Amos bit his tongue to keep from saying "about time". Instead, he fixed his face in what he hoped was a calm smile. "Stewart is a good man. I'll take you up on that cider, for sure."

The Perrys ran a thriving orchard that stocked most of the local markets. They also offered apple picking all season and made the best cider. The hard stuff was even better. Eliza was their oldest daughter, and she and Micah Stewart had been making eyes at each other for what felt like forever.

Amos had finally had enough and told the kid to volunteer at the bonfire tonight. Then he'd made sure to talk to Eliza about fire safety and the importance of having fire extinguishers handy. Oh, and someone knowledgeable to help.

Satisfied his matchmaking efforts were well under way, he headed to the cider booth. Maybe he'd go ahead and grab a hard cider. He was off duty for the rest of the day. He might as well make the most of it.

He stopped in his tracks at the sight of a petite goth fairy standing in front of the cider booth. *Katie Tilman.* He hadn't known what to make of his kid sister's bombshell revelation about Katie. Or if he should even believe it. He racked his brain, trying to recall every interaction he'd ever had with her and for the life of him, couldn't see it.

Grace was fucking with me. Nothing said he couldn't be friendly.

He stepped behind Katie and cleared his throat. "Go for the hard cider. It's worth it."

She jumped and whirled to face him. Her eyes went wide, then she broke into a smile that made him feel like a goofy kid talking to a cute girl. *Yeah, just friendly. Right.*

"Really?" She waved a hand at the sign behind her. "I was kind of thinking a hot cider. Or I guess I should save that for later at the fire. I don't know."

He stepped in next to her. The top of her head barely came to the middle of his chest. "Two hard ciders, please." He paid for their drinks then handed a brimming cup to Katie.

"You didn't have to…" She stopped and bit her lip, then looked up at him with a big smile. "Thank you."

She took a tentative sip, then another. "Oh, that is yummy!"

They walked down the hill toward the corn maze. Katie turned her head as if it was on a swivel and she was afraid of missing some sight.

"What brought you back here?" Maybe not the nicest way to ask, but he was used to being direct.

Katie stepped into the maze ahead of him and turned right. "Aside from a job?"

She had on dark jeans that hugged her tiny frame and sent his mind places he knew damn good and well he had no business going. You didn't chase after your best friend's kid sister. *Not sure it still counts if I haven't talked to Miles in over ten years. And he's sure as shit not my best friend anymore.*

"I missed home." She made another turn, then stopped and went back the other way, muttering quietly, "Always make the same turns."

Amos wasn't paying any attention to the maze. If he stood on tiptoe, he could probably see over the top of the swaying corn. The Perrys only had a small patch of corn, so the maze was stacked bales of straw topped with tied together sheaves of dried corn. It made everything smell like fall.

"Where'd y'all wind up? You went to college and all. Guess I'm surprised you'd come back here."

Katie paused at the next intersection. "What do you think? Left or right?"

Maybe she didn't want to talk about that stuff. "You've been going right every time. And you said it— you wanna get out of a maze, make the same turn every time."

She cocked her head to one side and gave him a tiny smile. "Who said I want to get out?" She turned left. *Wait, is she flirting? Or was that just teasing?*

"We moved around a lot," she said. "I went to seven different high schools. I got lucky and got into Drexel. In Philadelphia. My first teaching job was in the city."

She hadn't mentioned her brother. She skipped ahead and made a series of rapid turns until Amos had no clue which way they were facing. What he did know, beyond any doubt, was that Katie didn't want to talk much about herself, or the past.

She made another turn, then stopped so quickly he bumped into her. She whirled and put a hand over his mouth before he could say something. Over her head, he caught a glimpse of a young couple locked in a kiss. He caught Katie's wrist and they turned the opposite direction. Katie didn't pull her hand away. She moved down the path, giggling, and rushed through another couple of turns before she stopped, dropped his hand and lost herself to laughter.

"That coulda been awkward," Amos said.

Her laugh mixed with the rustling corn sheaves, reinforcing his impression of her as some dark fairy creature.

"We're in a huge orchard. On the edge of the woods. A corn maze was the most private place they could find?"

Amos shrugged. "It hasn't been that long since you were a teenager. Exactly how much critical thinking did you do back then?"

Her laughter trickled off. "Fair point. What about you? The fire department?"

She set off again at a much slower pace. Amos fell into step next to her. He wasn't sure how much she knew of what went on back then, and he didn't feel like dredging up old shit.

"I got a little wild during high school. Like a lot of kids. Chief Lawson pretty much told me to find

31

something constructive to do. One of the things he suggested was the fire department. I guess it stuck."

She reached out and stroked a finger down his forearm, sending goosebumps up his entire body. "Looks like the wild period didn't end there."

"Got my first tattoo the day I turned eighteen," he replied. Adding to his ink was an annual tradition and a constant reminder to never forget the past, but always strive for a better future. "And a lot more since. You have any ink?"

Katie shook her head, looking almost shy. "I can admire them on someone else, though."

They made another turn and Amos stopped. "Pretty sure we've been this way."

She spun around in a circle, then poked her head around one corner then the other. "How can you tell? It all looks the same to me."

He pointed to a brown can tucked in the corner. "Trash can—where we tossed our empty cider cups. Plus"—he pointed to the top of the sheaves—"some of those stalks are bent."

"Well, then you should lead the way, Mr. Tall Stuff." She crossed her arms and stared at him as if daring him to challenge her.

There's the bratty kid sister coming out. He turned down what he hoped was a different path and quickly made the next couple of turns before stopping at what had to be the center of the maze. He spread his arms wide and backed up until Katie smacked his shoulder with an open hand.

"Hey!"

Amos didn't budge. "Close your eyes and trust me."

He tipped his head over his shoulder to see her glaring up at him. Finally, she heaved a theatrical sigh and closed her eyes. Amos faced her, took her hands and led her into the clearing.

The Perrys had gone all out. Bales of straw covered in blankets sat along all four sides and the space was filled with twisting vines of fall leaves and glowing jack-o-lanterns. *That explains Eliza's questions about battery operated candles.* At least he hoped all the flickering lights were flameless candles. The maze was set against the trees and the jack-o-lanterns cast a warm orange glow in the deep late afternoon shadows.

"This better be worth it," Katie said. Her tone was chiding but she kept her eyes closed. "If there's like a killer clown or some stupid jump scare, you'll live to regret it."

Amos chuckled. "Just open your eyes."

Katie blinked, then gasped as she looked around. "Oh wow!" She wandered the small clearing, every now and then bending to inspect a pumpkin.

"They're all movies or books," she exclaimed. "This one's the Headless Horseman. And this one looks like the guy from *Scream.*"

Amos bent next to her. He'd been so amazed by the experience of walking into the space that he hadn't noticed the carvings. "There's Cthulhu. Who did these? They're pretty cool."

They circled the space, trying to identify all the images.

"What d'ya think? The Raven?" Amos pointed at a detailed carving of a bird.

"Definitely. There's Jason Voorhees over here," she said, pointing at a pumpkin bearing the classic mask covered face and a knife carved next to it.

"Balrog."

"Wednesday Addams."

"Jack Skellington."

"Pennywise."

Katie stopped and stared at one pumpkin. "I don't know that one."

"Venom," Amos replied. "Comic book character. And a couple movies."

She shrugged and sat on a straw bale. If he'd been here with anyone but her, he'd be sitting right next to her, putting his arm around her shoulders and maybe angling for a kiss. She smiled up at him, all wide gray eyes and rosy cheeks. *Screw maybe.*

He stuffed his hands into his pockets and looked up at the sky. "Got about an hour before sunset. You hungry?"

Katie rose and nodded to the far side of the clearing. "Judging by the traffic pattern on the grass, I'm guessing that's the way out."

Something Drea was always on about—observation at a scene. Amos looked around and didn't notice anything at first. On a second pass, he saw it. All of the other entrances to the clearing had grass matted in all directions. The one Katie pointed at, all the grass was bent away from the clearing. *Huh.*

It only took a few minutes to get out. Between Katie looking at the grass, and Amos cheating here and there by peeking over the top of the corn, they made good time.

"That was fun," Katie said. "Thank you. For the cider and the maze."

Her words sounded like a brush off, but it didn't feel like that. It felt more like she was uncertain. Maybe she hadn't been flirting earlier and he was making her uncomfortable. That didn't feel right either. Could be she was as confused as he was.

"Is that a no to an amazing dinner of whatever festival foods we can get our hands on?"

Her cheeks flushed and she half gaped at him, then the shy smile came back. "I just... Well, I don't want you to feel like you have to babysit me or something."

There it is. That makes more sense.

"Here I was thinking I was getting to know a pretty cool woman." *Fuck it. Might as well.* "I'll be honest, I didn't recognize you at the safety day. What I saw was a woman with a beautiful smile who had a great sense of humor and an awesome attitude. Same thing I see right now."

Katie bit her lower lip. "Oh, that makes me feel so much better! I didn't recognize you right away either. I just saw a hot fireman and..."

She sucked in a gasp of air and her eyes went wide as her hands clapped over her mouth. The pink flush that had started to fade raced back in, turning her entire face red.

Amos threw his head back and laughed. It was that or wrap his arms around her waist and kiss her.

"Someday, I'd love to hear the rest of that thought," he said. "We were kids. We've both grown up a hell of a lot since then. We seem to like each other's company. What's wrong with that?"

She dropped her hands, gave him a bright smile and pushed a lock of hair out of her eyes. "Okay," she said with a nod. "Okay. You're right. There's nothing wrong with that. So... is that offer of a dinner that's probably a bunch of deep-fried somethings still good?"

Katie

Amos' laughter filled the air. It was a deep throaty sound that at once recalled the teenager she'd had a crush on and reminded her that the cute but awkward boy she'd known had grown into a ridiculously hot man.

"More likely to find pepperoni rolls and plenty of hotdogs." Amos pointed out several food trucks lined up along the dirt road. "Best hit 'em up now before they get rushed around sundown."

If Katie had thought she was hungry before, she'd been wrong. Her stomach threatened to growl.

"With chili sauce and slaw and everything?" It had been forever since she'd had a proper hotdog. No one else seemed to get the chili right.

He didn't answer. Instead, he tipped his head in a 'c'mon' gesture then turned toward the trucks. Katie let out a tiny gasp. Somehow, they'd gone through the entire maze and she'd missed the fact that the view of Amos' backside was just as droolworthy as all the rest of him.

His T-shirt stretched tight across his shoulders and clung to the muscles in his back like it was painted there. Low-slung jeans lovingly hugged his ass and long legs. A leather cuff circled one wrist and he wore more than a couple of chunky silver rings.

Catnip, as far as she was concerned. Never mind that men who looked like that spelled trouble. She'd seen enough of it in her life — from her father and brother, to every guy she'd dated. Amos was exactly the kind of guy she needed to stay away from. She had a very unhealthy attraction to the wrong kind of guy. When she'd moved here, she'd promised herself that she'd take a year off dating.

Not that she had ever been good at heeding her brain's advice. Or keeping her promises to herself. *But there's nothing wrong with harmless flirting.*

Amos stepped up to the truck and Katie laid a hand on his arm.

"You got ciders earlier. I'll get the dogs." She didn't wait for him to agree. She turned to the teenager at the register and ordered three dogs with everything—assuming Amos would eat two himself. Someone called Amos' name, then a chatter of conversation erupted behind her. When she turned back around, Amos was talking with a dark-haired woman. When she looked up, piercing green eyes seemed to stare straight into Katie's soul.

"Katie Tilman." The woman extended her hand and Katie shook on instinct. "Welcome home."

Katie's confusion must have shown on her face because the woman smiled as she released Katie's hand. "It's been a while and you probably don't remember everyone. I'm Drea Hidalgo."

The brand new police chief. Katie had vague memories of Drea from way back. They were a few years apart and Drea had hung out mostly with the horse crowd, while Katie had lurked at the edges of her brother's circle of friends. The two groups hadn't mixed.

"Drea's been helping pitch the idea of a paid fire department," Amos said. "We're still all volunteer and while the county guys may not be that far away, they're coverin' a lot of territory and not always available."

This was definitely not the Amos she remembered. Miles and his group of friends were not civic minded. At all.

"Your food's up." Drea pointed at the truck. "Best decision Morrison's ever made—opening a food truck."

Amos stepped up to grab the dogs, leaving Katie smiling awkwardly. Something she'd gotten a lot of practice with since coming back. She still hadn't figured out how to deal with those who remembered her while she was drawing a blank on them. Hell, she'd been a child when she left. There was another whole layer of uncomfortable—who knew what Carl Tilman had told folks after his wife had packed up the kids and disappeared in the middle of the night.

Someone called Drea's name and she smiled at Katie. "Duty calls. Good to see you out in the community."

Amos handed Katie a cellophane-wrapped dog. "Did you mean to skip the jalapeños? Or did you forget they're optional?" He plopped a tiny plastic cup full of pickled peppers on top of her hotdog. "Just in case it was forgetting."

He held two dogs cupped in one large palm and the neck of two soda bottles stuck between his fingers. They found a spot to sit on a couple of straw bales and Amos laughed as Katie piled on the jalapeños.

"Totally forgot they're not part of 'everything'," she said. Amos sat across from her, looking amused. *Whatever.* She bit into her dinner. *Holy hell, that is so good!* She closed her eyes in bliss. This was what she remembered.

When she opened her eyes, Amos hadn't moved. His expression, however, had changed. Gone was the look of amusement. In its place was something darker and damn sexy. He looked like he was ready to skip dinner and have her for dessert first.

Not that I'd complain.

They didn't talk as they finished their food. Katie found most people needed to fill any silence with chatter. She liked silence. It meant no one was arguing or fighting.

"What did you mean when you said you got a little wild?"

Asking about his past would probably mean opening up about her own, but she had to know. She'd worked too hard to distance herself from her family and their problems to get sucked back into it by the hot man her childhood crush had become.

"Ah...ancient history," Amos replied. "You know the crowd that ran with me and Miles. I never quite fit in, but since I was his best friend, I was okay."

Oh, Katie knew that crowd too well. Most of them had arrest records by the time they were sixteen. Just like most were using, if not dealing, drugs. Even her alcoholic mother had seen the danger and for once had acted to protect her children.

"I never did drugs, but I drank. A lot. And got up to some stupid shit. Got busted for stealing a car summer after my sophomore year. Chief Lawson gave me a talking to — basically told me to choose my friends, then helped me get on a smarter path."

He held up his right arm and turned it so she could see the date inscribed on his wrist. Katie's breath caught. The same time they had suddenly up and moved away.

"My first tattoo. That was when I got arrested," he said, bringing her mind back to the present. He shrugged. "Every year, I start new ink in June. To remind myself."

He cupped both her hands in his and smiled. "It's no secret. This is a small town. Everyone knows everyone's business. In fact..." He looked down at their entwined hands then slowly let go and straightened up. "Safe bet there's gonna be some gossip here."

Oh shit. That had never occurred to her. She'd been a kid when they left. Sure, she'd been aware of gossip, but it wasn't like it ruled her world. He was right, though. They'd gone into the maze together. Grabbed hotdogs together. Now they were sitting together and he'd been holding her hands.

Did she want that? Did he? From the sounds of it, Amos had turned his life around. It was possible he didn't want to be connected to her, just like she didn't want any connection to Miles or her father. Maybe coming here wasn't such a hot idea. She could've picked any other small town and it wouldn't have had the landmines that Orchard Creek held. But she'd wanted to feel at home.

"I'm sorry. Does that mean we shouldn't... I mean, do we need to... Oh!" She couldn't get her thoughts straight, let alone her words.

"Your cheeks turn a pretty shade of red when you blush," he replied. "I don't have a problem with it if you don't. Might even give 'em something to talk about. If you're so inclined."

Katie sputtered. Everything in her was at war. Part of her brain wanted to get to know adult Amos better. Ideally in a way that involved getting naked. Part of her thought it was nothing more than her childhood crush rising up, and still another part cautioned that whatever he was now, he'd been Miles' best friend.

"What do you say to a couple of apple hand pies then we go find a spot for the bonfire?"

Amos stood and offered his hand. Katie slipped her fingers into his calloused grip and mentally told her teenage self to keep it together because she and Amos were holding hands. Maybe people would talk, but she wasn't sure she cared.

Chapter Four

Amos
September 25, Monday

A loud clang echoed through the garage. Amos jumped and his head collided with the propped-open hood of the beautifully restored Mustang he was tuning up. He turned to see his father holding on to the car fender and reaching for the ground. Pops moved slow, like he was in pain.

Amos wiped his hands and crossed the garage. He stooped to pick up the wrench his dad had dropped then handed it to his old man.

"Arthritis acting up?" The second the words were out of his mouth, he knew it was the wrong thing to say.

In predictable Roy Kimmel fashion, his eyes narrowed and his face set in a hard mask. "Don't matter none if it is. Won't do any good to complain about it and my good for nothin' kids don't see fit to do as I tell 'em."

Some things never change. It didn't matter that Amos worked at least fifty hours a week at the garage, on top of his time at the fire department. It mattered even less that Leah worked twelve-hour days six days a week, or that Grace stayed up later than she should have and gave up her weekends to handle the books.

Roy Kimmel only saw what he wanted. He'd inherited the garage from his father, and figured he'd pass it on to Amos. But he'd never handled the business side—that had been his mother, and later his wife. After she'd passed, Leah picked up that slack. He'd been bitching the same line for years—Leah shouldn't be in the garage gettin' all greasy and Amos should be doing what his old man had done, stepping up and taking on the family business. And Grace should be focused on landing a husband, not pursuing some degree he didn't understand.

Amos clenched his hands and clamped his mouth shut before he said something that wouldn't go over well.

"Daddy, c'mon in and have some lunch." Leah's voice rang out from the side door. Both men turned and their dad's face softened just a touch. This was what he expected. His oldest daughter coming out, wiping her hands on a kitchen towel and calling the menfolk in to lunch.

He laid the wrench down and crossed to the sink. "No need to nag, woman. I'll finish this beast of a thing later."

Lunch was not going to be a pleasant meal.

"Amos, you okay to run out to the Parsons? Lily called and said that old Harvester is acting up again. I'll save you a plate."

Leah didn't wait for his response. She didn't need to. She'd probably taken the call hours ago and held on to it, knowing their dad was in a mood.

"That truck is a damn relic, but money is money, I guess." The old man had a habit of grumbling into the air. Their mother used to chide him about it. His three kids only half paid attention. "Better you go out there than her." He nodded toward the house.

It wasn't that there was bad blood between the Kimmels and the Parsons, at least not that Amos knew. The Parsons were horse ranchers and the Kimmels were mechanics. To Roy Kimmel, that meant they didn't mix. When Leah Kimmel had gone out with Jake Parsons in their senior year of high school, everyone else had got starry eyed imagining two of the town's oldest families coming together. Not their dad.

Amos wiped his hands and waited until the old man had finished and gone inside, then he tidied the garage and put all his dad's tools where they belonged. If he didn't, sure bet Pops would be out here bitching somebody didn't do their job right.

He cleaned around the Mustang and put the hood down. He'd finish that tonight. He washed up and climbed into the garage truck. He sent a text to his sister so she'd know he was on the road.

It didn't take long to get to Parsons Acres, and Lily was waiting for him where the old truck always sat when it wasn't in use — right next to the main house.

The candy apple red 1955 International Harvester rarely left the ranch these days. Back when he was a kid, old man Parsons had driven it around town on the regular. After he'd passed, Annette had kept it, but it was pretty much retired to ranch use.

"She is a beauty, isn't she?" Lily Elkins hooked her thumbs through her belt loops and nodded at the Harvester. "Brian said something about the carburetor."

"Sluggish acceleration and rough idle?" Amos didn't bother to pull his toolkit out. If he was right, this could either be a quick afternoon job, or one that he'd have to bring more tools, and possibly parts, than he had on him. He did grab a towel.

"Yep, you know the drill. Been nursing this thing along for a while now."

Amos popped the hood on the old truck and laid the towel over the side so he wouldn't damage the paint. "Start 'er up for me, would ya?"

The hard start told him all he needed to know, but he listened to the idle for a few minutes to be sure.

"Shut it off!" He lowered the hood and gave Lily a slow smile. "Same as last time, and I told Danny and Brian then—it's an old truck, original parts, and it doesn't get used often enough. Things are gonna get gunky. Add in the dusty environment, and you're gonna be at least cleaning it on the regular. We can clean it, or we can do a rebuild—maybe, if we can find the right parts, or we can swap out for something new."

Lily harrumphed and crossed her arms. "Lemme get Danny." She grabbed a walkie-talkie from her back pocket and muttered into it. Within minutes, Danny Parsons came loping up the walk.

He crossed to Amos and hooked a thumb toward the truck. "Same ole thing, huh?"

Amos nodded, prepared to repeat his explanation, but Danny laid a hand on the truck's fender and smiled. "It's time for a major overhaul for the old girl." He straightened up and turned to Amos. "I mean everything. Rebuild or replace the engine and transmission if you have to. Whatever it would take to get her up and running the way she's supposed to be."

Amos swiped a hand over his face. "If you're not in an all-fired hurry, I'd like to get her into the garage for a thorough check up. Then I'd have to source parts and draw up some options for you. That part alone could take a week or two, tops, considering the rest of our workload."

Not to mention keeping his dad out of the process. He'd make it harder than it needed to be. Still, the Parsons had always been good customers, so it was worth it.

"I'm not in any hurry, and I always prefer to give business to someone local," Danny replied. "If you can swing it, just tell me when's a good time to bring her in."

The main garage was currently full, but the side garage bays were all open with nothing major lined up. A big, ongoing project might stretch them a little thin on man hours, but he could always call in help, or cut back his hours at the fire department for a while.

"You got it, man," Amos said. "Any day this week is fine—just call ahead to make sure Leah or I will be there."

Danny offered a hand to shake on it and Amos took it.

"How's your daddy doin'?"

The question Amos dreaded, but heard a lot. The truth was, Roy Kimmel was going down the same path so many had before—brought up to believe mental health issues were a sign of weakness, yet unable to accept aging, or a changing world, and struggling with loss.

"He's holding up," Amos replied. "We keep trying to convince him to retire. The arthritis has gotten bad enough it makes working hard for him. But he's a stubborn man. What can you do?"

He'd leave out the fact that his old man self-medicated with beer and whiskey every night, and that the Kimmel siblings were starting to suspect their old man's mind was slipping.

"I know that story," Danny said, and his voice was kind. "Thanks for takin' time to come out all this way. I'll get her in to y'all later this week."

Amos hopped back into his work truck and headed home. Halfway there, he pulled to the side of the road and slammed the gearshift into park. His fingers clenched on the wheel so hard his knuckles turned pale.

The garage was doing well, mostly because of Leah. She was a damn good mechanic and had a head for business. If their dad would retire, she could hire some help and have the place even busier than it already was. There was work to be had.

If the town council approved a paid fire department, Amos would take the job. He already knew that. So did Leah. But it would create a rift with his old man that wouldn't be easily healed.

Then there was Grace. She wanted to get out of Orchard Creek. The kid was wicked smart. She somehow managed straight A's in all her classes, despite working extra hours at the garage and barely having time to study.

Leah had tasked Amos with convincing their little sister it was time to move on and go to college full time. Maybe that meant in Charleston. Maybe it meant someplace farther away. If Leah couldn't get their dad to back off on the guilt trips, it wouldn't matter what Amos said to Grace, she wouldn't go. And she'd be miserable because of it.

He didn't know what magic his big sister planned on pulling, but unless their dad changed a whole lot of his attitudes, life was gonna suck for all of them. Either they could do what they wanted, and deal with the fallout, or they could do what he wanted and not be happy.

Amos didn't even want to think what the old man would say if he found out his son was flirting with Katie Tilman. Roy Kimmel had told Chief Lawson Amos could rot in jail for all he cared—he wasn't putting up bail. Even after nearly two years at the youth camp, Roy Kimmel hadn't wanted his middle child to come back home. It wasn't until Amos' mother had threatened to leave that the old man had relented.

He'd never thought too highly of Miles Tilman, or his father. Everyone knew Carl Tilman and Dwight Phelps dealt drugs and used kids from down and out families to help distribute the goods. It wouldn't matter that Katie had gotten a degree and was a teacher. She was a Tilman and that meant bad.

Well, fuck it. He figured he was pretty much destined to have his old man pissed at him for one reason or another. From the time he'd first volunteered with the fire department, he'd felt a sense of purpose and belonging he'd never had before. Not even with Miles and his crew.

No matter what his dad thought, the fire department had changed him for the better. He'd grown up, learned what real friendship was and found something he wanted to do with the rest of his life.

He shifted into drive and got back on the road.

He'd do whatever Leah needed to help with the business, encourage Grace to apply to university and do what he could to preserve his relationship with his old man.

As for Katie Tilman...

He blew out a slow breath. He had no fucking clue how to deal with that puzzle. What he did know for sure was that he should've gotten her number and he should've kissed her at the bonfire.

Chapter Five

Katie
September 27, Wednesday

A paper cup of piping hot coffee and a napkin with two homemade coconut cookies sat on the empty chair next to Katie. She'd taken a seat in the back so she could observe the Parent Teacher Association meeting, but not call attention to herself.

So far, it had worked. Bonus points, she'd gotten to know a few more people's names and faces as the parents gave their names when they stood to ask questions or participate in the conversation.

She sipped her coffee and nibbled on the surprisingly tasty cookies while listening to the PTA reports from the treasurer, the president and more. She perked up at a mention of the Safety Day, but they were just highlighting the success of the event, then they moved on to some other budget discussion. *Goodness, this part is boring.*

Thankfully, the coffee did the job of keeping her awake. Then the meeting moved on to new business and Cinda Gable stood up.

"Y'all know it's time to organize a decorating committee for the Halloween carnival," she said. "Last year, we had a lot of kindergartners who wanted to do the haunted house, but parents were worried it would be too scary. So this year we're looking for ways to address that so the younger kids can enjoy it as well."

Oh! Wait...that's something I know about.

Katie raised her hand and waited for the chair to call on her. She stood and all eyes turned to her. *Shit. Didn't think this through very well.*

"Hi, I'm Katie Tilman. I teach kindergarten. And ummm... At my previous school, we opened the haunted house an hour earlier and basically had it empty."

She wasn't doing a good job of explaining the concept. Still, everyone was looking at her as if she had something important to say.

"I mean, it was all set up with dim lights, but all the scary stuff was turned off and there weren't any ghosts or ghouls roaming around to scare the kids. It was just a spooky walk through darkened halls and some creepy decorations. Each hour, it got a little more intense. If that makes sense."

She sat down quickly, her face feeling hot, and hoped she'd been clear. The room erupted in chatter as people debated the idea. Then someone proposed they adopt that plan. Someone else volunteered Katie to head it up.

Lily Elkins dropped into the seat on the other side of her. She leaned in and smiled.

"Told you the PTA was the place to get reacquainted with everyone. You okay with organizing that whole thing?"

Katie nodded, and before she could say anything else, Lily raised her hand. "I second that motion."

And with another minute of parliamentary procedure, it was done. Katie was in charge of the planning committee for the haunted house.

The rest of the meeting passed in a blur, then Katie found herself cradling another cup of coffee and more cookies — apparently baked by Drea Hidalgo — while parents and teachers came to talk about the haunted house or just say hello.

Lily caught up with her as she headed out the door.

"Hey, I realize I may have kinda thrown you under the bus a bit. I'm sorry." Lily fell into step next to Katie.

"Oh, it's fine. You were right about this being the way to get connected with folks. I was surprised, that's all."

Lily nodded toward a beat-up Jeep in the lot. "That's me. Hey, umm…you and Amos?"

Katie stopped in her tracks and stared at Lily. Well, he'd said the gossip would happen. It shouldn't surprise her.

"We hung out at the Fall Festival."

Okay, so they'd flirted a bit. And they'd sat together at the bonfire. And Amos had scooted really close to her when she'd gotten a little chilly. And walked her to her car when the night was over. But that was it. He hadn't even asked for her number. Not that she'd offered, or asked for his, either.

"I know you were pretty young when you left, but you know what the rumor mill is like around here," Lily said. "If you don't, Amos sure as shit does."

Katie bristled. She liked Lily, and she had never expected this kind of thing from her. "So, Amos and I spent some time together. Last I checked, we're adults and it's a free country. What of it?"

Lily's shocked expression and raised hands hit Katie like a punch in the gut. She'd misunderstood somehow. Lily wasn't being mean or malicious, but that's where Katie's brain had gone. *Shit.*

"I just wanted to make sure you knew the rumors were already flying," Lily said. "Amos turned his life around after y'all left. Everyone loves him."

Katie threw her hands in the air and blew out an exasperated breath. "Yeah, yeah. And nobody wants to see him get tangled up with a Tilman. Is that it?"

Lily laughed as if that was the most ridiculous thing she'd ever heard. When she got control of herself, she wiped her eyes and shook her head. "Completely off base. Can we maybe go grab a drink or something? I get the feeling you need a friend."

The last thing Katie wanted to do was go to some bar in town. But home was down the street. "Leave your car here. We can walk to my apartment. There's only one parking space."

She kept her mouth shut as they made their way down the street, then up the stairs to her small unit. She pointed Lily to the two-seat bistro table that served as her dining space and surveyed her kitchen.

"Water, cider, coffee or tea. What's your choice?"

Lily smiled and wrinkled her nose. "I'm driving, so if it's regular cider, not hard, I'll take that, thanks. Otherwise, water or tea is fine."

Katie poured two glasses of Perry's spiced cider and sat opposite Lily.

"Okay, so I was off base. I admit I'm probably a little hypersensitive on that subject, but I know my brother was a Class A troublemaker, and my father is worse. And this town seems to have a long memory for people's fuck ups."

Lily laid a hand over Katie's and squeezed. "Except those weren't your fuck ups. Sure, there are some assholes who will judge a person by their family alone. Amos' dad is one of them. Everyone else is all about what you make of yourself. Look at Amos. Or hell, me—I got knocked up by some carnie whose real name I don't even know."

Katie tried to keep her shock from showing. She hadn't known that, and wouldn't have suspected it.

"So, if I misinterpreted it, what did you mean, then?"

Lily dragged a finger through the condensation on her glass and chewed on her bottom lip. She hauled in a slow breath and let it out even slower.

"Folks aren't gonna judge you by your brother, or your parents," Lily said. "But they will by your actions. Start sportin' around with Amos—folks are gonna talk. They'll be happy Amos found a nice girl. A kindergarten teacher and a firefighter, how cute is that?"

Katie couldn't suppress the laugh that bubbled up. Lily was right. It sounded like an adorable story.

"They'll be happy a hometown girl grew up and came back. Settled in. Took an active role in the community. And oh, hey, even better, finds love with a hometown hero."

It sounded like a Hallmark movie—girl leaves small town, moves to the big city but gets disillusioned and returns to her hometown where she meets the local hunk. Except none of those movies included heroines who had a father who was a drug dealer and an alcoholic mother. "Yeah, I get it," Katie replied. "Wholesome and sweet and lots of grist for the mill."

Lily spread her hands in a wide shrug. "People will be hearing wedding bells before you two have even decided that you're dating. Which brings me to the dark side of the whole thing."

Now it clicked. Katie closed her eyes and tipped her head back for a moment. "Great. We're just hanging out, being friendly, and folks are seeing something more... If that doesn't happen, or maybe it does and someone gets hurt..."

If people believed she broke Amos' heart, she'd be painted as the bad girl. Then they *would* care that she was a Tilman. Safe bet no one would blame Amos.

"So, again...you and Amos?"

Katie had spent too many years bouncing from place to place. She'd never had a friend she could really trust. She kept her personal life private, thank you very much. Except here that might not be possible. Lily was right, she needed a friend.

"I don't know," Katie said. At this point, she decided honesty was the best policy. "We flirted. A lot. I like his company — he's a great guy. And have you looked at the man?"

Lily scrunched her nose. "I was BFFs with his kid sister. Amos is like a brother to me. Also, he's not my type. I'm more into guys who ride horses, not motorcycles. But yeah, he's a good-looking man."

Understatement. And wait, he has a motorcycle?

"And if Grace is to be believed, which I think she is..." Lily's words trailed off and she looked at Katie with her eyebrows raised in question.

"Yeah, I totally had a crush on him when I was a kid," Katie replied. "Couldn't even tell you why. There were other boys who were cuter. Definitely ones who were more confident. But, I always liked Amos."

Lily sipped her cider, eyeing Katie over the rim of the glass. "Oh, I know why. Or at least, I have a good idea why."

Katie would love to hear it. She'd been trying to recall her reasons, ever since Cinda had pointed out the firefighter she'd been flirting with was Amos Kimmel. Just as she'd tried to figure it out when they'd left and she'd found herself pining for a boy who for the most part acted like she didn't exist.

"You saw Amos for who he really was," Lily said. "Simple as that."

She finished her cider and stood. "I was serious about the friend thing. And for the record—those boys who might have been cuter back then? They're not now."

Lily shouldered her bag and headed to the door with a wave. "Thanks for the cider."

The door clicked behind her and Katie stared down at the cider she hadn't touched, suddenly wishing it was the hard stuff.

Whether Lily was right about everything or not, Katie had a lot to think about. This was a small town, and Amos had pointed out the gossip would start. He'd even joked about giving folks something to discuss, then he'd taken her hand and they'd walked to the bonfire together.

No wonder folks were talking. Amos was hot as hell, she liked what she'd seen of him and she wanted to get to know him better. If it wasn't for her promise to herself to stay away from men, she'd go about doing just that without a second thought. Being in Orchard Creek added its own complication. Here, she had to think about the fact that being seen with him would start tongues wagging and heads speculating.

Her choice was to pretty much never be alone with him, if not avoid him entirely, or accept the fact that their every move would be scrutinized and people would jump to conclusions. In fact, they probably already had—she'd lay odds that folks assumed Amos had walked her to her car and kissed her.

Too bad he hadn't.

Chapter Six

Amos
October 6, Friday

Two weeks. Amos scowled at the calendar that hung on the wall at the fire station. Between his regular work at the garage, diagnosing and sourcing parts for the Parsons' old Harvester, and his normal volunteer shifts, he'd been going virtually nonstop for fourteen days.

His last day off had been the day he and Katie spent at the Fall Festival. He'd spent a lot of time trying not to think about how good she'd felt sitting next to him at the bonfire. Well, it was five o'clock on a Friday night and he had nowhere he had to be before Monday morning. A free weekend was a rare thing. If the nice weather held, he could do a long ride.

He cussed himself, again, for not getting Katie's number. Right about now would be a great time to text and see what she was up to. She'd have already left work, too. A sunset ride would be fun.

"You planning on hanging around for another shift?" Shawn Dubois smacked Amos' shoulder on his way through the station. Amos didn't even bother to flip Shawn off. He shouldered his bag and got his ass outta there.

Halfway home, he made a detour and pulled in at a local coffee shop. All of a sudden, he wanted an apple fritter something fierce. He stepped inside and his skin prickled as if brushed by the lightest touch.

"Hey, I was just thinking about you." Katie waved from a corner table. Amos didn't bother to order a coffee or a fritter. He was pretty damn sure she was the reason he was here. And pretty damn sure that was the most irrational and nonsensical thought he'd ever had, but it was right.

He pointed at the chair across from her. "May I sit?"

The chair slid out and for half a second he wondered if she'd somehow commanded it to move. Then he saw the pink Doc Marten settle back to the floor. *She kicked it out. She only looks like some mythical creature. She isn't magic.*

Katie slid her plate over. "Want some? I love these things, but I can't finish a whole one."

A neatly split apple fritter sat on the plate. One half had a few bites out of it. The other hadn't been touched.

Okay, maybe she is magic.

"So, you were just thinking about me," he said. "Good things, I hope."

Her cheeks flushed and her lips curled into a smile. She didn't have to answer. He'd guess her brain had been in the same place as his.

"There's something I regret not doing last time we saw each other," he said. Her eyebrows arched up, but the rest of her face stayed calm. "I'd like to get your number, if that's okay by you."

She pulled out her phone, tapped the screen and handed it to him. "Put in your number."

He added his digits and handed the phone back. Katie's fingers flew on the screen, then his phone pinged with an incoming text.

"Now you've got my number," she said. "That the only regret? No worries about the gossip that I hear is already making the rounds?"

Shit. He knew there had been some talk. Grace had repeated things she'd heard. He'd hoped somehow Katie wouldn't have gotten wind of it yet.

"Told you before, I don't have a problem with any of that." He reached across the table and covered her hand with his. Her gorgeous misty gray eyes went wide then crinkled as she smiled. He leaned forward so he could whisper, "Wanna add to it?"

She looked down at their hands, now intertwined on the table, then back up to him. "I think we already are, but what did you have in mind?"

Too many possibilities clamored for attention. A ride and a picnic. Dinner. A movie. Drinks and dancing. A concert. A hotel room, crisp sheets, a comfy bed and hours of uninterrupted time together.

That last thought sent a whole series of throbs and twitches below his belt. He needed to stop that right now if he wanted to be thinking clearly.

"Well, I was thinking a date."

The rosy flush was back in her cheeks. "I like that idea. But not tonight. I'm on my way to a meeting with the Halloween haunted house committee."

Halloween hadn't even dawned on him. It was just a night of a lot of accidental fires thanks to unattended jack-o-lanterns.

Katie, on the other hand, was wearing dangling pumpkin earrings and a shirt that read *'smiling pumpkins'* and looked like a vintage band tee.

"How about tomorrow night? We could go someplace local — Oak Bridge is casual and has decent food, plus darts and pool. Or we could go outta town if you'd rather not be on display around here."

He could almost see the wheels turning in her head as she considered the options. It didn't matter to him. He'd grown up here, gone through his shit and settled into a good life. The only negative might be his dad, but it wasn't like that was anything new.

She might feel differently. She was a kindergarten teacher. She had to think about the parents, the school and the fact that she had just moved back to town and had to find a way to fit in.

"Either way," she replied. "People are going to talk no matter what we do."

She squeezed his hand, then pulled away slowly. "I have to get going to that meeting. You have my number now. Let me know what, where and when."

She wrapped up her half of the fritter and waved as she walked away. Amos couldn't take his eyes of her perfect denim-wrapped ass. *When did teachers get hot?* His kindergarten teacher had worn baggy coveralls and flowery shirts with big bows at the neck.

Might as well get some work done. He scooped up the rest of the fritter and bit into it as he walked to the door. He could go home and keep trying to chase down parts for the Harvester, or he could brave his old man and tackle the backlog of work there.

He chose the garage. The universe must have been smiling on him, because the old man was nowhere to be found. From the looks of things, Leah had been at work—she always left the place spotless. The only car in the bays had an order of work attached that said they were waiting on parts.

Amos shrugged. Not much to do here, but it'd been a while since anyone had done an inventory. He grabbed a notebook and opened the supply cabinet. They always seemed to be in need of gloves and cleaners.

"Leah says we need to restock on oil." Grace settled onto a shop stool. "Dad had a rough day and banged his hand pretty good doing shit he shouldn'ta been. I got him bandaged up and Leah…well…" She waved a hand around the almost empty garage. Non-stop work was how Leah blew off steam.

"Old man needs to call it quits and let Leah take over," Amos replied. He checked the shelves where they stored the motor oil. Definitely getting low on some of the common weights. He added those to his list.

"You know that's never happening. Just like he's never going to approve of me going to school anywhere but here."

Grace liked to act tough, but inside, she was a marshmallow. After losing Mom, she'd spent a couple of years partying herself numb, but she had always been careful not to do anything that would alienate their father. Trouble was, it was making her miserable.

"You don't need to be worrying about that," he replied. "Leah and I can deal with him. You should be looking at university. Period."

She scoffed and spun the stool in circles. Same as she had when she was little and something was eating at her.

"I'm serious, Gracie Lynn." He tried to adopt the tone their mother used when she was being encouraging, but direct. She made a face at him then stuck out her tongue, but she was smiling.

"Yeah, I know. I'm just..." She sighed and spun the stool some more. "The advisor at the community college says at the end of this year, I'll have enough credits to transfer in as a third-year student, if I pick the right major. I've got good enough grades I can qualify for some scholarships. And I'm old enough I can maybe get some grants. But there's a lot to think about."

Amos didn't have to tell her the logistics. Grace already knew, but she was afraid of hurting her family. If he had to guess, he'd bet it was about their dad. She'd have to go to Charleston, at the very least. She could commute there, but it was still an hour's drive away. It would save her renting a place to live but would cost her in time.

He straightened up and crossed to where she was still spinning on the stool. He stuck the toe of his work boot out and brought the dizzying circles to a halt, then laid his hands on his kid sister's shoulders.

"You're fucking brilliant," he said. "You've got big dreams and you should one hundred percent shoot for the stars. You do your part — get the grades, put in the applications, do whatever you can do to get as much help as you can. The rest? You know Leah and I will help. You know we'll deal with Dad."

The way Grace bit her lip made it clear he'd been right about that being her biggest worry.

"Most of all, you know he can't stay mad at his baby girl. No matter how much he guilts you, or acts like you're doing him wrong, or anything else, you ignore it. Do what you need to do. Do what you want to do. He'll come around. I promise."

Grace was twenty-four years old. She should've been out and pursuing her dreams years ago, but when their mother died, she'd clung to their dad and ever since, any time she tried to pull away, he held her back. It didn't help that she looked like a carbon copy of their mother—all tall and lean with golden hair and blue eyes.

She stood in a rush and hugged him. She reached up and scrubbed her knuckles on his head.

"You're my favorite big brother."

Amos rolled his eyes as she practically skipped out of the garage. It wouldn't do any good to point out he was her only brother—big or otherwise. Grace was a study in extremes. She always had been. Of the three Kimmel kids, she was the most sensitive one, but she was also the most curious, with a drive that could take her places, if she wasn't being held back by a small town and unhealthy attachments to family.

Well, he'd planted the seed and done what Leah had asked—worked on convincing their kid sister to do something with her life. Hopefully, Grace would run with it, but he had no doubt he'd be repeating the whole thing at least a few more times.

Shit he didn't need to be dwelling on while he had work to get done. At least he had something nice to look forward to tomorrow night.

Chapter Seven

Katie
October 7, Saturday

Katie stuck the tape measure back in her bag and smiled. Last night at the haunted house committee meeting, she'd proposed doing more outside the entrance. The haunted house was really a short corridor with two connected classrooms on either side. A clever design by one of the now long-gone parents, it used temporary walls to create a meandering path.

It was brilliant, really, except the front was still the plain double doors of the school building. Katie had proposed decorating the doors and the path leading to them, so the spooky atmosphere started before students even entered the haunted house. Everyone had loved the idea, so of course, she'd gotten up early on a Saturday to come take measurements and sketch some ideas that could be done quickly.

She skimmed her scribbled notes and the rough sketches she'd made. It felt good to be involved. To be doing something other than just teaching. In the city schools, even her kindergarten classes had been overcrowded, and while the schools had activities, there wasn't this level of involvement between teacher and parents. She smiled again, stuffed her notebook into her bag and headed to her car.

Plenty of time to get herself something for lunch, then go home and have a leisurely shower before getting ready for her date with Amos. They'd chatted this morning and decided getting out of town sounded like the better option.

In the parking lot, Katie nearly dropped her bag when she caught sight of the man sitting on her car hood. *Miles.* It was tempting to turn around, go back inside and call the police. Not that she was sure what good that would do. It's not like her brother was doing anything wrong.

No, hiding wasn't going to make Miles go away.

"What the fuck are you doing here?" Katie saw no reason to be polite. Sure, addiction could drive people to do terrible things, but her patience and tolerance for her brother's shit had run out during her freshman year of college.

Miles spread his hands wide and smiled in a way she was sure others found disarming. She wasn't so easily taken in.

"After six years, that's how you greet your big brother?"

She'd long ago learned not to answer questions like that. "Get your ass off my car."

Miles didn't move. Not that she'd expected him to. He still wore that wide, aw-shucks grin that people usually fell for. Often more than once.

"Y'know, growing up, you were just bratty," Miles said. "Now, I'm getting bitchy vibes."

He hopped off her car and Katie saw the beat-up duffel bag on the ground.

"Fresh outta rehab," he said. "Weren't you the one always trying to get me to go? You gonna be a hardass when I'm on my first day out, clean and sober?"

Maybe if she hadn't grown up with him, and their father, and hell, their mother as well, Katie might have fallen for that routine. Instead, she recognized it for what it was. Manipulation. *Score points for therapy.*

"I'm thrilled for you," she replied. "Congratulations."

Katie had her keys in her hand. If she unlocked her car doors, there was a chance Miles would jump in. Then she'd have a hell of a time getting rid of him. She could manually open the driver's door and hope he would leave her be.

"Aren't you gonna ask why I'm back? I mean, earlier, you were all hot to know what I was doing here."

She had no intention of asking him anything. It was going to take a lot more than a claim of recent rehab to change her mind. Especially when he was behaving the same way he always had.

"Fine, I'll tell you." He rolled his eyes and sagged against her car. Blocking the driver's door. Of course. *Asshole.*

"I've got no place else to go," he said. "I had a place lined up, but it fell through. I don't know where Mom is anymore. I figured I could stay with you till I'm on my feet again."

It sounded so plausible. So believable. But Miles was barking up the wrong tree. He'd burned her one too many times in the past.

"I'm sorry, but no." She said the words firmly and without anger. Just as her therapist had taught her to do.

"Aw, c'mon. Just like that? What am I supposed to do?"

Katie pulled in a slow breath and blew it out. "I don't have an answer for you, but you cannot stay with me."

The urge to defend her answer, to give reasons for it dug at her. She clenched her hands into fists and counted to ten. She didn't need to give him a reason. No was a complete sentence and a complete answer.

"Seriously? You want me to go and stay with Dad? When I'm fresh outta rehab. Do you have any idea what that's likely to do to me?"

And there it was. The guilt trip.

"How did you even know I was here?" Katie replied and instantly regretted asking. Her old work wouldn't disclose that information. She didn't know where to find their mother these days, so she hadn't told her. She sure as hell hadn't told their dad, but it was a safe bet he'd heard things through the grapevine. Which would mean Miles had talked to their dad.

"What? You ask some really out-there questions." Miles ran a hand through his hair. He was still blocking the car door. "I'm not asking for much. Just a place to crash for a bit. Then I can find a job, get a place of my own. Y'know, all that shit."

His refusal to answer her question told her all she needed to know. Whether or not Miles had been in rehab at all, or if he was truly clean and sober, which she doubted, he'd talked to their dad. Which meant he was already plugging himself right back in to everything their mother had tried to get them away from.

"I said no," she replied. "I meant it. Now move out of my way. There's a place in Logan that has weekly rooms to rent and they're affordable. You can go there. Or there's a YMCA in Charleston."

The perfect, disarming smile flickered for an instant, but it was enough for Katie to know she had it right. This wasn't Miles turning over a new leaf. This was Miles being himself. Even if she was so inclined, her place was a small studio with a full-size bed tucked into an alcove. She didn't even have a regular couch—just her dining chairs and a loveseat that despite being deliciously comfy for sitting in, she couldn't imagine sleeping on.

"C'mon Katie." His voice took on the pleading whine he'd used as a teenager when he wanted her to do his chores, or finish his homework. "You're my baby sister. You know I can't stay at Dad's. Think about what that place would do to me. You don't want me relapsing."

Katie held her temper in check. Blowing up at Miles wouldn't do her any good.

"You are the only one responsible for your choices," she replied. "I did not invite you here. I gave you two affordable options. I cannot, and will not, do more. Now, please move."

Miles crossed his arms, spread his legs wide and glared at her.

"You come here asking for help, but you're still acting like your old bully self," she said. She forced herself to keep her voice level. "I am trying to build a life here. You and your choices have cost me dearly in the past, so no, I won't help you. Not when I see no evidence of real change."

She fished her phone out of her bag and thumbed it on.

"If you are really trying to rebuild, you would understand my position. I'll give you five seconds to get off my car and away from me before I call the police."

For a moment, she feared Miles would refuse. Years ago, he'd have believed she was bluffing, and he would have been right. Today, her finger hovered over the call button. She stared at Miles and waited.

He blew out a sharp exhale and shoved himself off her car. "When the fuck did you get so uptight? You used to be at least a little fun. Whatever."

He scooped up his bag and walked a few feet away, then turned to face her again. "Guess whatever happens to me next is on your head. Guess family doesn't matter to you at all. So much for you saying you care about me, huh?"

When she didn't respond, he waved a dismissive hand at her and sauntered across the lot as if he didn't have a care in the world.

Katie wasted no time getting into her car and locking the doors. She kept looking back as she pulled out of the lot. The last thing she needed was for Miles to follow her home. Not that he couldn't figure out where she lived if he asked around.

Well, there's one big downside of small towns in general, and this small town in particular.

Once home, she dropped into her very comfy – and very small – loveseat and stared at her phone, debating who, if anyone, she should call.

The answer was simple – there was no one.

The last phone number Katie had for her mother had been disconnected while she was still in college. Letters sent to the place Katie had known she lived came back marked 'no longer at this address'.

She had no desire to talk to her dad. Ever again. If her suspicions were correct, he already knew Miles was back in town.

So much for her relaxing afternoon. She'd been so flustered, she hadn't thought to stop for lunch. She rose and crossed to her fridge. Maybe some scrambled eggs and toast. Her fingers shook as she reached for the handle and Katie sank to the floor.

She leaned against the fridge and hugged her knees to her chest. This was what she had fought so hard to escape. What the hell was she thinking coming back here? She had a one-year contract with an option to renew at the end of the calendar year. It was still early enough. She could terminate the agreement if she had to. She had enough in savings to make a few months. She could move. Work as a substitute until she could land a new contract.

No. I wanted a place to call home. That's why I came back here.

She pushed herself up from the floor. She'd figure this out. Somehow.

Screw food. She needed a shower first. On the way to the bathroom, she stopped. Last night, in a fit of excitement about her upcoming date with Amos, she'd gone through her closet and picked an outfit. They'd decided to get out of town, not to avoid gossip, but to be able to relax and enjoy each other's company.

The vintage blue wiggle dress hung on the bathroom door. Maybe the dress was too much for a date in a small town—even if they were driving to Charleston.

She'd never seen Amos in anything but his work clothes or casual jeans.

This morning, she'd been looking forward to dinner and time with Amos. Now she was a bundle of nerves, thanks to her older brother.

Had he called Amos? They'd been best friends. It would make sense.

I should cancel.

Her stomach rumbled a rude reminder that she hadn't eaten anything since breakfast and as wonderful as a shower sounded, food was more important.

"Fine. No decisions until after I eat and take a long and very hot shower." As if there was anyone in the tiny space to hear her. Sometimes, she had to say things out loud for herself. Like thinking the words was very different from saying them, and hearing yourself say them.

Two hours later, after eating, cleaning the kitchen and taking a shower so gloriously long that the water was starting to go cold, she felt much more like herself. She wouldn't cancel. She would not give Miles that kind of control over her life.

Katie shoved the dress back in the closet and pulled out a bunch of other options.

Her alarm buzzed. Time to get ready. Katie smiled and gave a nod to her final outfit choice—a black pencil skirt and pink sweater. Her bed was piled high with discarded looks and she rushed through putting as much as she could away.

With the clock ticking before Amos arrived to pick her up, and no makeup on her face, Katie stopped and surveyed the still messy room.

She could deal with this later. A little makeup, her pink and black Chucks on her feet and she was ready to walk out the door right as Amos rang the bell.

Katie took a deep breath and hoped against hope her brother hadn't called his former best friend.

She opened the door and took in the man in front of her. Slim-fitting black jeans and a black button-up shirt highlighted his broad shoulders. The black leather jacket, sturdy black boots, and chunky silver jewelry made her glad she'd swapped outfits.

"Hi!" She breathed the word out and stepped onto the landing, pulling her door shut behind her. "Let's go."

Amos took a step back and whistled as he looked her up and down. Katie had to resist doing a spin for him.

"You look amazing," he said. "I mean, you always look good, but this? Wow." He offered his arm and turned for the stairs.

All of Katie's cares went sailing out the window. Amos Kimmel was taking her on a date. And grown-up Amos was oh-so-much hotter than his teenage self.

Amos

Katie smelled like incense and roses and she looked like a dream. Amos opened the door of his truck and she gave a nervous sounding laugh. Before he could figure out what was going on, she'd shimmied her skirt up her thighs and he had a hard time not scooping her up and suggesting they go right back upstairs and spend their date in her bed.

When she reached up to get a hold on the doorframe, he realized the problem. Short woman. Tight skirt. Tall truck.

"Hang on, lemme help." He stepped in close and Katie turned to face him. "Truck ain't even lifted, but I guess..." His brain was short circuiting too much to let him finish that sentence. "How about I give you a boost?"

He held his hands out near her middle. Katie nodded and Amos closed his hands around a tiny waist. Katie rested her palms on his shoulders and Amos lifted. He hadn't expected her to help, but she did a little knee bend and jump or something, and pushed her hands against him as she went up so she felt like she weighed almost nothing.

He managed to resist temptation once again and got her into the seat.

"Thank you," she said. "I guess pants would have been a better idea."

Amos let his gaze travel down her legs, still exposed by the hiked skirt then he looked back at Katie. A rosy flush colored her cheeks. "I'm not complaining."

That seemed to break the ice. Katie burst into bright laughter and everything felt easy and comfortable. He closed her door and went around to the driver's side. He didn't miss that she'd slid her skirt back down in the meantime.

"You can save the pants for when I get you on the back of my bike."

Katie arched an eyebrow at him. "Why does it not surprise me that you have a motorcycle?"

"Dunno," he replied. "Maybe it was the leather jacket? I'm serious about taking you out for a ride, though. If you want."

Katie turned in the seat and crossed her arms. "Depends. What do you ride?"

Her tone and expression said she was joking. Her bratty streak was showing. "Harley Fat Boy."

He started the truck as her laughter filled the cab. "Yeah, it suits you. I'd love to go for a ride, but I'm definitely a fair-weather rider."

"Not much of that left this year, but we can try to fit something in. Otherwise, I guess we wait for spring," Amos said as he pulled onto the road.

"I'm supposed to wait for spring to fit something in?"

Her throaty laugh sent blood rushing to his dick. *Seems to happen around Katie.*

"So where are we going tonight?"

Amos tapped his phone so she could see the restaurant. "There's a new tapas place in Charleston that I thought sounded good."

"That works," she replied. Despite her laughter and joking, something seemed off with her. There was a tension in her he hadn't felt before.

They passed the drive chatting about trivial things, and over time, she loosened up a bit more, but it was clear she was holding on to something.

The restaurant felt cozy and the host led them to a table by the window that commanded a view of the Kanawha River. They agreed on a bottle of wine and as soon as the server left, Amos laid his hand over Katie's.

"You're as tense as a live wire. What's going on?"

Her hand clenched under his, but she didn't pull it away. She let out a low sigh. "I'm sorry. I debated canceling tonight, but in the end, I didn't want to."

That hit Amos like a punch to the gut. He'd been so excited he hadn't slept much, and she'd considered canceling? Something was definitely wrong. Her hand shifted in his and she squeezed.

"I can see the gears turning in your head," she said. "It's a long story, and I promise, I'll tell you, but I need wine first. And a promise."

Well, that sounded ominous, but Amos nodded. "What's the promise?"

"When I tell you why I'm tense—no questions. Actually, don't even talk—don't tell me it's okay, or anything. I don't want to discuss it, or dig into it or examine it. I'll have one question for you once I've said my piece and all I ask is complete honesty."

Their wine arrived and they both ordered a few tapas plates. Amos captured Katie's hand again and smiled.

"That's a promise I can make. I'll keep my mouth shut while you talk. Then I'll be as honest as I can be about whatever question you have. Fair?"

"Yep." Katie took a long sip of her wine. Then another. Finally, she looked back at him, her eyes haunted.

"Miles showed up at the school today while I was taking measurements for the Halloween thing."

A rock dropped into Amos' gut. All at once he was too hot and too cold. He'd promised he wouldn't ask questions and he'd bite his tongue till it bled if he had to, but dammit, did he have a list.

"Short version—he claims he's clean and sober. Not sure I believe him. He claims he hasn't talked to our dad. I know I don't believe that. And he wanted a place to stay."

Now he was regretting his promise to stay quiet. The more Katie talked and told him about her interaction with Miles in the parking lot, the more he wanted to hunt down his former best friend and throttle him.

Miles had always had a selfish streak, but that was taking it too far.

"I don't know what y'all were into during high school but I know it wasn't good," Katie continued. "I know it was a big part of why we moved away so suddenly."

Amos clamped his mouth on the laugh that nearly came up. *Yeah, understatement of the year, there.*

"He kept having troubles, everywhere we'd go. There was a juvenile rehab center — thanks to that he graduated high school. Of course, he fucked up again. He was in and out of programs."

Katie fidgeted in her seat and didn't meet his eyes when she continued speaking. "None of them made a difference and Mom kicked him out."

Oh shit. He had a feeling he knew where this was headed. Miles had always liked to experiment with drugs.

"Eventually, he had nowhere else to go. He came back to live with us during my senior year of high school. Miles was...uhh... Shit..."

She fiddled with her napkin and cast her gaze at the ceiling. He wanted to say something, ask her what happened, but he'd promised to keep quiet.

"He was an asshole," she said, looking back at Amos. "There's no getting around it. He started dealing as well as using. I don't know what exactly, or how much. I do know that he stole from our mother. He stole from one of my friends, and that got him arrested."

Another sip of wine, this one smaller than the last. She looked down at the table, her fingers clenching on the smooth, white cloth.

"He nearly cost me my scholarship and admission to college, and in my freshman year, almost got me kicked out after breaking into my dorm, stealing and later dealing drugs on campus. The administration was sure I was a part of it for a while."

When she looked back up, there were no tears in her eyes. Only cold, hard acceptance. He'd seen that look on women's faces before—usually when the medics were getting ready to cart them to the hospital for the latest 'accident' that had happened.

The urge to throttle Miles grew.

"I cut off all contact then. It hurt and I felt shitty about doing it, but I knew it was the only choice. Before today, I hadn't seen or heard from my brother in six years."

Her eyes did tear up at that. She sniffed and pressed a hand over her face.

"Cutting him out of my life nearly broke me. If I had the tiniest shred of hope or belief that he was being genuine today, I'd have gotten sucked right into his drama. So, uhh…that's it. I'm done."

Their food arrived and serious conversation came to a halt as they settled in to try everything. Katie laughed and teased as if she hadn't just dropped a bomb. Not that it was all that unexpected. He'd known Miles was a shithead. He had his own stories on that front, including a juvenile record because of him.

All through dinner, Amos turned her words over and over in his head. Carl Tilman was a hard man. Amos knew that for himself. He'd come uncomfortably close to living that life. He'd gotten lucky—he'd been young enough, and had the right support and help thanks to Chief Lawson. He'd not only gotten out of it, but found community and purpose in the fire department.

Katie didn't know all of that. She didn't need to. The last thing he wanted was for her to think of him the way she thought of her brother.

After dinner, instead of going directly to his truck, Amos took Katie's hand and walked along the river path. They found a bench and sat.

"You warm enough?"

Katie had brought a jacket that she now had pulled snug around her like she was cold, but she nodded.

"I can see why you're tense. You said you'd have one question for me. What is it?" Amos took Katie's hands in his and waited.

She chuckled, a soft, bitter sound, and the smile she gave him trembled a little.

"Two-parter, actually. First—you planning on rekindling a friendship with Miles?"

Her directness surprised him, but he schooled his face to stay neutral, lest Katie see his reaction for something it wasn't.

"Hadn't given it a whole lotta thought to be honest. I didn't know he was back until you said something. We didn't stay in touch."

Chief Lawson had been pretty clear that he didn't think much of Amos' list of associates at the time, and even less of Carl Tilman and Dwight Phelps.

"I, uh… I was pretty steamed at him for a while. Now I realize he was a fucked-up kid. Like we all were, really. I can't blame him for being stupid back then." He shrugged. "I guess if he showed up wanting to talk, I'd listen. I believe everyone deserves a second chance. Do I see myself looking to hang out with Miles? No."

Her laugh this time was a little nervous sounding. "It sounds silly now, but after seeing Miles, I was… Well…I mean…back when we were kids, you and he were best buddies and I was just his bratty kid sister."

She was dancing around whatever was really bothering her, and Amos was pretty sure he knew what it was.

"You planning to make me guess what the second half of your question is?"

She bit her lower lip and damn, he wanted to slide his hands into her hair and discover if her lips were as soft as they looked.

"I think you know." Her voice was a whisper almost lost when she tucked her head down.

Amos put a finger under her chin and lifted until he had a clear view of her gorgeous gray eyes.

"You're worried I'm gonna think of you as Miles' bratty kid sister."

It wasn't a question. He knew beyond any doubt that he was right. Still, Katie nodded. He could tell her she was wrong. He could tell her how beautiful she was. Sometimes words weren't enough.

"Remember in the corn maze, when I said I wanted to hear the rest of that thought?"

Katie's eyebrows furrowed for a moment, then rose toward her hairline. She hadn't pulled away from the finger under her chin, so Amos slid his hand up to cup her cheek in his palm.

"You don't expect me to tell you that right now, do you?"

Her eyes had gone wide. Whatever it was had to be really delicious and he'd love to hear it, but it could wait.

"No," he replied, and her look of relief was almost comical. He leaned closer to her, close enough some soft rose scent washed over him. He placed his lips close to her ear. "But you will share it with me before..."

He stopped and pulled back. Katie's lips were parted and her breath came in short, fast bursts.

"Before what?" She leaned forward, bringing her lips inches from his.

Amos inhaled slowly, relishing the way she smelled — warm and soft, sweet flowers with a sharp tang of incense and this close, a hint of leather.

"The past is the past," he said as he slid his hand from her cheek and into her hair, until he cradled the back of her head. "I'm not interested in looking back. I'm interested in the woman sitting on this bench with me. Here and now."

Katie tipped her head back and arched closer to him. Everything about her body language and half-closed eyes said she wanted to be kissed, but Amos had never not asked before a first kiss. He'd caught hell about that from his friends, but fuck them. He brought his free hand up and stroked a lock of hair from her face.

"Katie," he whispered her name into her ear. A little shiver went through her and he didn't think it was from the cold. "I want to kiss you."

Her gasping intake of air could have been his answer, then Katie let out a soft sound that had him wanting a lot more than kisses.

"Yes, please!"

There it was. Permission granted. Amos tipped his head and brought his lips to hers. A feather-light touch to start. She hummed and her hands clenched into his jacket.

He traced her lips with the tip of his tongue and her mouth opened for him. She tasted of chocolate and coffee. She inched closer on the bench and wound her arms around him.

Amos slid his hands down her sides until he cupped her slim hips. With a gentle pull, she slipped sideways into his lap, never breaking their kiss.

He lost track of time just as he lost himself in Katie's kisses. When he moved a hand down her thigh and found chilled skin under her skirt, Amos reluctantly lifted his head.

"You're cold. Let's get in the truck."

He gave her his jacket even though they were only going across the street to the parking lot. Once inside the truck, he cranked the heater and turned to her. Her lips looked puffy and her cheeks were flushed with color.

"I think I answered your question."

Katie threw her head back in laughter. "Well, the original one, yes. But I still want to know when you're expecting me to tell you what I was thinking at the Safety Day."

Amos reached over and laid a hand on Katie's leg, then looked to her and raised an eyebrow in question. She placed her hand over his.

This felt too good. Too right. Not that he was going to complain. He pulled onto the highway and changed the subject to her favorite music. They talked bands and music the whole way back.

"Tell me this—when you saw me, and didn't recognize me, were you thinking thoughts that might make church ladies blush?"

Katie's leg twitched under his hand. All the answer he needed.

"That's what I figured. How blush-worthy were they?"

Katie caught her breath. "Uhhh...let's just say, if they were a movie, it'd get at least an R-rating."

That sent his thoughts careening even deeper into the gutter than they already were. He came around to help her out of the truck, then walked her up. At her front door, Amos stopped her before she put her key in the lock. He slid his arms around her waist and looked at her upturned face.

"I had a wonderful time, thank you," he said.

"Me too!" She raised up on her toes and kissed him.

God, if she keeps that up, I'm not walking away from here. "Tonight, I'm not gonna ask to come in. I want to. You have no idea how badly I want to. But...not until you tell me what you were thinking on Safety Day."

Katie's eyes went big and round and her lips parted on a soft exhale. "Oh, you're good. Evil, but in the right kind of way. So...I have to tell you that before..."

The look on her face said she knew what he meant. It also said she wanted him to say it. He had no problem there, but she'd have to ask for it.

He kissed her lightly, then caught her hair in one hand and held it tight at her nape. He planted tiny kisses from her shoulder, up her exposed neck to her ear.

"I want to hear every single blush-worthy thing that went through your head that day. In graphic detail," he said. He tightened the hand in her hair and a tiny moan escaped her lips. The sound nearly drove him to grab her keys from her hand and open the door himself.

"Before...what, though? I want to know."

Amos chuckled. He traced his lips along her neck. "You already do."

She let out a sharp exhale that almost had him laughing. It was the equivalent of stomping her foot and pouting. Even as an adult she had a bratty side. The difference was, these days, he found it sexy as fuck, and he could get into taming a brat who wanted it.

"But I want to hear you say it."

Close enough to asking.

"You'll tell me before I fuck you," he said. This time, her moan was deeper, throatier, and he wanted nothing more than to lift her skirt and pin her against the wall next to her door. Instead, he kissed her lips and slowly pulled himself away.

"Goodnight. I'll wait on the stairs till you get the door unlocked."

Now she was pouting. He wasn't sure he could refuse if she asked him in. Lucky for him, she took a deep breath and shot him a smirk.

"G'night." She whirled, unlocked her door and without a single glance back, went in and shut it behind her.

I asked for that. Bought and paid for, in fact.

The hell of it was, he liked it. He liked it a lot.

Chapter Eight

Katie
October 12, Thursday

Katie parked her car in the lot, as close to the school as she could get. Until Saturday, she'd parked as far from the building as possible — every opportunity to get a few extra steps in was a good one. That was before Miles had shown back up.

She hadn't seen him since that day, and while she was relieved, she was also worried. She'd been ignorant of the extent of the problems when they'd lived here. She spent her childhood vaguely aware that her father, and later her brother, were not exactly fine, upstanding citizens. Even after the move, she hadn't realized how bad things had been.

After the incidents during her freshman year of college, she'd slowly come to realize nothing about her life had been normal. None of her new friends worried about the police knocking on their doors. They didn't hide money from their siblings or parents, or refuse to own anything of real value lest it get pawned.

She double checked the lot before she got out of her car and walked into the building. She only had a half day of teaching then she'd work on the haunted house plans. Her phone buzzed as she got to her classroom and she fished it from her pocket. Amos' name popped up on her screen and she thumbed to open the text.

Finally off duty. I've got a full day at the garage, but if you wanna maybe grab dinner. Lemme know. Would love to see you.

She sent a thumbs-up emoji and closed her messages. She wasn't used to men who communicated. Ever since their date, Amos sent a good morning text every day. And a good night text every night. They'd made plans to go out on the weekend but he'd been angling for some additional time during the week.

She hurried through her morning routine, desperately trying to keep her mind from dwelling on his kisses, or the things he'd said. Not that she expected to succeed on either front. She hadn't yet.

The bell rang and she pushed open her door and counted heads as her students filed in. Nineteen. Someone must be sick. Katie started roll call and lost herself in the habits of the day. So much so that she was startled by the noon bell that announced lunch time and that her teaching day was through.

She grabbed her lunch bag and headed to Cinda Gable's room where the haunted house committee was meeting every Thursday.

Cinda, Lily Elkins, and sisters Sue-Ann and Patty Jenkins made up the rest of the committee and were spreading out at the big table up front. Katie took a seat and greeted the group, then hauled out her sandwich. Sue-Ann always had a smoothie for lunch and was an obsessive note taker, so she had a notebook and pen ready to go.

"Might as well jump right into it," Cinda said as they all got settled. "We've got plenty of room in the budget for the outside additions Katie suggested."

She pulled out Katie's basic sketches outlining the design for the building entrance. "Katie, can you get a materials list to Patty and Sue-Ann by tomorrow? They're doing all the shopping this weekend."

Katie already had the list done. It was one of the many tasks she'd busied herself with to keep from thinking about Amos. She'd give it a final check and send it over as soon as she got home tonight.

"How much extra time do we need for set-up? Plus how much do we need to back it up since we're opening an hour earlier?" Leave it to Lily to bring up the tough stuff.

"The outside should only take a couple of hours," Katie said and braced herself for a chorus of complaints. They didn't come. *Good.* "I convinced Principal Dubois and the two teachers whose classrooms are affected to have classes in the library the day of the Halloween carnival," she continued. That news was met with excited chatter.

"I'm taking Katie's class that Friday," Cinda added. "We've bumped up the carnival start time to five-thirty, and we'll open the haunted house to kindergartners and younger siblings thirty minutes before the carnival opens. So we need to be ready at five, instead of six like years past."

Katie and Cinda had gone over the possible timelines until they were both bleary eyed and tired, but they'd finally figured out a plan that worked and didn't create too much havoc with the set-up teams.

"We're going to start the day with the outside decorations," Katie said. "That should take about two hours, and we'll put yellow caution tape all around it once we're done. That will get all the students talking about it. Especially when they learn it's going to have different scare levels this year. Then we can take our time inside."

Lily sat back in her seat and whistled. Patty shook her head and Sue-Ann looked up from her notes. "That gives us more time than we've had before. How did you manage that?"

Katie shrugged. It hadn't been too tough to get the teachers to move their classes for the day, and with Cinda taking her students for the morning, it meant they could start first thing.

"Just puzzle pieces fitting together," Katie replied. "The haunted house cast can arrive at their usual time, since the first hour won't include any ghosts or ghouls. Like years past, they'll have a walk through on Thursday. The changes to pull this off are small but they have big impact."

"Okay then. On to the easy stuff," Cinda said. It took less than an hour to go through the rest of their agenda — who was handling costumes and makeup, the cast of ghosts and ghouls who were mostly older siblings of current students, the parents and teachers serving as chaperones, and the plan for taking it all down.

"That leaves one last thing," Cinda said. "We always have members of the fire department on hand just to be safe. We've got Shawn Dubois as always and he's bringing Micah Stewart. And Amos Kimmel called today and said he'd be here. Pretty sure that's thanks to Katie."

She winked. The other ladies laughed. Katie felt the heat rising in her cheeks. That explained the series of texts yesterday. Amos had asked about her schedule for the carnival. Katie figured he was looking to find some time for them and told him she'd unfortunately be busy the whole night but they could do something that Saturday, after they took down the haunted house.

Despite that moment of mild discomfort at realizing her relationship with Amos was not only gossip fodder, but the subject of open speculation, she walked out of the meeting feeling for the first time like she'd found home.

As for whatever she had with Amos — well, it was early yet. Just thinking about his kisses had her toes curling in pleasure. He was the perfect mix of cocky and a little demanding and she hoped like hell he wasn't the type to wait a long time before getting naked.

Because oh, how she wanted to see him out of his clothes.

* * * *

Amos

The bluesy rock vibe of the Ghost Hounds echoed in the side garage as Amos got the Parsons' Harvester up on the lift. It was time to start the work on the thing. Luckily, Leah and their dad were busy in the main garage.

"What the fuck are you listening to?"

Amos froze at the voice. Even years later, Miles Tilman still sounded the same. Laidback tones with a note of disdain for everyone and everything. To think, Amos had once aspired to be as cool as Miles.

He put his tools down and wiped his hands, then shifted himself from under the truck and faced his one-time best friend. The years had not been kind to Miles. He seemed much older than twenty-seven and his clothes looked a size too big. He still sported the same *Rebel Without a Cause* expression—a mix of boredom and condescension.

Amos tapped his phone screen and brought the music to a halt. "Band outta Pittsburgh. When did you get back in town?"

He didn't know what else to say. If his old man came out here and saw Miles hanging around, they'd have to call the police. No way Roy Kimmel wouldn't swing on him now that he was a grown man. Luckily, he never came out to the side garage.

"Been about a week, I guess. Hey, you still have that apartment over the shop? I'm looking for a place to stay that ain't my dad's."

Only Miles could do the shit he did, disappear for over a decade, then come back and act like they'd never lost touch, or that he'd done nothing wrong.

"Sorry, man. Leah's got that now. Besides, uh…"

Amos stopped. His brain couldn't land on the right words. Never mind what his old man would think, Leah would sling Amos' hide up a rope if she thought he was hanging out with Miles again. Grace would just stop talking to him as if he didn't exist.

Katie… *Ah, shit, Katie.* He couldn't tell her Miles stopped by. She'd been torn up over his visit and it was obvious she was feeling guilty about turning him away.

"Besides, what? You got something to say? You planning to blame me for you getting your ass in trouble?"

Of course Miles would know that. It wasn't a secret in town. Except most folks didn't talk about it anymore because Amos had not only done his time but had worked damn hard to prove he'd grown up and learned a few lessons. Plus, they'd never talk to Miles Tilman. The whole family name thing was exactly the source of some of Katie's stress over them maybe dating. She was a Tilman, and in Orchard Creek, that meant trouble.

One date does not mean dating. Fuck. He could tell himself that all he'd like, but his brain—and other parts—were telling him otherwise.

The only way Miles could know anything about all of that was if he'd been talking with the folks out in West Creek—the trailer park crowd. Carl Tilman. Dwight Phelps, whose son Charlie had gotten mixed up in the whole mess with Robert and CeeCee earlier in the year.

"I'm past blaming," Amos said, finally. "I made those choices. I owned the consequences and I've paid that debt."

From what Katie had said, it didn't seem like Miles had changed at all. If anything, he might have gotten worse.

"Hey, man, I'm just yanking your chain," Miles said. He was suddenly all smiles and charm. "We used to hang tight. Didn't figure there was that much water under the bridge. Guess I'll see if old lady Sykes still has the rooming house."

Amos snagged two bottles of water from the fridge and tossed one to Miles. "She died few years back,"

Amos said. "Been closed ever since. Dwight might have a place or two, but those still come with a cost."

Dwight owned a handful of trailers—mostly rundown campers—that he'd rent out on the cheap. But the low rent came with strings attached. As did everything with Dwight. He was Carl Tilman's right-hand man.

"Outside of that, you're not gonna find much here. Logan has some places."

Miles made some noncommittal sound and chugged half his water in one gulp. "Maybe I will look at Logan. Never thought I'd miss this hell hole. Good to see you, man."

Without another word, Miles turned and left the garage. Amos shook his head and put away his tools. He'd get no more work done this afternoon, and he needed to wrap his brain around the whole thing before he saw Katie for dinner.

No way in hell would he tell her about Miles' visit.

Chapter Nine

Katie
October 20, Friday

One student left. At least he was napping. The clock ticked another minute as Katie continued tidying her classroom, trying to make as little noise as possible.

Little Mark Hodges sprawled on a nap mat, his feet in mismatched socks barely poking out of the legs of the oversize sweatpants Katie had found for him. She glanced at the clock. Thirty minutes past pickup time.

Shaking her head, she moved to her desk and opened the incident report book to the page where she'd already entered Mark once today. His mother had dropped him off late, wearing filthy shorts that Katie had soon realized were not just dirty, but at some point, he'd had a toileting accident.

Not that it should have been a big deal. Kindergartners sometimes had accidents. Except, Mark didn't have back-up clothes and he was so small they had a hard time finding anything to fit him. Katie eyed the bag of soiled garments before jotting down the time.

She dialed Mark's mother and the call went straight to voicemail. Sighing, she left another message then moved on to his emergency contact. That one also went to voicemail. She pulled up Mark's file, hoping to find a second emergency contact. She had another thirty minutes to reach someone before she was mandated to call child services. Considering the state of the child's clothes when he'd arrived at school, she should probably file a report anyway.

Meanwhile, she would let Mark sleep. Katie finished packing her things and busied herself with going over the plans for the Halloween carnival next week. Things were coming along nicely and she was glad she'd jumped in with both feet. Her classroom door burst open as a harried looking young woman scurried in.

"I'm so sorry," the woman said. She stood just inside the door, wringing her hands and looking around as if she wasn't sure where she was. Erin Hodges looked far too young to have a school-age child, but there were a lot of teen mothers in the county. *That's the price of no sex education and nothing else to do.*

She chided herself for the uncharitable thought and rose to pick up Mark's things, including the bag of clothes.

"Mark's shorts and socks were soiled this morning," Katie said, trying to keep her voice gentle. "We found clean ones for him."

Erin took the bag as if it might bite her. She gave Katie a shaky, gap-toothed smile. "I tried to get him to go afore we left this morning. Guess he forgot an' couldn't hold it."

She crossed to her son and knelt down to pick him up. Her coat was threadbare and the sturdy work boots on her feet were so old the tread was worn flat.

"If you want to bring in a spare set of clothes, I can keep them in the classroom," Katie said as the woman lifted her sleeping son. Mark stirred and swiped at his eyes, but then dropped his head to his mother's shoulder.

"Oh, that'd be something," Erin replied. "Some days it's all I can do to get him here on time. Sorry I was so late. Work went over."

She didn't look at Katie when she talked and her hands shook as she shouldered Mark's bag.

"I'll bring spares," she said and hurried out the door before Katie could get her signature in the incident book.

Poor, overworked families were nothing new. She'd taught in the city at a school where every student was receiving some form of assistance. Somehow, she'd convinced herself she'd see less of that here, but she should have known better.

She'd come to school hungry more often than not. She'd wake up and clean the bathroom because the smell of vomit and alcohol was so strong she couldn't stand being in there with the door shut. Miles had never seemed to care. He'd shower and brush his teeth as if there was nothing wrong.

They'd find their mother passed out on the couch and Katie would pick up the empty bottles and cans and dump the overflowing ashtray. Their dad's snores would echo from the bedroom at the back of the mobile home.

Most of the time, there wasn't anything to make for breakfast, so Katie and Miles went without. Sometimes, if their mother had gone to one of the church food pantries, there might be bread for toast, or canned fruit.

Katie shouldered her bag and switched off the lights. *Time to shove those memories back in the dark where they belong.* She'd get home and make herself a hot cocoa and try to get in a less melancholy mood before the weekend. Not that she had any plans aside from more work for the Halloween carnival. Amos was on duty for the next few days.

Though they texted or talked just about every day, Katie longed for his company. *Who am I kidding? I want his kisses again.* If she was being honest, she wanted a lot more than kisses. On their first date, he'd made it clear he was on the same page, but during their dinner last week, he'd seemed distracted. The more she tried not to think about it, the more it all dug at her.

So much for swearing off men for a year. One look from Amos had sent that resolution right out the window. She'd had a giggly, girlish crush on her brother's best friend. Nowhere in her wildest dreams had she imagined he would grow up into the walking fantasy that was Amos Kimmel as an adult. Or that his mere presence would make her blush.

Her little car puttered to life and she drove off the lot. Maybe next year, if things worked out, she could invest in new wheels. Something a little better for driving in the mountains.

Her cell rang as she stepped into her apartment and she smiled at Amos' name on the screen, then swiped to answer.

"Hey, cutie." His deep baritone pulled a soft sigh from her and Katie sank into her loveseat. She'd put her things away and get to making hot chocolate later. She had Amos on the phone.

"Hey, yourself. You on your way to the station?" She couldn't imagine how he kept the schedule he did and found time to sleep.

"Getting ready to be, yeah. Pulling a full weekend," he replied. "Plus gotta run out for a bit to Danny and Drea's wedding tomorrow."

"Someone mentioned that at work this week. Guess I didn't realize they weren't married."

People in town got starry-eyed when they talked about Danny Parsons and Drea Hidalgo. Listening to the stories was like hearing a fairy tale romance — Drea had moved away, but she'd come back ten years later and she and Danny still had feelings for each other. Oh yeah, she also solved the mystery of a bunch of fatal fires, leading to the arrest of CeeCee Cobb, one of her childhood best friends, and Robert Moore, who had taken over when Chief Lawson had retired. And Drea had saved Danny from being CeeCee's last victim.

Yeah, fairy tale. In a twisted sort of way.

"Everybody thinks like that about those two," Amos said. "I feel like I dropped the ball on our last date. What d'ya say I make that up to you? You available Thursday night?"

Yes! Katie forced herself to pause for a slow breath before she answered. "Lemme check my schedule, but I think so."

She knew her plans backwards and forwards, but still pulled up her calendar to check. "Afternoon Halloween carnival planning. I can be free for dinner. Sure. What did you have in mind?"

A low chuckle reverberated in her ears, sending her brain into *very* not family friendly thoughts.

"Do I need to have advance plans?" Something in his tone made Katie's skin prickle in anticipation.

When...no, how did Amos go from gawky teen to panty-melting hotness?

"I just need to know what to plan for," she replied. "What if you decide ax throwing sounds fun, but I'm dressed for dinner out?"

Amos let out a hearty laugh and Katie couldn't resist smiling if she tried. She hadn't had this much fun flirting with a man in forever.

"Not gonna lie, the idea of watching you throwing an ax while all dressed up has its appeal." His voice had dropped into a sexy rasp that made Katie want to climb into his lap and wrap herself around him. *If only he were here.*

"It's a weeknight. Nothing super dressy. Nothing super casual. Outside of that, you'll just have to trust me. Can you do that?"

"My ability to trust men is not exactly the stuff of legends," Katie said. "But in this case, I guess I can make an exception."

They laughed and talked for almost an hour until he had to report to the station. After they'd hung up, Katie kicked off her shoes and padded into the kitchen to make her cocoa, then stopped and headed for the shower instead. Along the way she made sure her favorite toy was plugged in and charging. She needed stress relief after the day she'd had, and talking to Amos had put her in a mood.

Chapter Ten

Amos
October 21, Saturday

Golden afternoon sunlight turned the surrounding trees into a blaze of red and orange. An unseasonably warm day had Amos sweating in his uniform as he sat in a too-small folding chair on the sprawling grass in front of the big oak tree.

Danny and Drea stood under the boughs of the tree as the minister pronounced them husband and wife. The small crowd gathered around cheered and clapped. He'd expected the entire town to be at this wedding, but Drea had said they decided to keep it small. Just friends and family. Which still meant a good size crowd. It felt a little strange to be in that group, considering that when they were teens, he had definitely not been in their crowd. Now…well, life was different, and it felt good.

Wilma Davis stood next to Drea, just like she always had in high school. CeeCee was missing, of course. He still couldn't wrap his head around that one. Next to Wilma was a tall woman with ebony skin and a headful of short, colorful braids. Unless he was very wrong, those two were more than just friends.

Most of the guests were in pairs. Usually, Amos didn't care one way or the other. In fact, he preferred being on his own. He'd learned not to date local women, and didn't bother bringing any out of town dates home. Too much gossip. It was better to keep things private. Besides, weddings weren't the kind of thing you brought a casual date to.

Still, he found himself wishing Katie was here with him. He joined the line of well-wishers waiting to congratulate the bride and groom. A couple of dates and endless texts and phone calls and somehow he was thinking of Katie as a fixture in his life. After a year of not seeing anyone, and many years of keeping his dating life strictly out of view of anyone in his hometown, it was strange, but he liked it.

The more he thought about it, the more right it felt. She felt right. He'd known that even before he'd realized who she was. That day on the playground, when he'd flirted with her. It was like something in him had known she was special.

The line moved and Amos stood in front of the happy couple. The shit he'd seen since Drea had come back would haunt him forever, but he would be eternally grateful for the way she'd pushed to get the town talking more seriously about funding the fire department.

For the first time in his life, Amos knew where he belonged. Now if he could just get his dad to understand that, and figure out how Katie fit into it all.

"Congratulations," he said and stuck out his hand to Danny. Drea laughed and pulled Amos into a hug with Danny joining in.

"Thanks." Danny clapped Amos on the shoulder. "When are we gonna get you out here for a trail ride?"

Amos shook his head. "I prefer my horses mechanical, thanks. Not too keen on climbing on top of a critter that has a mind of its own and outweighs me by a long shot."

They convinced him to stay for food and he followed the group heading across the grass to a giant white tent set against the tree line. Dinner meant playing politics, and he knew that was part of why Drea had insisted he stick around. She was constantly telling him that he was the face of the fire department. Whether he liked it or not.

The jury was still out on that front. He loved his job, but despite having been 'in charge' for a few years now, he wasn't one hundred percent sure he was the right person to run the show once they switched from volunteer to fully funded and official.

Still, he played his part. He talked with the town council members who were around and answered questions from folks who asked. When the band started up, he figured he'd escape, then Danny's mother tapped his shoulder.

"I need a dance partner." Annette Parsons held her hand out to him. The Parsons made regular donations to keep the volunteer fire department up and running, and Annette was vocal and tireless in her support of a funded department.

Amos smiled, stood and walked with her to the dance floor. "Perfect day for the wedding," he said, his brain stuck in small-talk mode. Annette tossed her head back and laughed.

"They deserve it." She nodded to where Drea and Danny stood in the middle of the floor, arms wrapped around each other, her head tucked under his chin. "How is Leah?"

The question took him by surprise. His older sister had briefly dated Jake Parsons back in school. That was years ago, but Annette had asked after Leah like there was something he was missing.

"She's doing fine, ma'am." He fell back on childhood habits. Short answers. Always with a 'ma'am' or a 'sir'. Annette smacked his arm.

"And how is Katie Tilman?"

Amos stumbled the next step and stammered as he tried to recover without stomping on Annette's toes. She maintained a warm smile as if there was nothing wrong in the world.

"Uhhh…" He felt like a kid who'd been caught with his hand in the cookie jar. "She's… I've been… It's…" He trailed off, unable to think of how to answer that question without inviting a whole lot more.

"About what I thought," Annette replied. "Y'all do make an adorable couple."

Amos was saved by the emergency chime on his phone. He excused himself from Annette and made his way off the floor to check the text. The message dumped about a gallon of adrenaline into his system.

An all-hands call. He quietly let Annette know what was going on and left. The address wasn't too far from Parsons Acres, so Amos called in that he was on the way and would meet up at the scene. Once on the main road, he stomped on the gas and rolled up right behind the fire crew.

"Stewart, what have we got?" Amos stripped off his jacket, swapped his shoes for boots and yanked on his turnouts. Shawn Dubois was already getting the rig set to start pumping water and one of the other crew was talking to a group of panicked looking teenagers.

"Bonfire got outta hand." Micah Stewart handed Amos his mask. "Some outbuildings caught. There's a hog pen down the hill but the wind's in our favor."

Amos scanned the field. The wind might be in their favor but with no rain in the past couple of weeks and the grass dry and brown, it was a tinderbox waiting to catch.

"Grab Brant and Del and get a break going. I'd rather face this thing up here where we've got room and keep it away from any more structures."

Stewart nodded and jogged off to grab his teammates. A shrill whistle from Shawn Dubois told Amos they were ready with the tanker, but he held back and watched the flames. With only the one truck available, they'd have to go at it smart. He joined Shawn at the truck.

"No saving that shed," Amos said. "Best we can hope with what we've got is to contain this mess and let it burn itself out. Ya think?"

His second in command agreed then pointed at the origin—a pile of pallets surrounded by flaming lumps that he was fairly certain were once furniture.

"I'm thinking this is a watch and see and tamp down any flare-ups. Not much else we can do unless we can run a hose down the hill."

Amos scanned the hillside, mentally calculating distance. "There ain't that much hose in the whole damn station. County not available?"

"Hell no. Never are. Rest of the crew's on the way in. ETA about twenty minutes."

That was good news at least. That meant the second truck. More water. More manpower. Most importantly, retardant.

"Let's get the rest of these guys on some backfires," Amos said. "See if we can chew up this fuel before this beast gets outta control."

The teams worked into the evening and managed to keep the fire contained. They used the last of the tanker water to douse the still-burning sofas and deal with a few small flare-ups.

"Yo! Amos!" Shawn stuck a hand in the air and beckoned Amos to where he was breaking up the remains of what looked like a recliner. Shawn held out a gloved hand. Glass and metal flashed under Amos' headlamp.

"A fucking bong."

Not surprising. Saturday night. Mild weather. A bunch of kids get together, throw some pallets in a pile. Probably douse it all with gasoline or some shit like that. Perfect set-up for hanging out and getting high.

Except shit went out of control. Whether it was someone goofing around, or the wind blowing wrong, or just bad luck, it didn't matter.

"It gets worse," Shawn said. "One of the crew found a ditched backpack. Had a baggie of pills and who knows what all else."

Shit.

"You call the police station or Drea?"

"You think I'm calling the chief of police on her wedding day? Do I look like I've got a death wish? Someone's on the way to collect that shit."

At least there was that. Amos sure as hell couldn't leave the backpack out here for anyone to find and he didn't want to be responsible for the damn thing.

"Kids still around or did they all bail?"

"Fuck man, they bailed a while ago," Shawn replied. "You figuring on having a talk with the parents or something?"

"Not the parents. One of the kids." Amos tipped his head toward the hog pen. "That's the Connour's. The short redhead girl in that group. Joanna Connour. Their oldest. Her daddy'd tan her hide if he knew she was out here with a buncha boys. Never mind that and the other shit." He hooked his finger at the pipe still in Shawn's hand.

Too many things pointed to this being a party spot. This wasn't the first time the kids had hung out here. Usually, that'd mean somebody pinching a few beers from their parents' fridge. Seemed like this group was up to much worse.

Well, fuck. Doesn't that just make my night.

Chapter Eleven

Katie
October 26, Thursday

A thin stream of fog curled up from the machine on the ground. Katie poked it with her toe, as if that would make it more productive.

"I don't get it." Cinda squatted down and checked the fluid chamber. Again. "It worked fine last year."

Katie was sure the fog machine had worked just fine. Before it was stored for a year with fluid still in it, in an out of the way shed that wasn't temperature controlled. She was surprised the thing even turned on. She let out a grumble and unplugged the box.

"Well, then we get a new one. Wasn't in the budget, but I'll make a donation of it if I have to." Hell, she'd drive halfway across the state to get one if that's what it took. The long drive might do her some good.

"Lemme make some calls," Cinda said. "The community college has a theater department that might let us borrow one. I'll text you if I find anything."

Cinda bundled up the fog unit and took off for her classroom, leaving Katie kicking herself for not checking on the thing earlier. The Halloween carnival was tomorrow night, and they had no fog machine.

Not that she should be surprised. Ever since Miles had shown back up almost three weeks before, weird little things kept going wrong. The latest just today when two of the older kids who were playing ghosts and ghouls in the haunted house were no-shows for the walk through. Which was a big deal, since things had changed significantly from their original plans.

She scrubbed a hand over her face. If she hurried, she'd have time for a shower before seeing Amos tonight. There was another thing that had seemed off. They hadn't seen each other in two weeks thanks to conflicting schedules. Though he was great on the phone, the last time they'd had dinner, he hadn't been his usual self. Instead, he'd been quiet and distant. And his goodnight kiss was a quick peck.

To top things off, she'd started her period early. Which probably explained her extreme grumpiness. She'd figured it was the stress of seeing Miles again. Not that she'd seen or heard from him since that day in the parking lot.

She shook herself and headed to her car. *Nope. Not thinking about that at all.*

Once home, she got herself into the shower and took as much time as she dared. She'd just finished dressing when Amos texted to say he was on the way.

At least that hadn't changed. He'd sent daily good morning and good night texts. And sometimes pictures of whatever soup or chili the guys at the fire department had made. That had gone a long way to keeping her from feeling like something had gone really wrong with them.

She laughed at herself.

As if we're a thing.

Two dates. A handful of kisses. She was making mountains out of molehills. Maybe hanging on to some residual crush on Amos and wishing it were true. Well, it was time to grow up.

Her door buzzer pulled her from that train of thought. When she opened the door and saw Amos she knew two things, right away.

Whatever she was feeling was way more than a childhood crush and if growing up meant not seeing him, she had about zero interest in that, thank you very much.

"You look amazing as always." Amos held out a bouquet of dahlias and roses that were so deep red they looked almost black. "I saw these and thought of you. Plus I figured I owed you an apology."

Katie stepped to the side and waved him in. She wasn't sure what would cause her neighbors to gossip more—Amos Kimmel standing on her front step with an armload of flowers, or him coming into her apartment. Either way, folks would talk.

"Thank you." She took the bundle from his hands and went to the tiny kitchen to find a pitcher or something to stick them into. "But why do you owe me an apology?"

Amos leaned against the kitchen doorway, looking very long and lean in snug-fitting black jeans and a black turtleneck sweater. He shrugged.

"I was a little distracted the last time we went out," he said. "I wasn't great company because of it. I figured I'd make it up to you, but then our schedules…" He trailed off with another shrug.

Katie gave up trying to find something more suitable and plopped the flowers into her water pitcher. She turned to Amos and stuck her hands on her hips.

"Huh. I guess you did have something to apologize for," she said.

No sooner were the words out of her mouth than Amos had his arms around her waist, holding her close against his body.

"I suppose I should get busy with that, then." He kissed her forehead. Then her neck and along the edge of her ear. His lips landed on hers with searing heat and Katie's toes curled. She silently cursed the early arrival of her monthly visitor. Amos picked his head up and scowled down at her.

"What's the matter?" His hands gripped her waist and held her at arms' distance while his gaze focused on her face. Everything about his look made her wonder if he'd been reading her mind.

As if.

"I'll have to settle for the flowers and time with you tonight," she said. As soon as she said it, she wanted to take it back. Maybe he hadn't meant it that way. Some guys didn't like when women admitted wanting sex. Most guys didn't want to hear anything about why a girl didn't want it, either. *Damned if you do, damned if you don't.*

"As much as I'd love more than that, I wasn't assuming it was on the table yet. I was thinking dinner and whatever you want after," he said. "We can have some cuddle time on the couch, or go for drinks somewhere, or a movie. Your call."

Katie rose to her tip toes and kissed him lightly. "I like the idea of cuddle time."

Amos linked his hand in hers. "Well, all right then. And uh…I have two sisters. I think I understand that code."

Katie whipped her head up to look at him. He raised his eyebrows as if to say 'what's wrong?'

"I'm not sure what to make of that." She ignored his confused expression and grabbed her purse as they headed for the door.

Once in his truck and on the road, Katie turned to Amos and smiled. "There's a second half of that code, you know."

He laid a hand on her knee, sending pleasant shivers up her spine. "Oh yeah? I must never have learned it. What is it? Or is it some deep, dark secret?"

She put her hand over his. *Yep, definitely way more than a crush.*

"You're not supposed to talk about it."

Amos threw his head back and laughed. "That sounds like my dad talking. He didn't want to hear any of that womanly stuff. Then Mom would read him the riot act because he had two girls and how the hell did he expect to live in a household with three women if he was gonna go around acting like that."

Oh, how Katie wished her mother had been more like that. No, to Jan Tilman, a period was a relief—it meant she wasn't pregnant. But it was also a secret thing you didn't discuss with anyone. She didn't even keep her tampons or pads in the bathroom, but instead hid them in her dresser drawer and insisted Katie do the same.

"Men don't want to see those things in the bathroom, sweetie," her mother had said.

Dorm life had been eye-opening to say the least.

Amos squeezed her knee. "Hey. Where'd you go there?"

How is he so in touch with my every little mood?

"Your family is very different than mine," she said. It seemed like the safest answer. Or at least the one that didn't require her to dissect her dysfunctional family dynamics. "What's had you so busy the past couple weeks?"

She knew he worked full time at the garage, and still managed to volunteer nearly forty hours a week at the fire department. The fact that he had any spare time at all was surprising, that he had energy to do anything with it was nothing short of miraculous.

"Dad's gotten slow, so my older sister and I have been picking up the slack," Amos said. "Plus I've got the Parsons' old Harvester in for a total rebuild. That's a chunk of work. And we've had a drop in volunteers at the department, so I'm pulling extra hours."

He twined his fingers around hers and brought her hand to his lips before planting a kiss on her knuckles.

"I know, we had a great start and kinda hit a wall, and I'm sorry about that." He rested their hands on his thigh. Katie fought the mad urge to trace the line of hard muscle she felt under her fingers. "I'll be at the Halloween thing tomorrow night. I can lend a hand doing whatever you need. We'll find time for each other."

His words sent butterflies fluttering through Katie's stomach. Amos said all the right things, but she'd been on the receiving end of pretty words before. They were never backed up by real action. Even his seeming attention to detail was classic love bombing.

Katie took a deep breath and pulled her thoughts off that dark path. She was a piece of work herself — one minute thinking how great Amos was, and the next thinking he was just like every toxic narcissist she'd ever dated. *And what does it say about me that every guy I've dated has been like that? Who's the common denominator here, huh?*

"You okay?" Amos turned off the main road and pulled into the lot at Oak Bridge. Katie had been to the place once — the school had hosted a back-to-school lunch for the staff at the start of the year. She'd heard it was the local hangout. She glanced at Amos, unsure how to answer his question.

"It's been a long day," she said. Her phone buzzed with an incoming text. "I'm sorry, I need to check this. Cinda was looking into something for the haunted house."

She thumbed open her phone to see a three-word text from Cinda. *We have fog!* That was one big weight off Katie's shoulders. The most immediately pressing one at that. She smiled and slid her phone into her purse before looking back to Amos and deciding on honesty.

"Ever since Miles showed up, everything has felt off. I know most of it isn't related — like the job stuff can't be, not really. But it's still a lot."

Amos wrapped both his huge hands around hers then leaned forward and kissed her gently. He was tender and sweet and the butterflies went soaring around again. When he broke the kiss, she wanted to pull him back to her for more.

"I have a bit of a shitty history with dating. I tend to find exactly the kind of person who is wrong for me. I know that's partly on me. And I don't know why I'm telling you this, but you asked."

A slow smile curled his lips at the corners. "I think you might be pleasantly surprised here. You wanna go in to eat, or would you rather avoid a crowd?"

Katie looked across a parking lot filled with cars and trucks. "This your normal hangout?"

Amos shrugged. "I come in occasionally. Brian and I play darts sometimes. Most of the time, I'm too busy so it's just take out. You didn't answer my question."

The last thing she wanted was a noisy place with too many people. She'd have to be in school-teacher mode the whole time. If Brian was there, it was a safe bet Lily was as well, and likely others from the horse crowd.

"I'm sorry," she said. "I guess I'm more tired than I thought, and…"

Amos squeezed her hands, then put the truck in gear and pulled out of the lot. "We can stop and get barbecue on the way back to your place. That work?"

Katie nodded. She'd been so looking forward to their time together, but this was not an ideal date. Still, Amos was being so nice.

They got pit beef sandwiches and made their way up her stairs. Inside, Amos took the food to the tiny kitchen.

"Go change into something soft and loose and comfy. I'll lay this stuff out on the table."

Katie didn't have the headspace or energy to argue. She headed to her closet, wondering what stage of narcissistic love this was, because this wasn't like any love bombing she'd ever experienced.

Amos

Amos watched Katie's retreating form and shook his head. She was clearly tired, and if experience with his sisters had taught him anything, likely uncomfortable, but for whatever reason unwilling to admit it or express a real need.

It was also pretty clear there was something bigger eating at her and he had every intention of figuring it out. It hadn't taken him too long to accept that he had a whole complicated pile of growing feelings for her.

He got the sandwiches and drinks on the table right as Katie returned in a pair of yoga pants and a long, loose T-shirt. *And she still looks hot as fuck.*

She settled into the chair across from him and gave him a smile. "I'm sorry…"

"You don't need to apologize," he said. "But I would like to know what's going on."

Her face clouded for an instant. Her eyes narrowed and he could almost see the gears turning in her head.

"After food," she replied. "I just realized I'm starving."

They kept things light during dinner. Amos told her about stuff going on at the fire department and Drea's continued push to get the town council on board with approving a paid fire department at the December meeting. That was easier than talking about the garage and home. She talked about her students and only briefly mentioned the Halloween carnival.

As they finished cleaning up after dinner, she leaned back against the counter with her hands braced behind her as if she was holding on for support.

"I know this is all going to sound silly," she said. "And I know I'm overthinking everything. Probably going way too far down the road, and maybe even going down the wrong road, but…"

She stopped and bit her lip. He wanted nothing more than to wrap her in his arms and kiss away the worry that creased her face. He was going too far down his own road with those thoughts. He planted himself against the counter opposite her. In the little kitchen, it meant their toes were nearly touching as they stood just a couple of feet apart.

"How about you stop giving me all the caveats and instead draw me a map of where you're at."

That got a chuckle out of her. Then she nodded and pulled in a long, slow breath.

"You of all people know what my family was like. I thought I'd gotten away from all that." She bit her lip again and stayed quiet so long he figured she'd clam up. She closed her eyes and tucked her head down until he couldn't see her face. When she looked back up a moment later, she was blinking as if fighting tears.

"When Miles showed up, it shook me. He said some of the right things, but I can't trust any of that. He's good at those games and I'm afraid he's the same old Miles."

Another slow breath. Her head bobbed as if she was counting. Hell, she may have been. Didn't he count silently to ten when he needed to hold his temper, or think before he opened his mouth?

"All of a sudden, I've got folks asking me about you. Assuming we're dating, I guess. Then Miles. Then someone asked about my father — apparently he was in town and they wanted to know if I'd talked to him. The Halloween thing was going great until we realized nothing had been properly stored last year, so it's a mess and some of it's broken."

Her hands slid from behind her and fluttered in the air. He didn't think she was aware of doing it. She just had that much pent-up tension.

"The text earlier was about the fog machine," she continued. "And the past couple weeks, we've had some of the older students who were supposed to be helping drop out. Some were no-shows for the run through. And all I could think was — it's because of Miles."

Her hands dropped to her sides and she sagged back against the counter, looking defeated.

"It's silly, I know. What could he have to do with any of that? But at the same time, he shows back up and you suddenly don't have any time. And I know that's not fair, but..." She shrugged and let out a bitter sounding laugh that made him very glad he hadn't told her about his own visit with her brother.

"The last time we did have time together, you're right, it felt like you were distant, so it just... I don't know...fed that fear, I guess. And I told you I have a history of bad choices when it comes to dating. And tonight was...with everything...it felt like... I'm sorry, I'm not making any sense."

Except she was making sense. Probably more than she realized. He could think of any number of reasons teenagers would duck out on the Halloween carnival — Miles being back and possibly peddling drugs again was one of many possibilities.

Katie had been away long enough that she wasn't used to small-town life and the gossip chain. Not much he could do about either of those things, but there was one thing he could address.

"So, you're seeing me run hot and cold," he said. "All interested and intense. Then Miles shows up and I back off. Then tonight, it's back to hot again. I think I understand."

The expression on her face was one of long suffering. Whatever they might be in the end, he was determined to do at least one thing—show her what caring really meant.

"The rest of it—Miles, the kids, work, small-town talk—it's a lot and it's gotta be pulling you in all different directions. If you wanna talk about it, I'm here."

He took the half step to close the distance between them, then caught her hands in his and pulled her into his arms.

"You and me? This right here?" She let out a sigh as he tightened his arms and that tiny sound cut deep into his soul. *Yep, far enough down that road there's no turning back.* "You'll get no argument from me. The last few weeks have been a shit show, and I'm sorry. As for folks asking about us…"

He pulled back enough to lay a finger under her chin and tip her face up so he could see her eyes.

"They're gonna talk. Let 'em. Only thing that matters is you and me. I like you, I like spending time with you, and when you're ready and able, I wanna do a whole hell of a lot more than cuddle on the couch. So…what do you wanna call that?"

Katie wrapped her arms around his waist and rested her head on his chest. She felt so good and so right in his arms.

"I'd call that getting to know each other and seeing where things go," she said. "C'mon, let's go pick a show to watch."

Amos discovered Katie liked the same horror shows he did, and shared his twisted sense of humor. He also discovered that he could spend hours kissing her. Then her hand slid up his thigh until her fingers grazed his cock and he hissed in a sharp breath of air.

"Didn't think we were going there tonight." He managed to keep his voice steady even as her fingers were doing delicious things that made him want to drag her to bed.

"Well, I'm not, but what about you?"

Oh hell, she's been fed that line of shit.

"Ladies first," he said. "Always."

He laid his hand over hers then pulled her into his lap. He cupped her face in his hand and kissed her softly.

"You're gonna tell me all the things that went through your head when you first saw me at the school, then I'm going to explore every inch of your amazing body and see what it takes to give you so many orgasms you're begging me to stop."

Her cheeks flared with color and she wiggled in his lap, sending currents of pleasure straight to his throbbing cock. That part of him would have to wait.

"Like that idea, do you?"

Katie nodded and her cheeks darkened even more.

"We'll worry about me after that. Not before. Deal?"

"I can live with that," she replied. "If you're sure."

He clamped his mouth down to keep from laughing. Yeah, it was tempting to get a hand job or head, but he always felt like a selfish shit after and he wouldn't do that to Katie.

Chapter Twelve

Katie
October 27, Friday

Fog poured out from the hallway doors, spilling over the carved pumpkins lining the walk and Katie smiled. After finding much of the old decor ruined, they'd scrambled to come up with a new plan. Taking a cue from the corn maze she and Amos had been in, Katie suggested keeping the theme basic—haunted classrooms, decorated for the season.

With an hour to go before the haunted house opened for the younger kids, it was time to do a walk through to make sure all the effects were up and working. She glanced at Cinda and Lily.

"You ready?" The other two nodded and they marched through the double doors like they were going into battle. Lily's boyfriend Brian and a bunch of the crew from Parsons Acres had salvaged what they could of the walls and with Katie's suggestions, created a simple maze that felt easy when it was lit, but in flickering low lights and streaming fog was eerie and difficult.

The classrooms turned into nightmare images, stretched longer than they should, with desks and chairs on the ceilings and walls. Carefully placed mirrors made the spaces even more confusing. Thunder and lightning, strange sounds like nails on a chalkboard and a ticking clock added a disorienting feeling. Luckily, the animatronics had been stored well, so there were still the motion-activated effects—a bat that flew overhead, a skeleton that popped out of the wall, and Katie's favorite, the creepy hand that reached out from behind a partially closed storage closet door.

"Once we add the cast, this is going to be amazing," Cinda said as they got near the end. "We might want to leave the lights up for the younger kids."

Lily agreed, but Katie shook her head. "I'm thinking keep them dim. Not dark, just dim. We don't turn on any of the scary or flashy lights, and we have the parent helpers with flashlights. The younger ones are going in escorted groups anyway."

Lily stopped as she was about to open the doors. "You are an evil genius and that's brilliant."

"Do we leave the fog on?" Cinda pointed at one of the little black boxes on loan from the local college. "I kinda like it, but would it be too scary?"

They stepped out into the late afternoon sunshine. It had been a gorgeous day, but Katie had been inside for much of it, helping the crew of volunteers transform the space.

"I think a little fog would be good," Lily replied. "Not too much, but we can keep it low, right?"

Cinda pulled up something on her phone. "Lemme make sure. These can do a lot more than the old one. It looks like we can set them to like give puffs of fog at intervals, or just blow fog constantly."

"Puffs might be great for the start," Katie said. "The idea is to get incrementally more scary as the night goes on, so that gives us room to ramp up. For now, I'm starving and need to stuff my face because I'm not going to have a chance the rest of the night."

A hand holding a wrapped hamburger crossed into her vision, making Katie wonder if she was hallucinating. Then she heard the laugh. *Amos.*

"Gotcha covered," he said. "There's fries, too. And a chocolate-peanut butter shake."

"Well, now I'm hungry and want a shake," Cinda said. She waved at them and walked toward the food. Lily winked and headed for the front of the school, presumably to find Brian and Kyle.

"How did you manage to time that so well?"

"Stewart," Amos replied as they walked to the cafeteria to find seats. "He pointed out when you went in and told me about how long a quick walk through takes. Figured y'all would take a little longer since you were looking at stuff."

Katie bit into her burger and her eyes almost rolled back. *Heaven. Or maybe I'm just that hungry.*

Either way, she didn't care. Nor did she care about the teachers and staff, or parent helpers who saw her and Amos sitting together. After last night, she still didn't know what they were, or weren't, but she knew that was their business and she didn't have to worry about what anyone else thought.

She might not always be so sanguine about it, but for now, she was able to sit and laugh and enjoy her food with the best-looking guy on campus.

When they were finished, Amos reached across the table and snagged her hand. "I'm gonna give Stewart a break for a bit so he can get some food. Figured you'd be super busy with the little kids. Once he gets back, I'm all yours if you need an extra hand or anything."

Katie's chest tightened and a lump rose in her throat. She shook her head and stuffed a fry in her mouth. "You're a good man. Thank you."

That warm feeling carried her through the first set of students through the haunted house, and was buoyed by the happy squeals of the children and the praise from their parents.

Several younger children came through with older siblings instead of parents, and Katie loved seeing the older ones holding their hands and helping them when they got a little scared.

Sadly, the happy vibes didn't last when she came out and found Cinda waiting outside the classroom where the cast was supposed to gather and get into makeup and costume.

"We have two more no-shows," Cinda said. "And I think a couple of the kids are... I don't know...drunk or high or something."

Well, shit. They still had plenty of cast, though it would mean fewer breaks for everyone. She'd cut back how many were in the first hour so they could ramp up numbers as they went. But having students who might be impaired, that was a problem.

"Do we call the principal? Or what?" It wasn't Katie's first rodeo with students using drugs—she'd taught in the inner city where it was often much older siblings picking the younger students up. And those siblings were sometimes using something. They'd had to get police and child services involved more than once. She doubted that was the right choice here.

"Will you go check everyone out? Tell me if I'm wrong? I mean, I want to be wrong." Cinda looked like she was about to wring her hands. Her eyes were pleading and her mouth was drawn into a tight worry line.

"Yeah, gimme a minute. I'll be right back."

She pushed into the classroom and found the expected chaos of a half dozen parents all trying to sort out who was wearing what and who needed what makeup for a dozen and a half teens, most of whom were sitting with their phones in their hands. Typical teens, as far as Katie was concerned.

A couple of the students were actively helping, lining up costume pieces and laying out makeup. Then Katie spotted the ones Cinda must have been talking about. A pair of boys were goofing around with the giant scythe she'd decided not to use. For just this reason—she didn't know too many teenage boys who could resist horsing around.

Sure enough, one of them swung the thing in a wide ark and knocked over a folding chair. Luckily, the younger girl who had been sitting in it had just vacated the seat. Probably to get away from those two.

Katie put on her stern teacher face, marched over and grabbed the staff as the dark-haired boy prepared for another swing.

"Time to put this away," she said as she gave a firm tug. The boy did not let go. "You've already knocked over a chair. Swinging a six-foot staff around indoors is not cool. Let go, I'll put it away, and you two can get into costume."

Instead of letting go, the boy — young man, really — pulled back, almost taking Katie off balance. He and his friend both laughed. Whether Cinda was right and they were drunk or high didn't matter. They did not need to be in the haunted house if they were going to act up like this. Judging by the dilated pupils on the red-haired boy, who had so far remained quiet and at least tried to look contrite, they were on something.

"Okay, I'm going to make this simple — go home. Now."

The dark-haired boy laughed. "We're just having fun. Why are you so uptight?"

Oh, the standard defense when called on something — don't accept responsibility. Blame it on the other person. Yay. They're starting young.

"This is a school-sponsored event for the elementary students. If you cannot behave appropriately, you are not welcome to participate. So I'll say it again. Go home. Now."

The boy gave a hard yank on the staff. This time, Katie was prepared and didn't budge. He opened his mouth, but the red-haired boy cleared his throat.

"Dude." He nodded behind Katie.

The other boy dropped his end of the staff with a clatter. "Stupid bullshit baby thing anyway. Let's get the fuck outta here."

Katie turned as they passed, determined to keep them in her sights. The sight of Amos staring at the troublemakers did funny things to her heart. He stood a few feet behind her, legs braced wide, arms crossed over his chest and a deep scowl on his face as he turned his head to watch the boys leaving. As soon as they were out the door, he crossed to Katie.

"The high school resource officer is outside," he said. "His kid goes here and he's on my crew. He and I were talking when Cinda came to tell me what was going on. She got worried when you took more than a minute. You okay?"

Katie let out a nervous laugh. Sometimes small towns could be good things.

"Yeah, been through this shit before. Lemme check on everyone here."

One of the parents had already moved the other students to the far side of the room. Now they were marshaling the team into their costumes and moving ahead as if nothing had happened. Katie touched base with the woman who seemed to be in charge then she grabbed Amos and dragged him to her classroom.

Part of her wanted to be angry at him for barging in and acting like the savior. Part of her wanted to thank him. She didn't know which to give in to.

"First off, thanks for the help there." She closed her classroom door and paced, trying to work off the nervous energy. "Second, I could have handled that, but it was nice to have back up."

Amos put a hand on her shoulder, stopping her in her tracks. "I know you could have. I also know those two have been problems in the past. Jayce, the one who was swinging the scythe, he's like your brother. Popular with the right crowd. Troublemaker. Getting into things he has no business getting into. His friend, Kev, he's a lot like I was—he's just along for the ride."

Katie heaved a sigh. "Why does nobody tell me these things?"

Amos shrugged, but Katie didn't need an answer. She knew. It was the way things were. Folks would talk. The gossip was there. But unless there was something particularly juicy or nasty, it was small-town talk and she ignored it. Maybe she shouldn't.

"What's the rest of your night like?" Amos still had a hand on her shoulder, and Katie was tempted to lean into him for support. She felt like she needed it after that.

"I'm loosely on duty for the haunted house the whole night," she replied. "Keeping things running, making sure the next layers go into place on time. Not anything hard, just busy. Why?"

"Technically, I'm sort of on duty, but Stewart has most of it. So what do you need me to do?"

Katie had planned to station herself at the end of the walk leading up to the haunted house. That way she could count the folks going in, and hold groups back if it started to get too crowded. The effects were definitely better if there weren't too many people inside at once. Plus it felt scarier when you couldn't see someone right in front of you. While the younger students went through with chaperones, the older ones could do it on their own if they wanted.

Amos could sit at the table with her and help with that. She'd heard the last hour could get rowdy as many of the older kids were wound up, and some had older siblings. After the bit with Jayce and Kev, she wouldn't mind a hand. The question was, did she want to have everyone at the carnival see her and Amos together like that? Once again, Katie didn't need to ask herself the question.

"Wanna man the table with me?"

The rest of the night went off without a hitch. They got the cast loaded in and set all the effects, and every hour, the lights got a little dimmer and the fog got a little thicker. And the ghosts and ghouls went from silently standing in one place to roaming the halls with an occasional moan or groan to actively jumping out to scare people.

The screams, squeals and gales of laughter echoing up every time the doors opened told Katie what she needed to know. It was a success.

Amos hung around till the end. He even rolled up his sleeves and helped take down all the outside decorations and unplug all the effects.

"We'll take down the maze tomorrow," Katie said. "Thanks for your help. All of it."

He took her hand and pulled her into a quiet corner of the now-deserted space. "My pleasure."

He leaned down and brushed his lips against hers. Heat bloomed in an instant and Katie rose on her toes to wrap her arms around his neck. She pulled back before the temptation for more got any stronger. This was an elementary school, and it was her workplace.

"I'm free tomorrow afternoon," he said. "If you're not done, I can come help. If you are, wanna grab an early dinner? I have work at the garage in the morning and I'm on rotation at the fire department that night. Every night till the first."

She wasn't about to complain about more time with Amos. Then his words registered.

"Wait, you're working Halloween night? That sucks."

"Yeah," he replied. "We try to make sure the guys with kids get certain days off."

"Wow, you really look out for each other," she replied. "Tomorrow sounds great. Now let's get out of here before we get in trouble."

He leaned down and kissed her again, quick and hard. "Worried about getting caught?"

She laughed and pulled him along the hall. "Maybe a little. But don't stop."

Chapter Thirteen

Amos
October 31, Tuesday

Amos looked down at the worst poker hand that ever existed. He could fold or bluff. He was two mini Milky Way bars in and had a decent stash of candy. He could take the loss of a fold. Bluffing meant risking more. He'd have to give up the Snickers.

Everybody's phones buzzed at the same time. Incoming call. Amos thumbed his screen.

"We've got a fire at a trailer park in West Creek," he said. "County guys are too far out. Let's roll."

The entire team burst into action. Amos jumped into the truck and pulled out as soon as everyone was secure.

"You need GPS?" Micah Stewart was typing the address into the unit.

"Go ahead, but I know where I'm going."

It may have been years since he'd been there, but the second location came through, he could picture the faded green trailer where the Tilmans had lived when he and Miles went to school together. He'd spent enough hours hanging out there. He didn't know if Carl Tilman still lived there or not. He tried not to think about the man.

They pulled into the rundown park and Amos breathed a little easier when he saw it wasn't the Tilmans' old trailer, but the one right across the street. Wasn't uncommon to get wrong unit numbers in the trailer parks.

There wasn't a lot to do here. The trailer was fully engulfed already so putting it out wasn't an option. The best they could do was keep it from spreading. Normally, he'd be thinking about minimizing damage, but the broken glass and twisted siding painted a grim picture. This was an explosion. There was nothing to save. Luckily, the next lot over was empty, or they'd have a bigger problem on their hands.

Amos dropped his mask down and scanned the scene, looking for an exterior propane tank or any other major combustibles. The last thing they needed was for more shit to go boom. He found the tank and disconnected it then joined the team getting the blaze under control.

It was late enough that most of the trick or treaters were already done for the night, but a crowd still gathered, many of them in costume, making the whole thing seem unreal.

With the big truck pumping from multiple hoses, it didn't take long to get the flames out. One of the trailer walls collapsed under the spray of water and Amos shut his hose down. They kept one small hose going to deal with flare-ups while he and Stewart took a preliminary look.

"Shit." Amos shoved his mask back and spat on the ground. "Thought the air smelled off."

Even with the fire and water damage, the array of containers and tubes, a small propane tank and other paraphernalia combined with the blown-out glass said it all.

"Fucking meth lab," Amos said. "Cooking on Halloween, when there's likely to be kids around. That's some class-A shit right there."

Flashing red and blue lights announced the arrival of the police. Drea hoped out of the beat-up old Bronco, still twisting her hair into a tight bun.

"Sorry, I was already asleep and my one officer had to take his kid to the hospital." She walked the perimeter and came back shaking her head.

"Wanna bet there's no witnesses and nobody knows who owns the place, who lives here, or who comes and goes?"

Amos arched an eyebrow at her. "No bet. You could've just called. No need to be here in person for this. You know damn good and well Grace will be here to get photos of the scene, like she always..."

He stopped as his kid sister pulled up. Grace at least had the sense to come check in with Drea before she went stomping into a scene. She'd learned that lesson when she was taking pictures of the fires earlier in the year. Amos shuddered at the memory. He'd be happy to never see a dead body again in his life.

"You want me to get in there and take pictures? Anything you don't want me to do or touch?"

Drea shrugged. "It's not like any forensic evidence that might have survived all this is going to do much good. Document what you can see, but don't go in the building until fire clears it. You know the drill. And thanks."

She turned back to Amos and nodded toward the green trailer. "Tilman and son seem to be paying an undue amount of attention over there. I'll do my job—ask all the questions, but you used to be part of that crowd. Any chance they'd still talk to you?"

Amos raised his hands in a 'who knows' move. "Probably not. It's no secret police and fire have been much closer since you took over. But, I can be nice, go say hi and act like the concerned friend. See if it gets me anywhere."

Drea nodded, curt and unpleasant, as if he'd said something wrong. A bit of show for anyone watching. "Thanks. I owe you on that one." She turned away and all but stomped over to the closest group of people.

Amos checked with his team and took stock of the still-steaming building—didn't look like they'd have any flare-ups, but he wasn't willing to risk that yet. The guys could get in and check for hot spots in a bit. He did all his usual routines, then glanced up to see Carl and Miles Tilman still watching, their eyes glued to the chief of police talking to their neighbors.

Amos wandered over.

"Miles," he greeted. "Mr. Tilman. Sorry about your neighbor's place. That's gotta be rough. Anyone live there?"

He knew the answer. Just like he knew most of the smaller places in the back of the park were occupied by people who worked for Carl and Dwight. You could get a place for cheap rent, but it would cost you in other ways.

Katie had said Miles told her he didn't want to go back and live with their dad. He had been planning to go to Logan, or find someplace else. At least, that's what he'd said to his sister. Yet here he was with Carl, and dressed like he'd been at home — sweatpants and slippers. Not exactly the kind of thing you wore outside the house.

"Nah," Carl replied, his voice calm and his face placid. "Been vacant awhile. Prolly kids I' up to things they oughtn't."

Miles didn't have his father's mellow expression. He stared at the burnt-out trailer like it was a dog that had bit him. If Carl and Dwight were up to their usual tricks, it may well have been just that. If Miles was back with his dad, and was looking at the burned-up lab with such interest, maybe he'd been the one doing the cooking.

Those were thoughts that were way above his pay grade, but Drea had asked him to try. He couldn't be sure if it was the lingering chemicals in the air, or if Miles smelled slightly of ammonia.

"Look, not tryin' to be an asshole, and I know that one is gonna get around to asking questions." Amos waved his hand toward where Drea was talking with other witnesses. *Or non-witnesses.* "I gotta fill out my report, so I gotta ask if you saw anyone go in there? There gonna be bodies? I mean, that'd be a shit show."

He fell back into the shorthand speech pattern he and Miles used in school. Laidback, unaffected and fuck who had time for complete sentences or compassion.

Old man Tilman rolled his eyes, shook his head and went back inside. Miles darted his eyes to the side and Amos forced himself to not follow his gaze. He had a feeling he knew what was up. He'd seen Dwight Phelps lurking at the edge of the crowd.

"Place was empty," Miles said. "Not gonna find any bodies. There were kids around earlier, yeah, but guess they moved on. I dunno. Heard a car leave anyway. That had to be before the ex...uhh...fire."

Amos took the opportunity to look around as if he was regarding the burned-out structure and not catching the sight of Dwight Phelps as he crossed the Tilmans' driveway and went into the trailer without so much as a knock.

"Guess you got all you need for a report," Miles said. He turned for the trailer. Maybe he'd seen Phelps going in as well, or he expected it. Who knew?

"Hang on," Amos called out, not sure whether Miles would respond and unsure what he planned to do if he did. He scrambled for something to say, anything that might help. "You know how to reach me, man. If you need anything."

Miles' face softened for about half a second, then the hard look came shuttering down. "I figured you for a closed door, man. What gives?"

Amos shrugged. He didn't want to go down this path, but Drea had a point. There was a slim chance he could get information that she couldn't. Slim was being too kind, but he had to try. Years ago, Chief Lawson had told him he had an opportunity to make a change and be someone different. He'd taken that to heart. It was one of the driving reasons behind him joining the fire department.

"Time and a place for everything," Amos replied. "I've made my peace with shit. My old man? Not so much."

Miles clapped Amos on the shoulder. "I get that. Thanks."

That was as close to an acknowledgment of anything that Amos would get from his old friend. He made his way back to the truck, careful to avoid Drea. The last thing he needed was for any of the men in that trailer to see him go straight to the chief of police after talking to Miles.

Instead, he checked with his team and started to pack everything in. When he had a moment, he dropped Drea a text.

They claim the place was empty. Said there were kids partying there earlier – which we know is BS. Miles assured me there'd be no bodies. Not sure he wasn't the one doing the cooking. I am sure he knows something but isn't talking.

He hit send and stuffed his phone away. He tried to find some shred of remorse for ratting on his friend – *former friend* – but there was none. Amos was working to build Orchard Creek up and make it better, stronger and healthier. People like Dwight and the Tilman men were doing just the opposite.

He swiped a hand over his face and pulled his phone out again. He had to text Katie. Not telling her that her brother had visited him in the garage was one thing. This was something entirely different. She'd hear about the fire. She'd know the address. She'd know he was working. He couldn't outright lie to her.

He thumbed his phone and typed a message.

If you're up, can I call you in about 15? If not, call me first thing when you wake up.

He hesitated before hitting send. That message could send her into a panic, but he didn't want to say too much, and he wanted to talk to her before anyone else did. His phone pinged twice. Drea sent a thumbs-up. Katie's message was only slightly longer.

I'm up. You OK?

He sent a quick reply to Katie then put his phone away until they got back to the station and he could find a place where there was some privacy so he could call her and tell her that Miles was living with their dad. A trailer across from theirs had burned down, and unless Amos was very wrong, Miles had been the one cooking meth.

It had been a long time since he'd been faced with such a powerful reminder of how close he'd come to being trapped in that life. Katie had been an innocent victim of her family's activities, and now he wanted nothing more than to shield her from further harm.

Fuck, this is not going to be an easy call.

Chapter Fourteen

Katie
November 4, Saturday

The smell of fall was in the air — crisp leaves, wood fires and apples. Katie pulled up at Perry's Orchard intent on picking up a bunch of late season apples for pies. She came to an abrupt halt when she saw her brother stacking small baskets brimming with bright green fruit.

Every instinct told her to get back in her car and leave before he saw her. Instead, she stood rooted to the spot, trying to process the fact that Miles was working at the orchard.

"Hey, sis!" Miles waved a hand in the air. "I know what you're here for. Your pies were always the best."

Katie swallowed hard. Maybe Miles had been telling her the truth and he was clean and sober. She flashed on the phone call with Amos just four days ago. None of it made any sense. She stuffed her keys in her jacket pocket and walked down the gravel drive to the farm stand.

"You're working here?" Nothing like stating the obvious. Still, she couldn't think of anything else to say.

"Job's a job, y'know," Miles replied. "The Perrys are good folk and not too many people are willing to help out when you've got…well…my kinda history."

This wasn't the first time she'd seen Miles act contrite. He was an expert at it, in fact. If you pushed back, he'd act hurt, then indignant. Eventually, he'd drop the act and the real Miles would come out. But only if you dug deep enough.

"Long way to drive out every day from Logan, isn't it?"

Safe bet he wouldn't tell her he was staying with their dad. He'd come up with some semi-believable story.

"Couldn't afford a place," he replied. "Wound up staying with the old man till I could get on my feet again. Landed the job here two weeks ago and been saving up. Place just opened up, moving in tomorrow, actually."

Well, that was surprising.

"At the trailer park?"

It was a straight question and even Miles would be hard pressed to not answer it directly. Any place he could afford there meant only one thing — he was back to his old ways.

"Nah," Miles said. "Told ya, I'm trying to avoid that life. I just crash at Dad's. I don't hang around there. I work here as many hours as I can get. The Talbots had to put her mama in a home. Took her there on the first. Had to clean and repaint, I guess. So…"

He shrugged and for a moment she had a flash of her brother as a young teen, when they'd still been friends. Before he'd become too cool for hanging out with his kid sister. The thought she might get her brother back gave Katie the warm fuzzies. Then she shook herself. She knew better than to hope like that.

Nothing in her family had ever worked out that way. As a child, she'd been naive enough to believe things could change. People could change. Now she knew better. But hope was a hard thing to kill.

"I'm glad you're finding your way," she said. And she meant it. She wanted Miles to succeed, but not at the cost of her happiness and wellbeing.

His smile seemed genuine and even lit his eyes in a way she thought had long ago been lost.

"Thanks," he said, and his voice was a little rough. "So, uh...how many apples you want?"

She took a bushel and promised to bring him a hand pie. She also picked up fresh cider for her class and a small jug of their hard cider for her and Amos with dinner tomorrow. She planned to cook.

Miles even picked up the basket of apples and carried them to her car. Though she supposed that was his job.

"I hear you an' Amos been sparkin'," he said as he hefted the basket into her trunk.

The old term sounded odd coming from her brother, but still made Katie's cheeks heat. She could deny it, but Miles would never believe her. After the Halloween carnival, no one would.

"We've gone out a few times," she replied. "Seeing where things go."

Miles nodded and she braced herself for whatever was about to come out of his mouth. It could be sarcastic. It could be hurtful.

"My kid sister and my best friend. Who'da thunk it," he said. Then he patted her shoulder and turned to the folks who'd just pulled up in a beat-up old minivan. "Hey, y'all!"

Katie slid behind the wheel and watched in shock as Miles turned on the charm. He was all smiles and jokes with the young children the couple had with them.

Maybe he really had changed. But she wasn't getting her hopes up.

Back at home, she put the ciders away and started on her pie crusts. She'd peel and slice the apples while the crusts chilled. She'd learned to cook out of enlightened self-interest. During childhood, food might mean the same soup or stew for a week or more. Lunches were at the school, if there was money in the account, and if breakfast existed, it was whatever you could scrounge.

Once they'd moved, within a month, Katie had realized her mother was a haphazard cook at best and even worse at money management and keeping groceries in the house. So, she'd taken over. She'd demand money from her mother every time there was a paycheck and she'd squirrel it away, only buying a few days' worth of groceries at a time. Otherwise, Miles would get the munchies and eat everything, or her mother would decide to be domestic and cook a huge pile of food — most of which had to be thrown out because she'd ruined it somehow.

Katie had learned to bake after getting a bunch of flour, sugar, eggs and piles upon piles of bananas in a commodities box. They'd had banana bread for weeks, to the point where just the smell of it still made Katie want to vomit.

The kitchen was the one place at home where she'd been able to feel in control. After she'd moved out on her own, it had become her place of joy and relaxation after a hard day. And tomorrow, she'd get to share that with Amos.

Chapter Fifteen

Amos
November 5, Sunday

The bell dinged, indicating someone had driven into the service lane for the main garage. Amos pulled his head out of the Harvester's engine compartment and looked across the lot. Just Drea in the police Bronco. Probably coming by to arrange an oil change or something. Leah could handle that. He bent his head back to the old truck and cranked his music louder.

He'd had a few talks with the police chief after the trailer park fire. As far as he was concerned, his part in that mess was done.

"Leah told me I'd find you out here." Drea's voice was raised over the music and Amos swore. He straightened up and wiped his hands.

"You here about the Bronco, or the Harvester?" He didn't think her visit was for either, but it was worth a shot. She gave a short laugh that told him he was right.

"That Bronco needs way more than an oil change, but I'll donate a new car before I ask the town for money for it. There's things we need more." She didn't have to say what they both were thinking—like a funded fire department. They were overdue. Not that a new police car would break that budget, but he appreciated her making that sacrifice.

"You were spot on," she said. "That fire was a meth lab."

Big surprise. Amos managed to keep himself from rolling his eyes. The only reasons she could have for talking to him about it weren't good as far as he was concerned.

"There's been some problems at the high school," Drea said. "Starting about a month ago. I wouldn't think too much about kids skipping school, but there've been car break-ins, some thefts and a major jump in drug problems."

Nope, nothing good at all. Somewhere in the back of his mind came his mother's voice admonishing him to offer her a place to sit or at least see if she wanted a bottle of water. This was Drea Hidalgo—well, Drea Parsons now—they were friends. They were on the same team. He pulled a couple of work stools out.

"Sounds like this may take a minute," he said. "Have a seat."

The mini fridge was out of water and the last thing he wanted to do was head to the house where his dad would start asking questions about why the police chief was sitting in the garage jawing.

Drea dropped to the stool and sighed. "I'm stepping outside the bounds a little here, but you and I have always gotten along well and Chief Lawson sings your praises. Since you're currently dating Katie Tilman and used to be in Miles' crowd, that makes you my best choice."

Amos did not like the sound of any of that. Not one bit. He definitely didn't like the idea of involving Katie. Especially after she'd expressed some hope that her brother was turning his life around. He took in a deep breath. Drea wouldn't be coming to him with half-formed theories, though. If she was here, there was good reason for it.

"What did you have in mind?"

He didn't give it a second thought. He knew he was doing the right thing. Better to help solve the problem before it got any bigger. Just like it would be better to cause Katie the pain of it all now rather than later, after she'd let down her guard completely.

"I'm too new as the police chief to have developed any real connections," she said. "Doesn't help that I brought a whole team of federal agents around to deal with those fires earlier this year."

She was right there. While most folks understood and believed she'd done the right thing, there were some who didn't want the government around in any form. Even if they were actually helping.

"I need someone who Miles might talk to," she continued. "It's a long shot, I know, but it's that or wait for him to fuck up and frankly, a damn meth lab exploding in a crowded trailer park on Halloween was bad enough. I don't want to know what could happen next."

She didn't need to remind him of that night. He'd looked around the gathered crowd and seen the families with young children. They'd gotten lucky. Had there been a trailer next to the one that blew, or had the wind shifted the other way, things could have been much worse.

"I doubt Miles will talk to me," Amos replied. "It's been too long and that crowd will see me as part of…" He spread his arms and shrugged. The fire department was a gray area – he wore a uniform and was working with Drea to make the department paid instead of volunteer. That put him on the side of 'the government' as far as folks were concerned.

"He might not," Drea agreed. "Still, even talking to him a little bit, or being around him may give me more than I've got to go on right now."

She leaned forward, bracing her elbows on her knees. "You know the history there. You were caught up in it for a while. Chief Lawson did the best he could. He managed to find ways to give a few kids a chance to make something of themselves."

Yeah, like me. Amos couldn't discount that. Every good thing he had in his life right now was because the old chief had believed in him.

"He did at least keep the problem from growing, but Raymond…" She stopped and shook her head.

"Raymond was about as useless as they come," he replied. "No reason to sugarcoat that fact. So you're hoping to fix the whole thing?"

She laughed, short and bitter sounding. "There's no fixing the whole thing. Poverty, lack of opportunity and desperation will always be a factor in rural areas like this. That doesn't mean we should ignore it."

Amos knew the plan – the Parsons were doing new things at the ranch, creating more jobs and boosting the local economy. The high school had started a vocational tech program that placed senior students into apprenticeships that equipped them for decent jobs after graduation. The medical center had recently expanded and businesses were thriving.

Orchard Creek was growing. The fact that they could afford a paid fire department was testament to that, and he served to benefit from it.

None of that would work very well if there was a rampant, and growing, drug culture.

"Look, I don't want to know all the details, but I'll try," he said. He blew out a heavy sigh. "I don't know how much it'll help but you're right. We need to do something, and I'd rather be a part of the solution."

Drea rose and stuck out her hand. Amos shook on reflex. He'd barely known her in high school. She'd been two years ahead and her entire world had been horses and Danny Parsons. Not necessarily in that order. He'd gotten to know her when she came back, and found she was smart, no-nonsense and determined to do something good for her hometown.

"And don't worry about the Harvester," she said as she turned to leave. "Whatever it takes. However long it takes. It's part of the landscape at Parsons Acres and even I'll admit a soft spot for the old thing. Thanks for taking care of it."

Amos shared her sentiment there. The red truck had always been around. There were pictures of parades from way before he was born and that truck was there, decked out in flowers, leading the way.

"My pleasure," he replied, and meant it. Sure, it might be a pain in the ass, but he loved fixing things, and the old truck was a challenge. Once Drea left, he decided to call it a day. He cleaned up the work space and put his tools away then headed toward the main garage to check in with Leah before he went home to shower.

Katie was making dinner tonight then they planned on watching a movie. Or they'd see what else came up.

The thought of Katie in his arms sent his brain straight into the gutter and he turned for his truck instead. No way was he traipsing into the shop sporting a hard on. He texted his sister instead then started his truck and got home as fast as possible.

He wanted to keep his brain focused on time with Katie and not about Drea and Miles and the rest of the shit she'd brought up. By the time he was out of the shower, he had their conversation safely tucked away for the night, and when got to Katie's, the only thing on his mind was kissing her.

The smell of something delicious met him about halfway up her stairs, then she opened the door and Amos stopped dead in his tracks. Katie stood there in a black polka dot dress that looked straight out of a pinup dream with a crisp white apron tied on top. Her hair hung loose, held off her face by a headband that matched her dress. Whatever circuits were left in his brain shorted out at the red lips and matching heels.

Amos made the rest of the stairs in two steps, then he was in the door with his arms around her tiny waist. He bent his head to kiss her but stopped. She pouted, but he pulled back.

"I don't want to ruin your lipstick," he said. "You look amazing."

Katie smiled and preened, then she grabbed his face in her hands and kissed him deeply. When she pulled away, her lipstick was still perfect.

"Smudge proof," she said. "I know better than to wear smeary red lipstick. Unless, of course, that's your thing. I mean…it can be fun to look mussed."

As if he needed any help with the adult-rated thoughts. Now he was imagining all the ways he'd like to muss her lipstick, and her hair and everything else.

Katie's gaze traveled from his eyes to his toes and back again, lingering here and there. When she got back to his face, she smiled.

"You'll have to hold that thought," she said. "I'm starving and dinner is ready."

The delicious smell turned out to be roast chicken with carrots that had to be the most amazing thing he'd ever eaten.

Sitting at the tiny table with her felt so natural and so right. They talked about their weeks as if they hadn't spent hours on the phone the night before. When they were finished, Amos rose to clear the dishes and the two of them danced around each other in the ridiculously small kitchen.

The thought of sharing space with her came rolling in from nowhere, and instead of shoving it aside, his fucked-up brain considered it.

They could get a bigger place together. Something that had an office space for her. It would be good to have someone to come home to. The school and the fire station were close. They could find something halfway between the two.

The snap of a dish towel against his thigh pulled him out of that daydream.

"Third time I'm asking. Pie now or later?"

Amos took the dish towel from her hands and hung it up, then wrapped his arms around her. "Later."

If they sat down to pie right now, he'd be proposing or something. He bent his head and kissed her. Katie wound her arms around his neck and pressed against him. He slid his hands down her hips and hissed in a breath when his fingers ran over the telltale bump of stockings and garters on her thigh.

He scooped her into his arms, but instead of heading toward the curtained alcove that hid her bed, he sat on the small couch. Katie twisted in his lap then straddled his thighs. He slid his hands under her full skirt and past layers of fluffy slip until his fingers grazed the bare skin above the thigh-high stockings she wore.

"I think it's time you share what was going through your head on Safety Day."

Katie gasped and sat back a little. She pouted, but the twinkle in her eyes and the high color in her cheeks said she liked this game. Still, he needed to be sure.

"Am I misreading this?" He waved a finger between them and arched an eyebrow at her. She blushed even deeper and shook her head.

"I didn't think so," he said. "So tell me."

Katie wriggled in his lap, and damn it, if she kept that up he'd lose every shred of restraint he had.

"There's not much to tell," she said. "You're a tall, good-looking man and have amazing blue eyes. And you were in uniform. Not too many women could resist."

He traced the line of her stockings along her thighs, relishing the way her skin prickled under his fingers. He'd suspected she had a bit of a bratty streak and now he was seeing more of it come out.

He pulled one hand from under her skirt and hooked a finger into the low neckline of her dress then tugged gently until she leaned closer.

"Were you flirting that day?" He brought his hand around her ribs, then up her back to the base of her neck, holding her close to him.

"Maybe a little." Katie's breath came in short bursts and the bright flush on her cheeks hadn't faded.

"I was," he said. "More than a little."

A shy looking smile crossed her lips. "I figured."

Amos tipped his head and touched his lips to the hollow of her throat, eliciting a soft sigh from her. He kissed his way up her neck to her ear and planted a single kiss right below the lobe. A tiny shudder coursed through Katie and her fingers tightened on his shoulders.

"What was your first clue?" He murmured the words against her skin, still holding her with one hand gripping her thigh and the other holding the back of her neck. She swallowed hard.

"It was the possible innuendos about the hose." Her voice was breathy and low.

Amos kissed her jaw just in front of her ear. He'd take his time and plant kisses on every inch of her body if that's what it took to get her to let go.

"Oh? I was talking about a fire hose. What else did you think I meant?"

Her laughter rippled in the air. "I don't believe that for one instant," she said. "I mean, c'mon! Your hands were like this." She held her hands up and mimicked the way he'd been holding the small hose. "All that whispered talk about things being hard, and there's a lot of pressure, and how it can hit specific spots."

It was his turn to laugh. Then he leaned in and kissed the corner of her mouth. When she turned her face to him, he pulled back.

"You're being evasive," he said. "Maybe you're too shy to use your words. Why don't you show me what you mean."

Katie tipped her head to the side and her lips curled into a crooked smile. She slid one hand down his chest, over his belt buckle and cupped his crotch. His cock was already raging hard and it pulsed and throbbed as if demanding attention.

"Are you trying to tell me you didn't mean this?" Her fingers squeezed and Amos sucked in air. *Oh, this is gonna kill me.*

"Just like you're trying to avoid telling me all the not-fit-for-polite-company thoughts that went through your head that day."

Katie's hand withdrew. She crossed her arms over her chest and mock-scowled at him. It was such a cute expression he nearly laughed out loud. Instead, he shifted his grip on her thigh and pitched them sideways. It wasn't the smooth roll he'd wanted thanks to the small couch, but he got her sitting on one side and him on the other. Her skirt had hiked up to her hips, exposing creamy skin and a red and black garter belt.

Amos straightened her skirt then stroked a finger along the side of her neck. "You know what I'm asking for. You'll share all those naughty thoughts before I fuck you. Do you want that?"

Katie's tongue snaked out and wet her lips and she made a tiny sound like a whimper, but she held his gaze and nodded.

He stood, then took her hands and helped her up as well. Even in high heels, she barely came to the center of his chest and she was so small, he could wrap his hands around her waist and lift her easily. He continued to stroke a finger along the neckline of her dress, then her collarbones and down her back where the dress dipped almost to her bra line.

She shivered and let out a soft moan. He touched a finger to the top of her zipper. He cupped her chin with his other hand.

"Would you like me to unzip this?"

"Yes, please." It was a whisper, but clear as a bell in the quiet space.

Amos leaned in and placed his lips near her ear. "Tell me about Safety Day. What did you imagine me doing with my hands?"

Another low moan escaped her, then she inhaled slowly. Her body shifted. It was subtle, but her feet planted a little wider and her shoulders came back.

"I imagined you stroking yourself."

Oh fuck yes. He preferred more graphic language, but maybe she didn't. Whatever. He'd take what she wanted to give.

He tugged on the zipper, inching it down slowly to the bottom. Peeking out of the dress was a long-line bra and the top of top of her crinoline.

"Anything else?" He placed his hands on the shoulders of her dress and slid them down her arms an inch before stopping.

Her lips parted and her eyes closed. She tipped her head back and swallowed.

"I wondered how your hands would feel on my body," she said.

Amos slid the dress down her arms and over her hips until it puddled on the floor at her feet.

"Step out," he instructed and offered a hand for balance. She did as told and he took a moment to admire the perfection in front of him. He hooked his thumbs into the waistband of her slip.

"We can keep this up," he said. "However long it takes. Piece by piece until you're naked."

That might take all night, and test every bit of his patience, but it would be worth it. He was more than happy to spend the time and attention on Katie.

He stepped behind her and wrapped one arm around her waist and brought his other hand to her throat before hauling her hard against his body. She didn't stumble or reach for his hands. No, she relaxed into him and laid her head back to rest on his chest. He stroked her throat softly.

"Or answer one question honestly and I'll do my best to make sure you experience everything you were imagining."

Her stomach muscles fluttered under his hand. Katie laced her fingers with his and she pulled his arm even tighter around her.

"Okay."

"Katie, did you masturbate while thinking about me?"

Her exhale was sharp and short.

"Yes."

The urge to pick her up, carry her to the bed and fuck her senseless was nearly overwhelming. He brushed a lock of hair off her neck then pressed his lips along the shell of her ear.

"Good girl," he whispered, then he slid the slip down to join the dress on the floor. Katie looked amazing standing there in black and red lingerie, seamed stockings and high heels.

"Couple of things before we go any deeper into this." He took her hand and guided her to sit next to him on the couch. "I get tested for STIs every year at my physical. That was a couple months ago, and negative. I always use condoms."

She nodded and tucked her hands into her lap, sitting like she was about to be judged on her posture. "I'm the same. Every year before start of term. It was early August this year. All clear."

So much for the easy topics. "Do you know what a safe word is?"

Her eyes went wide, then her lips curled into a wicked grin. "You think I hadn't already figured out that you like to be in control?"

There was the bratty side again. "That wasn't an answer."

"Sure it was," she replied. "Just not the one you expected."

That was a challenge if he'd ever heard one. She might as well have said 'make me'. He cupped her chin and lowered his mouth to hers. At the first touch of his lips, hers parted, allowing his tongue to slip inside. She clung to him as he deepened the kiss. He cradled the back of her head with one hand and brought the other up her side until his thumb rested under the curve of her breast.

Katie arched into him and moaned into his mouth. Amos pulled back and rested his forehead against hers, enjoying the way her breath had gone ragged.

"What is your safe word? And I expect a straight answer."

Maybe not the most well-crafted, brat-proof approach, but he was beginning to suspect she used her bratty streak as a safety net and that it wasn't really her. There was something different driving her and he looked forward to finding what made her tick. It had been too long since he'd enjoyed this type of dynamic and Katie hit all the right buttons for him.

"I'm simple," she said. "Red works. Unless you want something ridiculous and complicated."

Amos kissed her lightly then sat back on the couch.

"Red it is," he replied. "Now stand up and let me see all of this, because, baby, you look amazing."

Katie

Katie stood without a second thought, then caught her breath as Amos rearranged himself on the loveseat. He spread his arms across the back and kicked his legs wide. A long, hard bulge clearly printed through his pants and tempted her to drop to her knees in front of him.

"Look all you want, but you're gonna have to wait to play," he said. He pointed at her then twirled his finger in the air. "Lemme see."

She'd chosen the whole outfit with this in mind, but still felt the hot flush creep up her neck. She stepped back from the couch and turned slowly, giving him a view of the vintage styled long-line bra and matching garter belt and panties.

Amos let out a low whistle as she completed her turn. She braced her hands on his knees, but he caught her wrists before she could sink down. His blue eyes stared into hers and his lips quirked into a smile.

"Ladies first, remember?" He kept her hands in his as he stood, then turned her to face the curtained alcove where her bed was.

"Do the curtains open up?"

His breath was hot on her neck as he spoke. Katie shivered in pleasure when his lips grazed her ear.

"Of course."

His chuckle sounded ominous, and it sent a thrill through her.

"Go open them up, then get those panties off before you climb into that bed. I want you on your knees right on the edge, with your back to me."

He released her hands and Katie crossed to the alcove and pulled one curtain back. She put one knee on the bed but stopped when Amos cleared his throat.

"Really? You can do better than that."

She stuck her tongue out at him and opened the other curtain before going back to the foot of her bed and standing there facing him.

"What was the rest of it?" She planted her hands on her hips and batted her eyes at him. Amos surged to his feet and was suddenly towering over her. She was already so aroused her panties were damp, but a whole new wave hit her at the dark look on his face.

His hands landed on her shoulders and he spun her to face the bed.

"You have a choice, Kitten. You can play this your way and maybe get what you want, or you can get your ass on that bed and get on your knees like I told you to, and I guarantee you'll love it."

Kitten? "Did you still want the panties off?"

Amos growled in her ear as he wrapped an arm around her waist and moved her until her legs were pressed against the edge of the bed, then his hands flashed to her hips. His thumbs hooked into her panties and hauled down. When he got them to her ankles, he twisted them around, pinning her ankles together.

He straightened up, tangled his fingers into the hair at her nape and held her gaze for a moment.

"Is this the game you want to play?"

There was a flash of uncertainty in his eyes that surprised her. She bit her lip, lifted her chin and stared straight into his eyes. *Gorgeous eyes.*

"You started this," she said. "Bring it on."

She was goading him, hoping to provoke him to stop being so cautious. He stroked his hands down her sides, then gently bent her forward until her elbows were braced on the bed in front of her. His hands continued down over her hips and thighs and down the outside of her calves before traveling back up to her waist.

She braced herself, expecting to feel a swat. Instead, he trailed a finger along the curve of her ass until he slid his hand between her thighs.

"Your panties were soaked," he said. "And so are you. Tell me what you imagined me doing with my hands?"

Katie wriggled, trying to open her legs to give him more room, but the panties around her ankles were wound too tight. She tried to grind down onto his hand, but he moved along with her and kept just out of reach.

"Did you want something? Tell me."

His hand slid up and brushed against her labia. Katie clenched and hissed in a breath. She'd played these games before and never cared what happened. But she'd never wanted another man the way she wanted Amos right now.

"I imagined you fingering me," she said.

"And is that what you want?"

Katie wanted to scream, plead and beg. *Yes! More than anything!* She took a deep breath and forced herself to wait for a count of five before answering.

"Yes, please!"

"Good girl," he replied as his fingers slid across her wetness. With unerring accuracy, he found her clit and stroked around it in slow circles, his touch feather light.

Maddening! She wanted harder. And she suspected the only way to get that was to ask directly.

"More please?"

His knee pressed into the bed next to her as he bent down and unwound the panties from her ankles. He straightened up and caught her hair in his hand again then hauled her up and against his chest.

"Get your ass on the bed. Now."

Katie didn't sass back this time. She clambered onto the bed and braced her knees on the edge.

"Down on your elbows, ass in the air."

She dropped to her elbows and arched her back. Anything to get his touch back. That teasing stroke had promised so much more and she wanted it all.

But it wasn't his fingers that caressed her thighs.

It was his lips and tongue.

He pushed her knees wider apart then his mouth closed over her labia. Whatever he was doing it was like nothing she'd ever felt before. He sucked her lips between his teeth and ran his tongue over every inch before he moved on to her clit.

His first touch was gentle, barely a breath against the swollen bud. Then he lashed with his tongue, flicking over and under until she was squirming and writhing. When he stopped, a wail tore itself from her throat.

"You are delicious," he said. "What do you want, Kitten?"

Fuck whatever game they'd been playing. She wanted his touch.

"Make me come, please? I want your fingers in me and your mouth on me."

"We're gonna have to work on your dirty words," he said. "Roll over, ass on the edge of the bed."

Katie flipped, eager to get in position for whatever he planned on doing next. No sooner was she on her back than Amos knelt between her thighs and lowered his head.

Any trace of taking his time was gone as he pulled her clit into his mouth and pressed a finger inside her. He curled into her G-spot as his tongue slid under the hood and stroked her clit. She ground down on him, wanting more. As if reading her mind, Amos slipped another finger into her. Or maybe more than one. He kept going until she felt like he was fucking her for real, not using fingers.

Every time Katie arched against him, his touch got harder and faster until she was panting and clawing at the bed. Her hips bucked and she cried out his name, begging for release.

He wrapped an arm around her waist and held her tight just as his teeth grazed the sensitive skin above her clit. When he sucked the swollen bud between his teeth and drummed his fingers inside her, the dam broke and Katie dug her fingers into his shoulders as she came.

She fell back to the bed as Amos stood and pulled off his shirt. Katie tried to focus on the display of gorgeous ink and taut muscles. He fumbled in his pocket, tossed a package on the bed then dropped his pants.

Katie pushed up onto her elbows and stared in open admiration. Amos was built like a god—broad shoulders tapered to narrow hips and powerful thighs. His arms were like corded bands and muscles rippled down his abdomen.

A dusting of dark hair traced from his belly button downward, drawing Katie's gaze to the thick shaft between his legs. He picked up the foil packet, tore it open and rolled down a condom.

"Did you want this?" His fingers circled his dick. "Can you guess what I want to hear?"

Katie did want that. Every bit of it. She'd expected to be giving head first, but if he wanted to go straight from giving her pleasure to sex, well, okay then. If she had to beg for it, she was fine with that, too.

"Please fuck me." It came out breathier than she'd expected, but the look on his face was worth it. His eyes narrowed and his lips curled up in a lopsided smile. He laid his hands on her knees and pulled her legs up and back.

Then he was hovering over her and his dick rested heavy against her pubic bone. Amos shifted, reached a hand between them and the head pressed into her entrance. *Good grief, the man is thick.*

She took a slow breath and Amos paused as if he was afraid of hurting her. He caressed her cheek.

"Stop being so gentle," she said. She laced her hands behind his neck and pulled him down for a kiss. She nipped his lip and Amos growled again, his fingers clenching into her hair. She wrapped her legs around his waist and tightened. Amos got the hint and pushed forward.

The pressure was intense and Katie arched her head back. Amos lowered his mouth to her bra-covered breasts and closed his lips over one nipple.

"Yes," Katie gasped. "More, please!"

He tugged her bra strap down and sucked her nipple between his teeth, flicking his tongue against it as he pushed his hips forward again, driving himself deeper into her.

"Don't stop. Please don't stop." Katie clutched at him as the pressure increased. He pulled back and gave a few short strokes then drove forward again and it felt like it would never end.

Amos pulled the other strap down, trapping her arms as he lowered his head to kiss and nibble on her other nipple. She managed to bring her hands up and clenched her fingers in his hair. The more she tightened her grip, the harder he sucked on her nipple, sending electric jolts straight to her still-swollen clit.

He pulled her legs up higher around his ribs and with one more push was all the way inside her. *He should come with a warning label.* Then he ground against her, setting up a slow rhythm that sent delicious friction over her hypersensitive parts.

He had her bent almost double and between her bra straps trapping her arms and Amos pinning her legs to his side, Katie could barely move. She was at his mercy as he continued to grind. He felt amazing, but she wanted to feel him pounding into her. Even if she wasn't sure she could handle it.

"Harder!" The word shot out of her mouth without thought. "Fuck me!"

Amos lifted his head and held her gaze as he pulled out slowly so she felt every inch. He took a few short strokes, then slid all the way in and Katie tried to arch herself up to meet him.

"Please." She was ready to beg. Whatever it took.

Then Amos drove forward hard. Their bodies slapped together with a sound like a clap. He drew back and did it again, and again. Each stroke, Katie felt like it was the first one. She expected her body to adjust to his size, but it never happened.

He punctuated each thrust with a grind and kept speeding up until his strokes were short but deep and hard and Katie was babbling in incoherent pleasure as another orgasm ripped through her.

This was what she craved. Being lost in the sensations of two bodies coming together.

He shifted, pulled out and slid her to the middle of the bed. With a single tug, he got her bra straps down a little more, completely trapping her arms, then knelt between her legs and pulled her up so her ass rested against his thighs.

He spread her legs wide, exposing her to his view. And he looked. His gaze roamed her body with obvious pleasure.

"This is an amazing sight," Amos said, and his voice was rough and low. "Are you ready for more, Kitten?"

There was already a dull ache pounding between her legs that said she'd be stiff and sore tomorrow, but Katie nodded. Whatever magic Amos was weaving, she wanted more of it.

When he lifted himself and slid into her, Katie gasped. If she'd thought he felt big before, in this position he was huge. He moved his hand down her thigh until his thumb pressed on her clit. He stroked in time with each thrust, sending Katie chasing yet another orgasm.

Amos sped up and Katie wanted to grab him, grab something, but her arms were trapped. She clenched her fingers into the quilt beneath her. She opened her eyes and focused on the beautiful, sweat-slicked man fucking her better than she'd ever had in her life.

His muscles stood out, tense and tight. The tattoos on her arms, shoulders and chest glistened in the soft light and his chest rose and fell in ragged breaths.

Between her legs, where their bodies joined, he moved his hand so his thumb and index finger held her clit between them.

He rolled her clit between his fingers and sped up, thrusting deeper and harder. Katie let out a scream as the orgasm crashed over her. Something warm and wet cascaded down her ass. His fingers clenched, sending her into more spasms and he ground out her name as he pounded into her in a frenzy of hard strokes.

Katie felt limp as Amos eased himself from her and lay on his side. He pulled her to him, cradling her in his arms as aftershocks coursed through her.

Amos stroked her hair and kissed her forehead while her breathing slowed. Without a word, he rose, scooped her from the bed and carried her to the bathroom where he started the shower. Katie was in a blur as Amos removed her lingerie, lifted her into the shower and gently washed and rinsed her body, then his. He dried her off, wrapped a throw blanket around her and tucked her into the couch then he pulled the quilt from her bed.

"It's wet," he said. "But everything under it is dry. Do you have another blanket or anything?"

Katie lifted her head and scowled. "Wet? What? Ummm...yeah... Box under the bed. There's a purple thing. Why is it wet?"

Amos arched an eyebrow at her then rummaged under the bed. He made quick work of spreading her purple comforter out before carrying her to the bed.

"I can walk, you know," Katie said as he slid her between the sheets.

"Uh huh, I'm sure you can," he replied and sat on the bed next to her. "I'm going to get us both a water and then you're going to tell me whether you want me to stay or not."

Katie reached out and grabbed his wrist before he could get up.

"Stay," she said. "And I think I need...ummm..." She didn't know what she needed. The sense of emptiness when he pulled away was deep and strange.

Amos leaned down and planted a gentle kiss on her lips. "Kitten needs aftercare," he said. "Be right back."

He stood and Katie was treated to the magnificent view of his backside.

Kitten? She wasn't sure what she thought of that nickname.

The refrigerator door opened and she heard a soft gasp.

"Oooh, yes!"

Something clinked in the kitchen. A cabinet door opened then closed.

"Hey, Kitten, how about pie?"

Katie rolled to her side. Yeah, okay, she could get used to kitten. From Amos.

"Sounds great. There's ice cream in the freezer."

Chapter Sixteen

Amos
November 6, Monday

The garage loomed in the heavy morning mist. Still dark. On any other day, he'd take that as a bad sign. Today, it could help his plan. Amos pulled up next to the house and stretched. Katie had woken him up in the middle of the night, then he'd woken her up just before sunup. His body was ready to have words with him over all the activity. Not that his cock cared—it was stirring to life again at the thought. If he had a few aches, he could only imagine how Katie was feeling.

All the pleasant thoughts were driven straight out of his head when the side door opened and Leah poked her head out, a scowl painted on her face. He sighed and got out of his truck.

Leah shoved a cup of coffee in his hands the moment he was inside the house and Amos took a sip before following her into the kitchen.

"Dad's doing poorly," she said. "Damn fool did too much yesterday and his back is out. I gave him some muscle relaxers and he's back in bed. We've got a mountain of work this week and you're on duty. Grace has classes so she can't even step up."

Much as he hated hearing the old man was in pain, the whole situation could help.

"We need to hire someone," he said. They'd had this discussion before. Leah and Amos were on the same page. Their dad was not. He didn't want to accept that he couldn't physically keep up with the work, or that Amos didn't want to take over the garage.

"You say that like you have someone in mind," Leah replied. "Out with it."

Amos took in a slow breath. "I need you to promise to hear me out before you say anything."

Leah's eyes narrowed into a glare. "I'm not gonna like this, am I?"

"Probably not," he said. "Just...trust me."

He laid it all out—that Miles had come back and was claiming to be clean and sober. He was working at Perry's Orchard. The fire at the trailer park. Everything Drea had asked Amos to do. He even told his sister about Katie and how she was struggling.

"Orchard work's about to dry up." Leah refilled their coffees and sat back down at the worn kitchen table. She hadn't blown up like he'd expected. Then again, he hadn't discussed his whole plan.

"You're thinking we could bring him on to handle the routine stuff," she said. "You know what Dad would say?"

"What I'd say about what?" Their dad stood hunched in the kitchen doorway. The pain etched into the lines on his face made him look far older than his years. Leah cast a pleading look at Amos.

"We're gonna hire someone to help a bit," he said. "Business is good, thankfully, but we can't keep going like we are. Leah's busting ass too many hours a day. I'm working full time here and full time at the fire department and that's not gonna change. And you..."

He rose, filled a cup of coffee for their father and handed it to him. The old man's slow movement and deepening scowl said it all—just standing was a challenge for him right now.

"You've been overdoing it and your body is paying the price. There's no reason for it. We can swing enough to hire a basic mechanic and that alone will lighten the load enough for Leah and I to manage for a while."

His sister was perched on the edge of her seat, one elbow on the table, the other hand clenched on her knee as if she wasn't sure whether to remain seated or stand in a rush. Her eyes darted between Amos and their dad.

"Who you plannin' to bring on? Some kid who took a vo-tech program and thinks they're a mechanic?"

Leah bit her lip and shook her head. Looking at his father, his shoulders stooped and crooked from the pain in his back, holding on to the doorjamb for support, there was no doubt if they didn't get help, things would get worse. If there was work to be done, their father would break himself trying to do it, just as he had always done to provide for his family. Amos couldn't lie to the man. Not outright. He couldn't tell him the truth either.

"That's one possibility," he replied, keeping his tone light and trying to avoid a direct answer without outright fibbing. "Figured I had to talk to Leah about it first. See what she thought."

Aw fuck, wrong thing to say.

Roy Kimmel rolled his eyes and let out a sharp laugh. "You keep talkin' like your sister's the one runnin' this business. You know damn well what I think about that."

He drew himself up, wincing and shaking with the effort, and slammed his hand to the kitchen counter. "Kimmel and Sons," he said. The same refrain he'd sung every time the subject of his children taking over the garage came up. "It's been that for generations. Can't help it I've only got the one son and he's not interested in the family legacy. And you can be damn certain it will never be Kimmel and Daughter while I'm alive."

He thumped his coffee cup onto the counter and stormed off. It might have been a glorious exit in the past, but his slow gait and shuffling steps made it painful to watch.

Amos and Leah waited, counting the footfalls down the hall until the primary bedroom door slammed. Leah let out an audible sigh and sagged into her chair.

"Well, that was better than him going off about Miles Tilman, I guess." She spun her cup on the table and looked up at Amos. "You might as well tell me everything. Starting with how you plan on dealing with him finding out?"

Just like that, Leah was on board.

"Haven't given it too much thought," he replied. "I knew if you weren't okay, it would never work. We can run the routine stuff out of the side garage. Dad never goes out there anyway. You can say it's to keep the main garage for the bigger projects. Grace runs payroll, so that's not a problem."

His big sister nodded. "Given it more thought than you admit, I think."

He wasn't about to tell her the whole idea came to him in the shower this morning after he'd rolled around in the sheets with Miles' kid sister. *For the third time in one night.*

"Still," Leah continued. "What happens if, no, when, he does figure it out? Someone says something to him? Or he sees Miles around?"

Amos hadn't gotten that far in planning this out. He was about to own up to it and hope Leah had some sort of idea when his eyes fell on the tattoo on his wrist.

"Second chances," he said. The moment the words were out, he knew they were right. He sat at the table across from Leah and smiled. "Everyone deserves one."

He laid his arm on the table and turned it so she could see the ink.

"That's to remind you not to fuck up again," Leah said. Amos leaned back and waited a bit before answering. Leah made the same assumption most folks did.

"No," he said, finally. "It's to remind me not to squander the second chance I was given. Maybe to you, that means the same thing, but to me, it's very different."

Leah's gaze snapped up to his. She and their parents had encouraged him to fight back. To throw anyone and everyone under the bus if it would save his ass. Even as a teen, Amos knew better. Chief Lawson, Amos' attorney and the minor's rights advocate the court had appointed all made it clear — if he didn't have enough information to help them go after the bigger fish, it was his ass on the line. Amos had taken the plea offer and vowed to turn his life around.

"Okay, little brother," Leah said. "Yeah. I can buy that. Plus having Miles work out of the side garage means he has limited access. Which, considering the circumstances here, I think is a good thing."

Amos had given that some thought and he was glad Leah brought it up. Saved him the effort.

"Why are you so willing to help Chief Parsons out?"

He supposed eventually he'd get used to her married name. Hell, back in school, everyone had figured Danny Parsons and Drea Hidalgo a done deal. They'd just taken a while to get around to it. Life could be funny that way.

"Next year, we are likely to have a fully funded, paid fire department," he said. "And she's been a big part of making that happen. Plus…"

He heaved a sigh. He didn't have the words for all the conflicting thoughts swirling in his head.

"Maybe I can keep one kid out of the kind of trouble I got into," he replied. "If we're lucky, there's a chance of putting an end to Carl and Dwight's little drug empire, or at least making a big dent in it. Either way, I think it's worth the shot."

Leah stood and clapped him on the shoulder. "Don't get killed. I mean that."

She rinsed her cup, grabbed her jacket and headed for the door, leaving Amos stewing in his thoughts. He didn't think the stakes were that high, but then again, he'd been wrong about Miles before.

Amos had been a naive kid back then. He was a grown man now, and nowhere near as naive. The only possible trouble was, he was falling head over heels for Katie, and he never wanted to be the reason she experienced pain.

Chapter Seventeen

Katie
November 8, Wednesday

The door closed behind the last student and Katie closed her eyes to savor a moment of stillness. A kindergarten classroom was rarely quiet and she'd learned to cherish the little things. She sank into her chair and scowled at the November folder open on her desk.

She'd come in late in the planning process, so Katie had been grateful the previous teacher had left all of her resources. That gratitude had quickly ended when she'd seen the curriculum the woman had been using was beyond outdated.

The folder full of instructions for making handprint turkeys and crafting pilgrim hats from construction paper was proof enough of that. Teaching social studies was required, and that included covering the early colonists. Katie had never taught the same white-washed mess she'd been fed during childhood and she wasn't about to start now.

Luckily, by the end of her first week, she'd given up trying to use any parts of her predecessor's curriculum. Instead, she used it as a guide for general expectations.

The woman had kept meticulous records, which was a great help. Katie had already run into a few cases of parents who were confused about why kindergarten was different than it was for their older children.

Katie scooped the scattered contents into the folder then headed for the door. She didn't stop until she got to Cinda Gable's classroom. Katie knocked before opening the door and found the first-grade teacher sitting at her desk with her head in her hands. She looked up as Katie came in and the stress on her face was evident.

"Should I leave you alone?" Katie shifted the colorful folder emblazoned with a turkey out of Cinda's sight.

"No, I'm just… Gah! I hate this season." She threw up her hands and sat back, then eyed Katie. "What's up?"

She pulled a chair over to the desk and tossed the folder down. Either she and Cinda were on the same page, or very opposite ones. Katie was about to find out.

"I accept the fact that I'm going to piss off some parents every November," Katie replied. "Is this really the expected curriculum around here?"

She waved her hand at the folder then crossed her fingers as Cinda leafed through it. After a few pages, she closed the folder, picked it up and tossed it into the trash.

"In a word, no. Mrs. Watts had been told repeatedly to update her lessons, and she had improved them a little. It was a constant struggle. Until three years ago, she was still having the kindergartners do a Thanksgiving pageant."

Katie wasn't surprised at that. Older teachers were loath to let go of their tried and true plans. Plus, the old narrative was easier, especially with younger students. No one wanted to tell a bunch of five-year-olds that the Native Americans and the early colonists were not exactly friends.

"So, Principal Dubois isn't going to have a fit if I don't teach that stuff." Katie pointed at the folder now sticking out of Cinda's trashcan.

"She'll probably be grateful," Cinda replied. "Parents on the other hand? They'll be about a fifty-fifty split."

She pushed a book across her desk. The cover featured the typical, old-fashioned image of the first Thanksgiving. Katie didn't need to read the blurb to know it was not something she'd ever present in her classroom.

"A gift from a parent," Cinda said. "Do you have something else to work with? If not, I can help."

Katie set the book back on the desk. "Thanks, but I do have a good curriculum that focuses on unlearning some of the common misconceptions."

"Oh hell, share!" Cinda laughed. "Maybe we need to send that out to parents. Though most of ours are better than you'd think for being a small town. The fifth and sixth graders are doing a cooking module this year. They've been researching authentic recipes."

Katie shuddered. They'd done similar at her last school. "Remind me to bring a lunch that day. If memory serves, the dishes are not all that appetizing."

Cinda leaned back in her chair and folded her hands across her waist. "You still trying to claim you and Amos aren't dating?"

The days of being able to deny it were gone. The Halloween carnival had made it clear to everyone at the school that he and Katie were an item. Then he'd cemented that privately on Sunday. She'd barely made it to work on Monday and struggled to keep her mind on her students and not on the hours she'd spent in her bed with Amos.

"Yeah, thought so," Cinda said with a laugh. "You know he dated Larry's cousin — well, cousin-in-law I guess — back when she was Missy Talbot."

Katie didn't know who Missy was, and she hadn't known Amos had dated her. They hadn't discussed dating history in detail. He was clearly experienced, and since he'd grown up around here, it made sense he'd gone out with local girls. And that threw her head into a whole new place.

"Relax." Cinda reached out and patted Katie's hand. "It was about the time he came back to town. They met at some fire department event. Her daddy's Bruce Talbot. Didn't last too long. Back then, Bruce was in charge of the volunteer crew and Amos was a kid fresh out of youth camp."

That relationship may not have lasted long, but he must have dated other women over the years. The thought twisted her stomach into knots.

"Far as I know, he hasn't dated anyone else local," Cinda continued as if she'd read Katie's mind. "I did kinda bring that up for a reason."

Oh shit. Yeah. "I think I get it," Katie replied. "Everybody loves Amos and he's been unattached for almost ten years. Now we're going out."

"With Danny Parsons off the market, Amos is the town's most eligible bachelor," Cinda said with a nod.

There it was again. The reminder of small-town life. Everybody knew your business and felt it was their right to poke their nose in anywhere they saw fit. And a good-looking man nearing thirty whose family owned a moderately successful garage and who was working hard to ensure the town had a functional fire department was a catch.

And Katie had swooped back in after being gone for so long and snatched him up. An alarm beeped on Cinda's phone and she stabbed the screen with her finger.

"Fertility alarm," she said. "Time to go home and pounce on my husband."

They walked to the parking lot together and Katie waved as Cinda climbed into her car and drove off. Katie loaded her bag in the car and glanced at her watch. Amos had said his schedule was packed this week. They texted every day, but wouldn't have time together again until Friday.

Except now the need to see him gnawed at her. The memory of his kisses sent a wave of heat up her neck. Amos was an amazing kisser. She clambered into the driver's seat before she started thinking about all the other things he was oh so good at.

Her fingers hovered over Amos' name on her phone screen. She tapped the text button.

Hey. Just thinking about you.

She hit send. It was a simple enough message. Nothing demanding. Not like she was checking up on him or asking for more of his time or something like that. Her phone buzzed with an incoming text from Amos.

Naughty thoughts I hope. Share with the class...well, with me.

Katie tossed the phone into the passenger seat, buckled up and sped home. She parked and hurried up her stairs. As soon as the door closed behind her, she sat, hiked up her skirt and maneuvered herself to get a sexy shot up her legs that showed off a flash of panty. She sent it to Amos before she could second guess herself. His response came almost immediately.

Take off those panties and show me more, Kitten.

His words sent coils of heat coursing through her body, tightening her nipples and making her clit throb with the memory of his touch. She removed her panties and snapped a picture of them sitting on her couch and sent that to him.

Three flashing dots appeared in her text message. Then they stopped, then came back again, and stopped again. Amos was typing something, then deleting it and starting fresh. Katie kicked off her shoes and socks then shrugged out of her sweater as she made her way to her bed.

You know that is not what I meant.

A frowning emoji followed. Katie sprawled face down on her bed. She held the phone up high and angled it so she got her face and down along her body in the shot. She hit send then wriggled out of her skirt. Something about lying in her bed in nothing but her bra and camisole while she sent Amos sort-of suggestive pictures pushed her from semi-aroused to oh-I-need-to-get-fucked-now. Her phone buzzed.

I was about to jump in the shower and planned on sending you a nice soapy picture, but if you're going to play like that, I guess that's off. Unless you're angling for a spanking next time we see each other.

Forget tightening and throbbing, Katie's body demanded to be touched. She wanted release. She also wanted a picture of soapy Amos. The idea of his hands on her ass, turning her cheeks pink had her wishing he was here right now. She grabbed her phone and typed.

Dilemma. Should I be a good girl and send the pic you want so I can see naked you in the shower? Or do I keep teasing since you're threatening a spanking?

Katie hit send and reached into her nightstand for her vibrator. Her phone rang and she swiped to answer the video call as she rolled onto her back. Amos' face and bare shoulders popped onto her screen. *Damn, he is fine.*

"You're half dressed," he said. "I like it. Now put the vibrator back, Kitten."

Katie frowned at him and held up the small toy. "I was already thinking about you, then you went and made it worse. What else am I supposed to do?"

His laughter echoed from the tiny phone speakers. "Oh, I want you to please yourself while thinking about me. But you have to earn it first."

The toy tumbled from her fingers as Katie sat up in bed. "And how do you expect me to do that?" She fixed him with her best bratty glare and waited.

"Switch to a headset so you can really hear me then prop yourself up on pillows and get comfortable," he said. "And keep both hands on your phone. I just got home from the garage and I need to shower, but I've got time before I head to the station."

While Katie popped her earbuds in, he stuck his phone on something and the background came into focus — a white and gray bathroom and the shower was already on. Amos moved into the frame, naked. Katie's breath caught as he stepped into the shower and faced the camera.

"Hands on the phone, Kitten." He grabbed a washcloth and soaped his body. When his hands cupped his balls then ran the soapy cloth over his dick, Katie let out a moan. The urge to touch herself was nearly overwhelming as he got hard and memories of that thick shaft filling her flooded her brain.

"You like what you see?" He dropped the washcloth and slid a soapy hand up and down his length.

"Yes." The word spilled from her lips in a breathy whisper that she doubted he could hear, but he smiled and winked.

Amos ducked his head under the water, rinsed then shut off the shower. He crossed the bathroom dripping wet, making Katie want to run her tongue over every single droplet clinging to his perfect body. She pouted when he wrapped a towel around his waist, then giggled at the tent his still hard dick made in the fabric.

"Show me what I wanted to see, Kitten." His voice was a low growl and the look on his face said there would be no arguing. She could tap out and end the game or do as he said. Or she could be a brat and see what he did about it. She shifted on the bed and angled the phone until Amos could see most of her body.

"Spread your legs like a good girl," he said. She didn't think, she parted her legs. "That's it, Kitten."

His voice reverberated in her head and sent shivers of pleasure down her spine.

"Do you want to come for me, Kitten?"

Katie's entire body was thrumming at his voice. Her nipples ached to be touched, licked, pinched, anything. She didn't need to put a hand between her legs to know she was slippery wet with arousal.

"Yes, please!"

Amos moved into a darkened room and sat, then a small light came on, clearly outlining his hand moving on his hard dick.

"Get yourself to the edge of the bed and put the phone on the nightstand. I want your legs spread wide so I can watch you touch yourself."

When given instructions in the past, Katie's first instinct was to push back. Question. Tease. Anything but obey. Something about Amos was different. She wanted to hear him say 'good girl' again. Her body hurried to do exactly as he instructed.

"Just like that," he purred. "Now show me how you touch yourself, but don't come without asking. Is that clear?"

The way she felt, she'd likely explode the moment she touched herself. Still, she answered. "Yes."

She reached for her vibrator.

"Ah ah ah."

Katie stopped and tipped her head to see her phone.

"Start with your fingers."

Amos filled her phone screen—from the top of his head to just below his dick. His hand stroked and slid, pausing at the head before gliding back down. A flutter of nerves settled in her stomach. She'd masturbated in front of a man before. This wasn't anything new or different.

Except it was. Somehow it was very different. She moved her hand down and slid her fingers alongside her clit. Everything was slick and wet, as expected. A moan escaped her lips.

"There ya go, Kitten," Amos said. "You seemed to like my mouth on that pretty pussy. Tell me what you want to be doing right now."

Katie whimpered. She wasn't good at talking dirty. It made her feel silly and self-conscious. Her fingers stuttered and she lost her rhythm.

"Hmmm, okay. Close your eyes and keep touching yourself, but don't come. Just listen."

Katie closed her eyes. Suddenly the sounds coming through her earbuds seemed much louder, as if he was in the room with her. The rhythmic stroke of his hand on his dick. His breathing — deep and strong.

"I loved eating your sweet pussy the other night."

Katie shivered at the low growl of his voice in her ears and her fingers sped up.

"Next time we're together, if you want that again, you'll have to beg for it. So today we're going to practice. Let's start easy. Say my name."

That was easy. "Amos."

Her clit twitched under her fingers and she pulled in a sharp breath.

"Very good," he said. "Tell me where you want my mouth."

"Oh god," she whispered. "Ummm…on… I want… Oh…"

The pressure built and Katie needed to come. She slid her fingers closer together.

"Not yet, Kitten," he cooed. "Tell me where you want my mouth."

Her legs shook and her stomach muscles trembled.

"On my pussy," she whispered. A deep moan of pleasure filled her ears.

"That's what I like to hear," Amos replied. His voice was raspy and tight, hinting he might be on the verge of his own orgasm. That thought nearly sent her over the edge. Her back arched and she let out a low keening wail.

"Get your vibrator."

Katie fumbled on the bed, found the little toy and turned it on.

"Keep up with your fingers, Kitten. You can switch to your toy after you get permission to come."

As if she wasn't already about to. Every muscle felt tight and her toes curled so hard they hurt.

"Please, Amos, please may I come?"

He hissed in a breath then let out a soft groan. "Good girl. Yes, Kitten. Come for me."

As soon as the vibrator touched her skin, Katie exploded. She cried out as the orgasm came in waves. She thumbed the toy off and lay on the bed gasping.

"Look at me."

Katie opened her eyes and rolled to her side. Amos was back in the bathroom with a washcloth in his hands. *Oh, he must've come, too. Wow.*

"That was beautiful," he said. "And you are amazing. Are you okay?"

The question surprised her. She gave it a moment of thought. She'd been uncertain, but never uncomfortable, and she trusted Amos.

"Of course," she replied. "All good."

"I need to get moving," he continued. "Make sure you eat tonight. Take care of yourself — have a bath or whatever makes you feel good."

He leaned in so his face filled the screen.

"If you're not done, make yourself come as many times as you'd like, but I want a picture each time."

Katie rolled her eyes at him and barely stopped herself from sticking out her tongue. Amos threw his head back and laughed.

"Have a good night, Kitten."

Her phone went dark. Katie stared at it as her brain struggled to process the entire phone call. She and Amos just had phone sex. At least she was pretty sure that was phone sex.

And dammit, she never got around to asking him about Missy. *Well, shit.*

Chapter Eighteen

Amos
November 10, Friday

Bare trees dotted the drive as Amos pulled down the lane leading to Perry's Orchard. Katie had said her brother was working there and catching him at work seemed a whole lot easier than risking running into Carl Tilman or Dwight Phelps at the trailer park.

He parked at the end of the gravel drive and gripped the steering wheel. The idea of offering Miles a job at the garage had seemed solid at first. Hell, he'd even managed to convince his sister.

After a few days of letting it stew and figuring out all the logistics, he wasn't so sure. What he was certain of was that it was his best option. He'd promised Drea he'd try to talk to Miles, and this was the only way he could see that working.

Amos' fingers clenched tight on the wheel as Miles Tilman sauntered out of a low building and walked toward the truck. Amos got out and Miles stopped and crossed his arms over his chest.

"What are you doing here?" His old friend was never one for polite greetings.

Amos stuffed his hands in his pockets, mostly to keep himself from climbing right back in his truck and driving off.

"Figured you might be interested in some work," he said. He'd thought long and hard over how to do this, and blunt seemed like the right idea. "Perry's Orchard shuts down this month. We've got enough guys on the crew who work the season that I know that schedule like the back of my hand."

He'd also talked to Eliza, who confirmed it and told him Miles had been great. No trouble at all. Miles shrugged and looked down at the ground.

"Seasonal work is what it is, man." He lifted his head and the despair was clearly printed in his features. That, or it was a show for Amos' benefit. You never knew with Miles.

"I need someone to handle some basics — oil changes, tire balancing, winterizing, that sorta shit." It was a gamble and Amos knew it, but Miles had the skills, or at least used to.

"You're serious?" His eyes narrowed. "Your old man wouldn't be too thrilled."

Amos dug deep, trying to recall his teenage attitude. Anything that would read right. He shrugged. "You interested or not?"

If he gave an explanation, it was an opportunity to fuck up and say the wrong thing. He'd made the offer but he couldn't sound too invested in the answer.

Miles bit his lip and looked around. His eyes squinted in the thin morning sunlight. Amos could practically see the wheels turning. If Drea was right, and Miles was back at selling drugs and targeting high school students, he'd be worried about spending too many hours at the garage. Still, money was money, and having cash but no regular job looked suspicious.

"Sure," Miles said. "Could use the income. Startin' when?"

Amos shrugged, as if it didn't matter. "Finish out the season here if they need you. Gimme a shout when you're ready to come in. We're fixin' to have a whole lotta work what with winter prep and all."

It was so easy to slip into the way he talked as a teen so he would fit in with his peers. The language that would reach Miles. His mother had insisted they all 'speak proper' in the house. She didn't want her kids sounding like they came from the mountain. *Guess that's what comes from being ashamed of your roots.* Those lessons had been reinforced during his time in the youth camp.

"Good deal." Miles tipped his head to the side. His eyes narrowed in a way that sent a cold shiver through Amos. That look said Miles was calculating something.

"You and Katie, huh?"

Amos nearly sighed in relief. This was a question he could handle. "Been over this before, ain't we? That a problem?"

Miles shrugged. "Prob'ly not. She, uh... We had some rough patches and she's still mad at me."

From what Amos knew, disappointed would be a better description. That and a healthy dose of fear for the havoc her brother could bring into the life she was trying to rebuild. Amos knew all about that challenge. All the more reason to keep Katie as far from this whole mess as possible.

"That's between y'all. Not my business." It very much was Amos' business. Anything that hurt Katie was, as far as he was concerned, but Miles didn't need to know that. *Time to get the fuck out of here.*

"We good?"

Miles pulled a cap from his back pocket and shoved it down on his head. "Yeah. Catch you later."

He didn't wait for a response before heading toward the gravel lot where staff parked. Amos didn't relax until he was in his truck and well on the road back home. He didn't know how he was going to get any work done if he had to spend his days sweating over every little word.

Drea might not like having to wait, but getting Miles to trust him enough to really talk would take time. If it worked at all.

Back at home, he threw himself into getting the side garage set up so Miles could have a full bay to himself. He didn't like lying to his old man, but his outburst earlier in the week proved what Amos and his sisters had suspected for some time—their already stubborn and uncompromising father was edging into irrational. Lately, he'd been prone to episodes like the one he'd had in the kitchen.

If they had any hope of keeping the business running, they'd have to go behind his back and do whatever it took to make it happen. It was that or continue doing nothing while he worked himself, and his precious family business, into the ground.

The rumbling in his stomach reminded Amos he hadn't been doing a great job of taking care of himself. The three kids took turns cooking and there was almost always food in the fridge, ready to heat up. Leah had started that habit when she'd realized their dad wasn't eating regularly, and they'd all liked having easy meals available, so they'd made it part of the routine. There was always food at the station, so Amos had no excuse for not eating. *Except stress and worry.*

He checked his watch. Just after noon. High likelihood of running into his dad. Plus he had work to do on the Harvester and plans with Katie tonight. There weren't enough hours in the day. He stared across the lot at the weathered sign — *Kimmel and Sons.*

There was still the old single pump that everyone thought was the start of the business. Amos knew the business had started well before Eli Kimmel had installed the first gas pump in the thirties. Eli's great-great grandfather Virgil had started as a mechanic at the railroad, then had taken a job with the mining company — keeping machines up and running.

The Kimmel family business had been around since the mid eighteen hundreds, if not earlier. Back when Logan was known as Lawnsville. Amos let out a short laugh. There had been Kimmels in the holler before there were Parsons, but the mechanics didn't mix with the wealthy horse ranchers. Or so he'd always been told. A fact made even more clear when Leah and Jake had dated and she'd asked Amos to cover for her with their dad.

They'd split up that summer, but remained friends. Leah was the only one who seemed unsurprised when Jake suddenly moved away. She had never really dated anyone after Jake. There had been some gossip that she was pregnant and Jake had run off, then Leah had gotten an abortion. Amos knew that wasn't true. Leah claimed they'd never gotten beyond a few kisses.

That was about the same time Amos got arrested, so it wasn't like he heard much.

A knock on his window startled him from those thoughts. Leah stood outside, a plate in her hand. He got out of the truck and took the food from her with a nod of thanks.

"Saw you out here and figured I'd save you the trip inside," she said. "I suggest you stay away from the house. He's…ahh…he's on a tear and talking to Mama as if she's around. I told Grace to stay with friends."

The lines around his sister's mouth and eyes said things were worse than her words implied. Which meant shit was bad.

"You going back in there?"

Leah gave him a wide-eyed stare. "Hell no. There's work to be done and he's bound and determined to get his ass to it. Never mind that he can't stand up straight and if he takes pain pills, he can't think straight. Not that he's thinking straight anyway. Luckily, he's not foolish enough to try the stairs, so he'll sit inside and stew. All the more reason to stay outside if you can."

Amos crossed his fingers she was right on the stairs. He held up the plate. "Thanks. I'm starving. Miles agreed to come to work here once the season closes. I'll eat, then help you out. The Parsons aren't in a hurry for the Harvester, so it can wait."

Leah tipped her head to the side and eyed him. The expression was so like their mother it gave Amos a twinge of sadness.

"What had you out here all spaced?"

He shook his head. "Everything. Nothing." He waved a hand at the old pump. "Dad and his stubborn shit. History. The family."

Leah gave a knowing smile. "Yeah. It's a lot." She smacked his shoulder and cocked her head at the main garage. "Eat, then get to work. I know you've got a hot date tonight, so let's see how much we can cram into a few hours."

Five hours later, Amos marveled at how much easier it was working with his sister than with their father. With the old man, everything was a battle — *why did you do it that way? Why'd you put the tools away already? Why haven't you put the tools away yet?* A never-ending barrage of criticisms and complaints where nothing he did was ever good enough.

Leah worked in her own little world. She'd emerge periodically to share a joke or check in. The two of them were seamless and fluid. Which meant they were also much more efficient. Leah dried her hands at the sink and surveyed the garage. Tools away. Floor clean and swept. Paperwork neatly in envelopes labeled with the car's info.

"We've gotten busier," Amos commented. They'd always had steady business, but over the last year, steady had turned into near crushing. Hiring Miles wasn't just a way to get the answers Drea hoped for. It was a necessity for the garage.

"I started advertising again," she replied. "Dad had stopped everything. He was getting so slow, local folks were going elsewhere, and you know he hasn't updated his skill set. It took a damn near miracle to get him to invest in new equipment."

Amos was only dimly aware of that end of things. He made no secret of his desires to get out and focus on the fire department. Leah was happy to handle it — this was her passion. Despite their father doing everything in his power to cut her out, he needed her.

"Is he trying to kill the business?" Amos couldn't imagine why. The old man saw the garage as his family legacy. Leah shot him a pointed look.

"You think he's joking when he says the shit he does?" She flicked the lights off and pulled the door shut behind them. "He's made it very clear he has no intention of leaving the business to me. Or even letting me take it over. So, unless he can change your mind about the fire department, Kimmel and Sons dies with our dad."

Amos tried not to wince at her words, but Leah caught some reaction from him and clapped him on the shoulder as he headed for his truck.

"This isn't on you. It's on him. He's letting me do more, mostly because he's not willing to let go and I think he's convinced you'll come around. As far as I know, he's still planning to leave the place to you. Fine by me. I'll wait and buy you out."

"Yeah, for a dollar," Amos replied. It was their ongoing joke. All three of the Kimmel children knew who should inherit the garage. That was Leah.

He shoved thoughts of family and business aside as his older sister climbed the porch steps and waved at him.

Amos put his truck in gear and headed home to clean up. The idea of spending time with Katie sent all his other stresses and worries scurrying into the dark. She was a bright ray of sunshine in his world.

* * * *

Katie

The bright pink glittery ball sparkled in the flashing lights as it rolled down the lane in a perfect hook. Katie crossed her fingers, hoping for a strike so she could tie Amos. The ball crashed into the pins and nine fell. The front pin wobbled, but didn't tip over. *Well, at least it's an easy pickup.*

"Oooo, tough luck." Amos tapped the score console and shot her a smile that had her ready to forget the game and the deal they had riding on it. She'd rather be back in bed, riding him. The ball return chugged and the pink thing appeared, looking closer to a deep purple in the blue-tinged light.

They had one set left after this. If she could pick up this spare and distract Amos on his next, she still had a chance. Katie picked up her ball and didn't allow herself to overthink it as she stepped to the line and released. The tenth pin dropped neatly and she bit her tongue from celebrating too soon.

"Nice," Amos said. He stood and picked up the other bowling ball. He bowled with a casual ease, looking like he wasn't even trying. There was no assessing, no aiming, no complicated approach. He just walked up, almost lazily, and the ball went curling down the lane.

Except this time Katie squeezed his ass as she moved by him to the console and Amos wrapped his free hand around her waist, pulling her to him for a quick kiss.

"Trying to distract me?"

Katie gave him her most innocent smile and batted her eyes at him. "Why would I do that?"

Amos chuckled and nuzzled her neck, sending goosebumps up and down her arms. "Let's see... What was our deal? You win and I'm yours to command all night—you get whatever you ask for. I win, and I get to play with that delicious ass of yours."

His fingers slid down her hip to cup her ass, then he pressed his lips against her ear. "What's the matter, Kitten? You worried about that and wanna back out?

You can, of course. You'd have to offer up some consolation prize, but I'm sure we could figure it out."

If he kept this up, she'd be dragging him home and agreeing to whatever the hell he wanted, so long as it got him out of his clothes and inside her as quickly as possible.

"As if," she replied as she turned so her back was to him. "You don't wanna lose because you know I'll expect you to lie still while I ride your face."

Being so direct was not her norm, and she felt the heat rushing to her face as soon as she spoke the words, but the results were worth it. Amos nuzzled her neck and growled softly in her ear. The slight hardness she'd felt pressing into her back twitched and pulsed and went rock hard. If she stepped away now, anyone near would be able to see how aroused Amos was. Katie wriggled her ass against him, eliciting a soft groan.

His grip on her waist tightened. "You are welcome to do that any time. In fact, please do."

She slid a hand behind her and cupped him and the soft groan became a low growl. She needed to distract him enough to throw off his game. When he'd proposed the challenge, her bratty self had risen up and accepted. Now she wasn't so sure, but she'd never admit that to him.

"You worried about taking all of that in your ass?" His breath ruffled the hair behind her ear as he spoke. In fact, that was exactly what she was worried about. "I said play with, Kitten. Not fuck."

Relief and disappointment went to war in her mind. One side wanted to cry out with thanks. The other wanted to make some smart-ass comment that could end up upping the stakes.

She squeezed her fingers around him again. "Oh? I thought they were the same thing. Well, you can back out, if you want. Guess you better start figuring out your consolation prize." She gave another squeeze then stepped away and nodded to the timer ticking down on the console.

"Twenty seconds left," she said. Amos darted his eyes to the screen, then he flashed a grin at Katie.

He turned and took two rapid steps before releasing the ball. It rolled down the lane and crashed into the pins a split second before the timer ran out.

One pin still stood. Katie still had a chance to tie, she just had to roll a strike on her final turn. Amos shook his head as he turned to face her. His eyes were full of heat and his mouth set in a lopsided smile that dimpled one cheek. The hard bulge in his pants hadn't gone away. By the expression on his face and the way his chest heaved as he took in his next breath, if she touched him now, he'd be dragging her off to a dark corner somewhere.

"Aww," she cooed. "You messed up your streak. Too bad."

Amos snatched his ball the moment it rolled out of the return. His chest rose and fell slowly before he faced the lane again and threw. The remaining pin dropped and Amos crossed back to Katie, his expression smoldering.

He stuck his hands on the arms of her chair and squatted in front of her. "Well played. You still have to score a strike on the first frame to tie. What will we do for a tiebreaker?"

Katie hadn't given that too much thought. She'd been trying to reel in her mouth from writing checks she wasn't sure her body could cash. No matter how much she might want to. She wasn't about to gamble that on a single frame of bowling as a tiebreaker.

"I'm sure we'll think of something." She pushed against his wrist as she stood, forcing him to move his hand and let her pass. She didn't dare look at him as she picked up her ball and turned to the lane. She bent and swung her hand around.

"Miss Katie!" The high-pitch squeal echoed even in the noisy lanes and Katie's hand twitched. The ball skittered off at an angle then landed in the gutter.

Kyle Elkins ran up and Katie bent down to say hi, then was nearly knocked off her feet by his hug.

"We're bowling, too! That's my Aunt Penny and Papa Brian."

Katie rose and walked with him to where his mother stood with a nice-looking redhead who wasn't that much taller than Lily, but was built like he moved rocks for a living, but Katie knew he was a veterinarian at the ranch. A small built, shy looking carbon copy of Lily stood on the other side of the man. Katie didn't remember too much about the younger Elkins kids, but she knew from gossip, Penny had spent some time in a mental health facility.

"Hi, nice to meet you." Katie offered her hand and shook. She barely registered Kyle chattering on about Papa Brian, and her hand shook on autopilot. Amos came up and rested his hand lightly at her waist as they all chatted. It felt so normal, and so surreal at the same time. Not that Katie could focus on what was being said.

I botched that throw. And now the time is gonna run out. Shit.

The timer buzzed as Lily and her family moved down to their lane. Amos had that smoldering look on his face again, which made Katie want to grab his hand

and leave. The faster they could get home, the better. She could ask for a reset. It would be fair — she'd been interrupted, and they talked so long her time ran out. Amos would agree to that, she knew it.

"What's it gonna be, Kitten?" His finger hovered over the reset button, as if he'd read her thoughts. She could take it, but the odds of her tying Amos were slim. She'd thrown two strikes the whole night and this was their third round.

Amos had won the first round by a long shot, and Katie had barely beaten him on the second. Then he'd offered the challenge for their third set — winner take all. After all their banter and teasing, she was more than ready to go home and have some private time. Still, she had to try.

"If you're willing, sure." She hefted her ball as Amos nodded. She took her time on the approach, aimed carefully and did her best to achieve a solid release. She took out eight of the ten pins on her first frame and only one pin on her second.

Amos punched the button for a final score. He'd beaten her handily. He offered his hand as they went to turn in their bowling shoes and get their coats. The cold night air did nothing to soothe the desire that had been building in her all night.

When she slid into the passenger seat, Amos leaned in for a kiss. Katie clenched her fingers into his jacket and pulled him closer, relishing the low growl that came from him in response.

"Let's get home," she said when he broke the kiss.

"Want something, Kitten?"

She wanted his mouth. His fingers. His dick. She wanted him touching her. Fucking her. But those words were hard to say.

Amos chuckled, pulled back and shut the passenger door. In seconds, he was in the driver's seat and they were on their way back to her place. Wordless, they climbed the stairs. Once inside, Katie wrapped her arms around him and tipped her head up for a kiss. She lifted her legs and locked them around his hips.

He turned and pinned her between his hard body and the wall. The idea of Amos claiming his prize — her ass — sent waves of pleasure through her. Her nipples pebbled and her clit throbbed at the thought of him having every part of her.

She tugged at his shirt, desperate to get skin to skin with him. When he kissed her again, she nipped at his lips and tongue until his kisses turned savage and primal. With a growl, Amos whirled them away from the wall and carried her closer to the bed.

She pulled his jacket off his shoulders, then concentrated on unbuttoning his shirt. Her fingers fumbled and Katie gave up and yanked, sending buttons flying. Amos lifted her sweater over her head and somehow unhooked her bra in the same move. He sank his teeth into the curve where her shoulder and neck met and Katie gripped his hair, holding him tight against her.

In seconds, he had her out of her jeans. His touch was firm, demanding, and her panties tore as he yanked them down before plunging his fingers between her thighs. Katie spread her legs to give him greater access.

Amos shifted, tumbling her to the bed before he pushed her legs wide and lowered his head. He closed his mouth over her as if she was a tasty meal he was bent on devouring. He thrust fingers into her and she cried out in pleasure at feeling so full of him. The orgasm hit hard and fast and before the shaking had stopped, Amos rolled Katie over.

He grabbed her hips and pulled her up until her ass was in the air. His lips were warm on her skin as he kissed the curve of each cheek.

"Time to pay up, Kitten," he said. He slid one hand under her and pressed his fingers back inside her. Katie ground against him, wanting more. She felt teeth on her ass, then a warm tongue sliding along the crack.

"You're so fucking wet."

He punctuated those words by sliding another finger into her until Katie felt stuffed full. There was a click, then the feel of warm lube trickling over her ass before Amos circled his thumb around the entrance.

"Relax, Kitten," he whispered. "I promise, you're not getting my dick in your ass tonight. Just a little warm up to see how you like me playing with this beautiful peach of yours."

He pressed and his thumb popped in. Katie tensed, but there was no pain. Only pleasure. She arched her back, enjoying the feeling of Amos thrusting his fingers in and out of her pussy while his other thumb pressed into her asshole.

The frantic sense was gone, but she was still wound up tight, shaking and clutching the sheets as he shifted to working a finger into her ass. He moved slowly, but there was nothing gentle about his touch.

"Finger your clit for me, Kitten."

There was no denying that command. Katie reached down and laid her fingers against her swollen clit. Her body rocked with his rhythmic thrusts and she timed her strokes to match.

The finger in her ass withdrew, leaving her feeling empty. Amos applied more lube, then it was two fingers pressing into her ass. Katie moaned in pleasure.

"Do you want more?"

"Yes, please!" There was no thought to it. She wanted whatever he had to give. A primal longing to be claimed as his own filled her. More lube then he pressed three fingers against her ass. He took his time. Slow and insistent pressure until her body relaxed and he was gliding fingers in and out of her pussy and her ass.

It was too much. It was not enough. Katie trembled and shook. Nothing existed except Amos and how he made her feel.

"Come for me, now, Kitten."

His command was her release. Katie cried out his name as she came, gushing over her own hand. The sound of a belt buckle, then the crinkle of a wrapper. Then the feel of rough denim against her ass. When had he moved his hands? When had he stopped fingering her? Katie arched against him, desperate to have him filling her again.

One hand gripped her hip as his dick slid into her wetness and Katie sighed at the now familiar pressure. Then a finger pressed against her ass again and she whimpered.

"It's okay, Kitten. You can take it."

One finger and she moaned in pleasure. Two and she gasped. Three and she was incoherent as he fucked her so hard and deep she couldn't stay up on her knees.

Katie collapsed to the bed, but Amos shifted again and pulled her to the edge of the mattress. He tugged until she was kneeling on the floor and bent over the bed. Then he was back inside her, filling pussy and ass and fucking her until she was ready to come again.

"That's it, Kitten. Come on my cock." He wrapped his free hand in her hair and tugged until she lifted up from the bed. His lips grazed her cheek.

"You are mine," he growled the words into her ear. "Your pussy is mine. Your ass is mine."

Katie exploded again at his words. Then Amos pulled out and stood.

"Turn around, Kitten," he commanded. She did as he instructed, and Amos pulled off the condom and laid the head of his dick against her lips.

"Suck this cock like a good girl. I want to come in that pretty mouth."

Katie opened her mouth wide and took as much of him as she could. He clenched a hand into her hair and held her head. She reached down and fingered herself as his dick slid over her tongue, mimicking the same slow, deep rhythm of him fucking her.

"That's it, make yourself come again for me." His voice was ragged and his breathing fast and uneven. "Come for me, now."

Katie shook in another orgasm as Amos exploded in her mouth.

"Good girl, Kitten. Such a good girl for me."

Amos slid out of her mouth, then he bent and scooped her into his arms. "We both need a shower."

Katie laid her head on his shoulder, lost in the feel of his strong arms supporting her and the hard wall of his chest cradling her body.

In the shower, he washed them both, then held her under the hot spray. He grasped her chin and tipped her face up to his.

"Checking in that you're okay?"

Katie nodded.

"Good." Amos kissed her gently, then held her face in his hands. "Okay with everything?" He traced his fingers over her lips, then slid down to brush her nipples, then over her belly and down until they grazed her still swollen labia. He slid along her cheeks until his fingertips rested against her tender asshole. "Because all of this is mine. I'm laying my claim."

Katie reached up and grasped his hair, pulling until he bent so she could kiss him. "Yours. Just like you are mine."

Amos pressed her against the shower wall, then touched his forehead to hers.

"Someday, I'm going to fuck your ass," he said. "And you're going to beg me to do it. In the most graphic, naughty way you can."

Chapter Nineteen

Amos
November 14, Tuesday

Early morning light turned the eastern sky into a thin band of pale orange that was quickly swallowed up by the still night sky. Amos got out of his truck and stretched, trying to stifle a yawn. He'd worked all weekend at the fire station, and when he hadn't been there, he'd been with Katie. A late-night call meant he'd been up all night.

None of that would matter to Leah. They had cars to take care of. Sometimes, being the biggest independent mechanic shop within a hundred miles was as much of a curse as a blessing. At least there'd be breakfast.

He pushed through the side door and the smell of burnt toast and what could only be described as incinerated bacon assaulted him. It was so strong, he looked for signs of a fire, but there was no smoke or heat coming from the kitchen and the smoke detector flashed green.

A door slammed upstairs. Grace's room, from the sound of it. He moved slowly into the kitchen to find the old man sitting at the table, arms across his chest and scowling. A beat-up coffee mug sat in a puddle of water and a soggy cigarette bobbed at the edge of the mug.

The clank of a pan in the sink pulled his attention to Leah as she wrapped a towel around the handle of the cast iron skillet and marched toward the side door. The smell of burnt bacon followed in her wake.

"What the hell happened?" Amos had never known Leah to burn food. Let alone turn bacon into whatever the hell that was.

He got no answer from their dad. The old man just fished another cigarette from his pack and looked around for his matches. He made a disgusted sound when he picked them up from the puddle of water on the table.

"Don't even think of lighting up in the house." Leah stormed across the room and snatched up the cup. She threw a towel at Amos and pointed at the table. He knew better than to open his mouth. He got to work mopping up the mess.

"You said you'd quit." Leah upended the toaster over the trashcan, shaking a bunch of burnt pieces of bread loose. "And if you decide you can't live without smoking, at least do it outside."

She sounded so much like their mother that Amos nearly said "yes'm" before he remembered she was chastising their father. For Leah to go that far, shit had to be bad.

"It's my house. I'll do as I please."

The door upstairs slammed shut again and footsteps thudded down the stairs. Fast and angry sounding. Grace popped her head into the kitchen. Her eyes were red like she'd been crying and she had a backpack slung over her shoulder.

"I've got to get studying done. I'm gonna stay with Lily for a bit."

She didn't wait for a response and she didn't cross the room to kiss their dad on the cheek like she normally did. She lifted a hand and waved, then hurried out the door.

Leah arched an eyebrow at Amos then followed their little sister, leaving him alone with their still-scowling dad.

Amos finished wiping up the mess and poured two coffees. Mercifully, the coffee pot seemed untouched by whatever chaos had unleashed itself in the kitchen. He took a sip and spat it in the sink. *What the hell?* He was all for strong coffee, but whatever was in his cup tasted like someone had dumped half a can of grounds on top of yesterday's used stuff. In a word—nasty.

Ignoring his father, he dumped the pot, scrubbed it out for good measure and made fresh. Only when he had two steaming mugs of something drinkable did he sit at the table across from his father.

"So, ah…" Words failed him. All Amos could do was wave a hand around the room. The toaster sitting sideways on the counter. The pile of messy looking paper towels overflowing the trashcan. Plus whatever the hell was in the other skillet in the sink. And the cast iron that was who knows where now.

"I wanted breakfast and the lazy bones in this house wasn't up to make it," the old man replied. "So I made it myself."

Amos glanced at the clock on the wall. Six-thirty. Judging by what he could see and smell, he'd bet Leah or Grace had walked into a smoky mess around six. For years, their dad woke up at six on the dot. Every single day. He'd make it to the kitchen by quarter past, and if there wasn't coffee already brewing, the man would be in a grouchy mood.

How their mother had put up with it was beyond Amos.

Amos took a sip of coffee to keep from saying anything. He stood and peered into the sink. A lumpy, blackened mess filled the small skillet. A hint of yellow suggested they were supposed to be sunny side up eggs. He downed another swallow of coffee and turned back to his father.

"So what had Grace so upset?" Amos didn't want to bring it up, but he had to. He'd understood Leah's pointed look. She might as well have screamed, "you talk to him."

Sometimes, Amos could get through to their dad. Sometimes Leah could. Usually, Pops had a soft spot for his youngest.

"How'm I supposed to know what goes through her head?" The scowl was back. He pointed a finger at Amos. "And where the hell were you? Day starts at six. Always has. You look like you were up all night. Partyin' like as not. What d'ya think you're doin' sneakin' home afore dawn?"

If his dad slipping into lazy speech wasn't clue enough that something was wrong, the fact that he seemed to think Amos was somehow sneaking back home like a teenager was a gut punch.

"I was working at the station, Dad," Amos replied. "We had a late-night call. Car rolled out on the four lane and hit a tractor trailer going the other way. Took a few hours to clear."

The old man nodded and took a slow sip from his coffee. "Don't know why you insist on working as a damn firefighter if they ain't paying you."

At least he seemed to be back in the present. Leah came in and made a disgusted sound at the sink. She shook her head and grabbed a cup of coffee before sitting at the table.

"What the hell, it's been a morning. Might as well make a meal of it." She squared her shoulders then reached across the table and laid her hand over their dad's.

"Daddy, I want you to listen to me for a minute," she said. "I know you don't like hearing this, but please, talk to your doctor. You haven't been yourself lately and this morning is a perfect example of that."

Amos racked his brain trying to recall if he'd ever heard Leah speak so gently. Maybe when she talked to Grace. Maybe.

This wasn't the first time they'd had to confront their dad. He hadn't dealt well with his wife's death, and it was Amos and Grace who had finally gotten him out of the room the two had shared their entire marriage. Not that it had been much improvement. He'd just poured himself into work, essentially ignoring his hurting children. Over the years since, it had usually been Leah who'd pulled him out of a funk, or convinced him to listen to reason.

"Watch your tone, missy."

Aw shit. The old man pushed himself up so hard his chair slid back into the wall. He dropped his cup to the table with a clatter and grabbed the pack of cigarettes he'd dropped earlier.

"Y'all are gettin' way too big for your britches, if ya ask me. I tol' y'all afore, I'll close this shop down."

Leah took a deep breath and planted her hands on the table, her face a tight mask.

"Okay, go ahead. I'll pack my things and move out of the apartment. I'm sure I can get a job in Charleston. Find a place for me and Grace, so she'll be close to the university."

She glanced at Amos, then back at their dad.

"I know Amos has money saved up, the way he lives. He'll manage until the fire department gets a budget and starts paying. We're busting our asses to make this family business work, but hey, you wanna shut it down because it's not the way you imagined? Go right ahead."

Leah didn't lose her temper often, but when she did, she pulled no punches. No surprise, the old man didn't back down. He slammed both hands into the table and leaned in close to his oldest child.

"If your mother was alive, you'd be breaking her heart right now. Get outta my house."

Leah didn't flinch. She didn't even bat an eye. She rose slowly and stepped to the kitchen door.

"No, Dad," she whispered. "You're the one who'd be breaking her heart right now."

The door didn't slam as Leah left. It closed with a quiet click that seemed somehow far worse. Amos toyed with his coffee cup, unsure what to say or where anything stood. He always figured one day the old man would push Leah too far and it seemed like that day had finally come.

Pops grabbed his keys from the peg on the wall and slammed the kitchen door on his way out. Amos leaned into the window and watched as his father clambered into his truck and tore out of the lot. No sooner was he on the road than Leah came back inside with the cast iron skillet in hand.

"Let's clean up this mess and get to work," she said, her voice tight. "I don't know about you, but if I walk away from here, it's going to be with a clean slate – no outstanding jobs."

Amos nodded and they set to work on the kitchen. Desperate as he was for answers to a million questions about the morning, he kept his mouth shut. Leah would talk in her own time. In the meanwhile, he busied himself scrubbing charred eggs from the pan.

"Grace called about a quarter to six." Leah scanned the now clean kitchen and handed Amos a bowl and a box of cereal. "I don't want to even smell an egg or bacon right now. Anyway, she was freaked out. Said she woke up to the smell of burning food and came into the kitchen and found Dad sitting at the table smoking a cigarette, staring out the window. The bacon was on fire and the eggs were... well, you saw them."

The scene played out in Amos' head as if he was seeing it – Grace, always cool under pressure, would have grabbed a lid and clamped it down on the bacon pan. Then she'd have turned off the eggs. He imagined the toast was already charcoal – likely because their dad had pushed it down more than the usual two times. She must've caught it before it flared too much, or else the smoke alarms would've gone off.

"Wait." Amos looked around the room. Their dad had been sitting staring out the window. "He'd opened the window, hadn't he?"

Leah nodded and poured herself a bowl of cereal. That explained the smoke detectors not going off – open window, lots of air flow prevented smoke build up and kept the heat low. Still, he'd have to test the thing to make sure it was working properly.

"Think he'll shut it down?" In a way it would be a relief. Leah was right, he had enough saved that he could get by for a bit. Plus he could always take odd jobs. He'd have to find some other way to get Miles talking, but that was somewhere at the bottom of his worry list.

"Not a chance in hell. He's too invested in the business and the history. There is a chance he'll kick us all out of it and run it and himself into the ground, yeah. But I think he'd come around before things got that bad. I'd rather avoid that path."

Me too. Fuck. That was some shit he didn't want to think about. "This isn't the first time he's acted…uh…like he's not really aware of when we are. If that makes sense."

For a year after their mother had passed, the old man had talked as if she was still around. They'd chalked that up to grief. He'd finally gotten past it and things had been normal, or as normal as they could be with Roy Kimmel. Then, for the past year, Amos had noticed their dad slipping a little. When he talked to his sisters, they said the same things.

Their dad would talk like Grace was still in high school, not well into her twenties. Recently, he mentioned he was planning to work on Paul DeJarnet's old truck, but Paul had passed in July after the big fire at Parsons Acres. Sometimes Amos forgot how much had happened over the last eight months.

"Makes total sense and you're right. I've talked to his doctor, but there's only so much he can tell me unless Dad gives him the go ahead. But I can tell the doctor a lot," she said. "And I have."

At least that was good news. They ate in silence. Amos tried not to think about where their father may have gone. He'd found him in a bar a time or two. Leah said after Amos' arrest, the old man had taken to following Dwight Phelps or Carl Tilman around, as if his presence would mess up their business. Their mother had put a stop to that behavior by reminding him that if those two were up to what he feared, she didn't want to be a widow because her husband stuck his nose where it didn't belong.

"So we just carry on like nothin' happened?"

"Until he actually kicks us out, or closes shop? Yep. Figure we need to get the garage all set. You said Miles was making noise about starting earlier than planned?"

Amos rinsed his bowl and stuck it in the dishwasher. "Yeah. Figure I'll call the Perry's and make sure they're okay with that. I don't want to find out he left them in a lurch."

She finished putting the milk and cereal away. "Well, let's get to it then. If the old man isn't back by lunch, we can start making calls."

Between extra coffee and the stress of the morning family shit show, Amos had gone from tired to laser focused and they got through two big jobs, leaving the rest for Miles, who'd agreed to start Wednesday.

Right before lunch, Amos called the Perry's and Eliza confirmed what Miles had said. Business was light, so they'd done what they always do—give staff the option of leaving early. Many would take it because working at the orchard was extra and they were being kind to those who relied on the orchard as their primary income during the busy months.

He'd just hung up from that call when he got a text from Drea, asking about progress with Miles and letting him know the drug related complaints were still on the rise. As if he couldn't see some of that on his own—the medic reports he turned in every week had more transports for drugs than usual as well.

Leah finished the tire balance she'd been working on and pointed a finger at the wall clock. *Lunchtime.* They cleaned up and headed to the house as the old man's truck pulled into the drive. Leah marched into the house as if it was any other day and Amos followed suit.

The old man came in reeking of beer and Amos had to bite his tongue to keep from lecturing the man on driving in that condition. *Come to think of it, maybe next time he pulls this shit, I should call Drea and get him picked up for a DUI.*

Leah handed Amos cans of tomato soup and told him to get busy while she threw together grilled cheese sandwiches. Their dad fished a beer from the fridge then took his usual spot at the table as he opened the can.

"Fine. Y'all wanna bring someone on for the basics. You do that. I don't want to see them. You work them outta the side garage so they're not getting in my way. Be nice to not bother with the busy work."

Amos shot a grateful glance at Leah, who seemed to be suppressing a smile. *Well that solves one of our worries.* If the old man didn't want to see the new hire, Amos had less fear of him finding out it was Miles.

"Help means you'll have more time on your hands for what you oughta be doing, Leah."

The pan she had in her hand banged against the stove as she took in an audible breath. "You want straight cheddar or mixed with jack, Dad?"

Their dad scratched his chin as if it was a question for the ages before he replied. "A mix. If you're not working so hard in the garage, you'll have more time to cook proper meals and think about finding yourself a man. You're not getting any younger, and I wanna see grandkids."

Amos reached over and squeezed his sister's shoulder. Her mouth moved as she silently counted to ten, then counted backwards. There was no changing their dad's mind on some subjects. To him, women belonged in the home, not turning wrenches. Never mind how good a mechanic Leah was. Or that she had a great head for the business. Or that the only person she'd ever gone out with more than once or twice was Jake Parsons.

His phone buzzed with an incoming text and he glanced at the screen. *Katie.* It was lunchtime — she often called or texted when she had a break. He'd get it later. Right now, he needed to keep his sister from throwing a skillet full of grilled cheese sandwiches at their dad.

"I'll share some of the blame there," their dad continued. "I should never have let you start working in the garage to begin with."

Amos' phone buzzed again. Two messages. One from Miles confirming the start time on Wednesday, and another from Katie. He sent a thumbs-up to Miles and opened Katie's message. He'd barely glanced at it, noting only "*rough day*" before Leah snatched the pot of simmering soup from in front of him and demanded everyone get to the table.

He blew on a spoonful of soup, then had to put it down as the emergency tone chimed on his phone. *Dammit.* He wasn't on call today. He shouldn't even be on the roster. Still, he excused himself and checked in with Shawn at the station. He also sent Katie a quick *"what's up"* and was about to type more when raised voices in the kitchen pulled his attention back to his family.

"If you didn't want me working in the garage, why did you ever teach me the skills?"

Leah and their dad sat at opposite sides of the table, their lunches forgotten as they engaged in the argument they'd been having since she'd given up her dolls and asked for a toolkit for her birthday.

"False alarm," he said as he sat back down. "Somebody paged everyone instead of just today's roster. Be nice to get it so we can have a full team staffing all the time."

A series of buzzes sent his phone clattering across the table and Amos slapped his hand down on it before his dad could bitch about phones during meal times. Though at the moment, the old man was yelling back at Leah and probably hadn't even noticed the phone.

Amos chanced a glance at the screen. More messages from Drea, Miles and Katie. They'd all have to wait. His priority was reining in his sister and their father before the fragile peace that had formed when he'd come home and agreed to hire some help was completely shattered.

* * * *

Katie

The little boy sat in the reading corner playing a game on Katie's tablet. She turned to Principal Dubois and shook her head.

"The social worker actually suggested sending him home?" She pointed out the window where sheets of rain battered the glass. "A five year old is supposed to walk alone to the other side of town in this? He has no jacket and came to school in a T-shirt and soiled shorts."

They'd had a cold snap and the mild temperatures had dropped dramatically. She could understand sending a child out without a coat on occasion, but this wasn't the first time Mark Hodges had come to school completely unprepared for the weather. It had been raining all night, so it wasn't like it had been sunny when he left the house this morning.

She could even understand soiled pants, up to a point. Kindergartners had accidents. It happened. But this had happened before with Mark and his shorts were crusted and stuck to his legs. When she hadn't been able to reach his mother, and social services hadn't responded right away, she'd found clean pants and called in another teacher as witness then taken him to the staff restroom to clean up and change.

"I left an urgent message for the supervisor," the principal responded. "Of course we aren't sending him home alone."

The classroom door swung open and a harried looking woman rushed in. "I apologize, I just got your message. I'm Rachel Linz with Child Services. I'm so sorry for that earlier response. That was... inappropriate, to say the least. We'll be addressing that internally. May we sit?"

Katie pointed at the large table she used for groups and the three women perched on small chairs. Katie was dressed for working with five year olds, but Principal Dubois was in a polished-looking pants suit. Still, she didn't complain and managed to look poised, even with her knees all bunched up.

"A team responded to the home and had a conversation with the mother," the social worker said. She slid a paper across the table. "I'll be taking the child home and completing the home inspection then. I do appreciate your calling on this."

Katie scanned the page. She didn't know what she expected to see, but the report seemed cursory at best. She hated the idea of coming between a child and their parent, but as far as she was concerned, the child's welfare came before anything else.

"I get the conservative approach here, but..." Katie paused and glanced over at the little boy. "This is not the first time. We've documented a pattern—he comes to school hungry, has no lunch and no money in his account and the family isn't on the free plan. We still feed him, of course."

Rachel Linz offered a tight smile that didn't reach her eyes. "I understand how frustrating it is."

"Do you?" Katie leaned forward and shook her head. "I am very tolerant. We all have bad days. I've worked in an inner city. I've seen families who simply don't have enough. But this child comes to school dirty nearly every day. He is hungry every day."

She took a breath and pulled out her notebook. "His mother is repeatedly late for drop off and pickup. On three occasions, he came to school with soiled clothing. By soiled, I mean he had dried feces and urine inside his clothes. We reported all three incidents and heard nothing back."

She turned her notes so the social worker could see them. The woman gave the page a quick glance then looked back to Katie. "They were all investigated and we found no cause to take action. We cautioned the mother about ensuring he has clean clothes. I appreciate your passion, and I assure you we are taking every step possible to guard the child's welfare."

Katie opened her mouth but stopped when Principal Dubois shook her head. The principal stood, somehow making the move graceful despite her high heels.

"Thank you, Ms. Linz," Principal Dubois said as she extended a hand to the woman. "We found some clean sweat pants in the lost and found and luckily they fit Mark. Kindly let his mother know he can keep them. And please keep us posted."

The woman shook their hands then crossed to Mark. He smiled and stood, brought the tablet back to Katie and waved as they left.

"I hate having to do that." Katie stood and paced the room. "Is it usually that bad?"

The principal shrugged. "Honestly? It varies. We've had some social workers who are overzealous and some who aren't zealous enough. Like that one. Are you okay?"

Katie stopped pacing and stood in the middle of the room, hugging herself. "I will be, thanks. I've seen worse, but you never get used to it. I don't want to ever get used to it."

As soon as the principal was out the door, Katie grabbed her phone. Amos' responses had been terse. Not like him at all. But maybe he was just tired. He'd said he'd had a late-night call and hadn't slept and he had a lot of work to do today.

She pulled up his number and hit the call button. He picked up on the first ring.

"Hey. I'm sorry you're having a shitty day. I haven't even had a chance to read everything you sent. Are you okay?"

That deep voice rumbling through her phone was a balm to Katie's nerves, but something was off. He didn't sound right. She reasoned it must be that he was in the garage. There were loud noises in the background making it hard to hear him.

"I'm...uh...yeah... I mean it's just..." Katie took a deep breath and tried to gather her whirling thoughts. "I had to call..."

A loud clang echoed over the phone and Amos cussed. "Hang on, sorry." He said something, obviously talking to someone at the garage with him. There were raised voices and another loud clang. "My dad's not doing well, but he's insisting on working in the garage and he's fucking shit up. I gotta go. Can I call you later?"

Katie swallowed the tears that threatened to rise up. "Yeah, um...sure. See ya."

She hung up before she sobbed into the phone. Katie rushed through getting her things together and drove home on autopilot. She made it upstairs and into her apartment before the real tears started.

With them came fear and uncertainty.

So much for taking a break from men. She was falling in love. Maybe had already fallen. But Amos was still running hot and cold. Just like every man she'd ever dated. He'd be all showy and affectionate one day, then turn around and be distant and cold the next.

No amount of logic or reason could change the facts. Katie had gone and done it again—fallen for a guy who loved being with her when it was convenient for him and ignored her when it wasn't.

Stop it! Amos isn't like that.

She stared at her phone as if she could will him to call her back. She plugged the phone in then turned the ringer off. *No. Turn the whole thing off.* She needed to not think about it. If her ringer was off, she'd still be constantly checking. She pressed the button and held until the phone powered down, then she made herself a cup of chamomile tea and went to draw herself a bath.

She'd soak in the hottest water she could stand, drink her tea, then crawl into bed and sleep. She tried not to think about little Mark Hodges, so cheerful and smiling in a child-size fireman's coat that was still far too big for him as he was the first of her students to take his turn with the fire hose.

Nope. Nope. Not thinking of that.

Those thoughts would only lead to more on Mark or Amos—neither of them a very cheery path at the moment.

She settled into the water, hissing as the heat prickled her skin. The first time she'd had to call child services, she'd cried for hours. Then she'd gone to a bar on her way home and drank until she couldn't see straight. The hangover the next day had been something spectacular. It was a pattern she'd repeated a few times that first year.

Then one morning, she'd looked in the mirror and saw her mother's face staring back at her. Bedraggled hair, dark circles under her eyes, and a drawn, haggard look. Katie had called a therapist before going in to work.

After that, she tried to find better ways of dealing with her frustrations. That had led her to discover more of her not-so-vanilla side. Which brought her right back to thinking about Amos and how their needs seemed so perfectly matched.

Okay, maybe she could think about him a little. Especially the things they'd done Friday, and the promise Amos had made about fucking her ass. A thought that caused a little squeeze of erotic tension and a tiny shiver of fear.

But she trusted Amos. She sighed and slid her hand down her belly until her fingers grazed her labia.

"Good girl, Kitten. Such a good girl for me."

She could hear his voice in her head. Katie stopped and rose from the bath. She needed to be on the bed with her toy. She needed to come.

She needed Amos.

Chapter Twenty

Amos
November 15, Wednesday

"So, shit like oil changes, right?" Miles stuffed his hands in his pockets as he walked the garage floor. Not like the space wasn't familiar to him. Amos' mother would've had a fit if she'd caught them smoking, so they'd go to the side garage. Even then, the old man had rarely used the building and he never cared if there was smoke on top of the usual shop smells.

"Yeah," Amos replied. "Just tryin' to be more efficient. Leah's got a whole system figured out."

The three Kimmel siblings had spent hours working out logistics while their dad cussed and muttered in the main garage. He'd taken the entire afternoon and late into the night to handle a tire balance and a couple of oil changes. Amos hadn't realized how slow the old man had become.

When Katie had texted yesterday, he'd had to put her off, then he'd done it again when she'd called later in the afternoon. He felt like shit about it. She needed someone and he'd not only failed, he'd lied to her about it. *Well, more like didn't tell her the whole truth. Which amounts to the same thing, asshole.*

"Tickets for the day will be on a clipboard on the desk." Amos pointed at the battered desk in the corner near the door. "Keys hung in the cabinet—all labeled. Cars lined up outside. Completed tickets go in the red folder. Simple shit."

Miles scanned the desk and nodded. If he noticed that the whole system was compartmentalized and isolated, he didn't say anything. The computer was locked to allow access only to things needed for the job. Even the visible client information was limited. Grace had set that up. Amos had hated getting their baby sister involved, but Leah had insisted Grace had the skills to do the job quickly and more thoroughly than either of them could.

"It's good to have the help early. I figured you weren't comin' in till after the holiday," Amos said. Miles lifted a shoulder then picked up the clipboard and flipped through the tickets.

"Shit got slow," Miles replied. "Had more staff than customers last weekend. Figured I had something else lined up, so I could bounce early."

That at least tracked with what Eliza had said. *This shit's way above my pay grade.* He had no clue what he was doing or how to go about getting Drea what she wanted. All he knew was how to be a friend, and maybe that would be enough.

"Listen to whatever you want," Amos said. "Finally replaced the old system. Connect via Bluetooth. I guess you could plug in or use earbuds. I'll be in and out and if you need anything, text me or Leah."

Miles picked up the clipboard and flipped through the tickets. "What hours do you want me here?"

Good question. Amos and Leah had gone rounds on that subject. During the day risked their dad coming out. At night risked him noticing lights in the garage. Amos needed to be here for at least some of the time. *Too many fucking possibilities.*

"Mostly weekdays are best," Amos replied. "But you've got flexibility within reason. We really need at least twenty hours a week, and up to thirty for now. Clock in on the desktop and log your job numbers for the day. So long as shit's gettin' done, it's all good."

Amos had convinced Leah to give it two weeks and see how it went. If Miles worked well and managed his time, great. If he didn't, well...they'd cross that bridge if it came to it.

"Sounds like a cake walk," Miles said. He looked uncomfortable — hands locked onto the clipboard, eyes darting the room as if he was afraid of eye contact. "Thanks, man."

Something in Miles' tone tugged at Amos. Maybe his old friend really was trying to rebuild his life and didn't know how. Or didn't have the opportunity. It would be nice if Drea was wrong, but Amos suspected that wasn't the case. He'd seen enough on Halloween to recognize that. The shit they'd found cleaning up after the fire at the Connour's place erased any doubts.

He got Miles set up with tools and everything he needed then figured the best thing for him to do was get out of the man's way and let him settle in. Hovering wasn't going to get the work done any faster and it wouldn't loosen Miles up any, either.

"Hey, one other thing." Amos waited until Miles looked back at him. "I haven't told your sister you're working here."

The smile that crossed Miles' face did not make Amos feel any better. It was a smile that said 'I have something on you now' and it gave Amos the creeps.

"I figured as much," Miles replied. "Maybe after a while, she'll get over the shit from the past. Nah, man, it's our secret."

Amos nodded his thanks and headed for the door. Everything in him wanted to reach out to Katie. Keeping things from her made him feel like an absolute slime. The fact that it was over her brother made it even worse. If he hurried, he could catch her before lunch. He was in his truck before he thought to at least text. He pulled out his phone.

I've got some free time. Can I bring lunch by?

He hit send and sat staring at his phone, waiting for the message to be read. Should he have been nicer? Maybe the message was too short. Or he could have apologized again for yesterday. He'd tried texting and calling after dinner, when shit had settled down, but Katie's phone was either off or on do not disturb. Three dots appeared. Katie was responding.

Another shitty day. Would you mind grabbing something that can hold for later? Like fried chicken or something? Meet in my classroom.

Amos replied with an *OK* and headed for the Chicken Shack, trying not to imagine what in the hell was going on. Twenty minutes later, he pulled into the school with a bag of fried chicken and a few sides. He checked in at the office and headed to Katie's class.

The last thing he expected to find there was Principal Dubois, Drea Parsons and a man and woman he didn't know. Katie sat on a low bench, hugging herself as if something terrible had happened. When he came in, her gaze shot to him and a thin smile crossed her lips, but didn't reach her eyes. He held up the bags of food as everyone in the room turned to him.

"Should I just put this on a desk and leave?"

Drea shook her head then tipped her chin toward Katie. She laid a hand on his arm and leaned in close. "One of Katie's students lost their mother today. Overdose. She's going to need a friend."

Amos laid the bag of food on Katie's desk then went to sit next to her. Everything in him wanted to wrap her in his arms and protect her from this kind of pain.

"This is the district superintendent Dave Clements, and our district social worker Lucille Ellis. They arrived just before you did, Amos."

Principal Dubois twisted her hands in front of her as if that could somehow contain the emotions she was clearly struggling with. "On Tuesday, Ms. Tilman called child services regarding a student in her class. Considering the nature of the complaint, they sent someone to the home. They spoke with the child's mother and determined they did not need to remove the child from the environment."

The woman's tone said she wasn't thrilled with the outcome. Katie's body shook as if she was stifling a sob. Amos put an arm around her shoulders and she leaned into him.

"Today, that child didn't show up for class," she continued. "Katie...ah... Ms. Tilman expressed concern after the incident yesterday and we tried to contact the parent. After we got no response and the emergency number went unanswered, we contacted law enforcement."

Drea looked sad as she turned to the superintendent and social worker. "I went to the home, a small unit in the back of West Creek trailer park."

Amos tuned the rest out. He didn't want to hear the details. Hell, he'd seen enough of them over the years and he knew the units Drea was talking about. The places Dwight Phelps rented out cheap.

"The child is currently with a foster family," Drea continued. "I asked to meet with you all like this because we have a growing drug problem in Orchard Creek and it's hitting our poorest families particularly hard. This used to be a problem for high school and maybe middle school students, but we're seeing a lot of young parents getting caught up in heavy usage as well."

Katie's hand, cold and trembling, slid into his and Amos wrapped both of his hands around her tiny one and squeezed gently. As if he needed any more reason to feel like shit about not being there for her yesterday, now there was this. *Chalk up another reason to throttle Miles as well.*

He sat silently while the superintendent suggested closing the school the next day. The principal argued against it, but she and the social worker agreed that Katie should take the next two days off.

"No." Katie raised her head and pulled her hand away as she stood. "I understand why you think that, but gossip spreads. It's likely some of my students will hear this news and it's important they have a familiar face at school to help support them. There will be fear. Uncertainty."

The room exploded in discussion, but Katie stood firm and in the end, got her way. The principal and school officials took their leave and Drea raised an eyebrow at Amos. He stifled a groan. His first concern right now was Katie, but there was no way Drea missed the significance of where the family lived.

"Why don't you get your stuff together and I'll take you home? We can pick up your car later. Or hell, tomorrow."

Katie nodded and went to her desk, moving as if on autopilot as she stuffed files into her drawer and started packing her bag.

"I just started Miles working at the garage. He hasn't said shit. Hasn't had a chance to. But yeah, I know." He kept his voice low so only Drea could hear him. Her lips pressed into a tight line.

"I can use this as an excuse to do some digging," she said. "Just try your best. I know it's outside your comfort zone and I appreciate it."

Drea said goodbye to Katie, leaving Amos alone with the woman he was falling head over heels for, and whose trust he was breaking every minute he kept silent about the fact he was spying on her brother.

I ought to tell her. There's no love lost there. She'd understand.

She would also fear Amos getting sucked into her brother's world again. She'd fear losing Amos to the whirlwind that was Miles. She'd fear the damage her brother could do in her life—just as he had before. Considering what she'd been through to distance herself from all of that, she'd probably tell Amos to go to hell rather than risk it all.

She shouldered her bag, but Amos slid it gently from her. "I got this. Grab the chicken and let's go."

His heart ached at the pain in her eyes, then soared when she slipped her hand into his again and held on tightly.

Katie

Katie tossed the last bone into the empty chicken bucket and reached for a wet wipe. Amos had kept up an easy chatter as they drove back to her place, then continued while he laid out dishes for dinner.

"You remember the first kid on safety day?" She picked apart a napkin, shredding it into tiny pieces that scattered over her plate. "The little boy who was too small for even the smallest coat?"

Amos took a moment and she could almost see him thinking back to that day. "Mark Hodges. Not likely to forget that one. His mother went into labor during gym class. Think she was in eleventh grade. Nobody knew she was pregnant until her water broke." He smiled and shook his head. "Mark came into the world blue and not breathing, but we got him tur..."

He stopped mid word and grabbed Katie's hand. "Oh, shit. It was Erin?"

"When the police showed up after we called social services, they found Mark sitting on the step outside the trailer, crying." Katie swiped at the tears on her cheeks. She was supposed to protect her students from shit like this.

Amos swore and slid out of his chair, knelt on the floor and wrapped his arms around her, cradling her against his chest.

"I should have seen the signs," Katie said, her words muffled by Amos' shirt. Her gut wrenched even as her mind struggled to make some sense of everything.

"He started the year out strong, but then started coming in late. Or with no snacks packed. Or his hair not brushed or even washed." Katie had brushed it all off. *He's a kindergartener. Maybe neurodivergent. The family wasn't well off.* All perfectly reasonable explanations. But she was his teacher.

"He came in after Halloween and still had candy smeared on his face. I figured he'd gotten into it in the morning until I found candy smushed into his hair and he said that's what he'd had for dinner."

Even then, she hadn't been sure. Kids had vivid imaginations after all. At pickup, Erin had been mortified about the mess. She said they'd had soup and Mark must have gotten into the candy after she'd gone to bed. She'd promised to hide it better.

Then he'd come in with soiled clothes and Katie had reported it, but never heard anything back. She shook her head. She needed to stop dwelling on something that was out of her control.

"What are we?" Katie blurted the words out as she pushed out of Amos' embrace. Maybe not the best way to bring up the subject, but right now, it was the only way.

"We've gone well past the seeing where things go stage," Amos replied. He took her hands and stood, then headed to the couch and pulled her to sit next to him. His gorgeous blue eyes focused on her face. "We've both known that for a while now, I think."

It was a non-answer. He'd given her a few of those lately and it felt wrong somehow. Once they'd started seeing each other regularly, Amos had been super communicative, even when he was busy. Lately, he'd often go silent or give vague answers.

"I'm serious," she insisted. "I'm not asking for a declaration of undying love or anything, I just…" Katie shrugged. She was trying to sort out exactly what she felt and wanted to say, but her brain was a scrambled mush after the last two days.

"Everyone figures we're dating," she said with a soft sigh.

Amos chuckled, and there was the warmth and openness she was used to from him. "I'd say everyone is right."

"But I mean, what are we? What do I say when people ask?" She heard the whine in her own voice and didn't like it.

"What label do you need?"

Another non answer.

"I need to know what I am to you. Are we just fuck buddies? Are you seeing other women? I dunno…we haven't talked about this stuff.

Amos' eyes narrowed. His fingers squeezed on hers. "Kitten."

That one word brought her whirling thoughts to a halt. The silly pet name that she'd first chaffed at but then embraced soothed frayed nerves. He slid a hand into the hair at her nape, his fingers gentle.

"I thought we made that clear last Friday in the shower," he replied. He leaned close and placed his lips near her ear. "You're mine, Kitten. I don't share, and I don't expect you to, either."

Amos sighed and brought his forehead to touch hers. He lifted her hand and laid it in the middle of his chest, then placed his hand over hers. His breathing was smooth and even under her fingers. The thumping of his heart steady and strong. Katie's own breathing slowed, matching his.

"I've got a lot on my plate right now, and I realize I wasn't there for you when you needed me." Amos kissed her forehead then pulled her closer into his arms. His strength and warmth enveloped her. "I'm here now. The next few weeks might be a little rough, but we can make it through it."

His words washed over her, calming fears and settling into her soul. Still, some part of her brain whispered that she shouldn't trust him. This was just another case of bombarding her with attention when she cried out she was starving.

"Cinda said you and Missy Talbot used to date?" Katie's traitor brain had to go there. Had to dig in to some stupid thing that was probably meaningless. Amos' chest rumbled with his laughter.

"Yeah, we did," he replied. "About ten years ago. I think she liked the idea of dating the bad boy, hoping it would piss off her parents. That's how Missy was back then."

He hadn't asked her why she'd brought it up. Or why she and Cinda were talking about it. He hadn't even blown it off as ancient history. He answered her. *Huh.*

"What happened?"

This time his laugh was sharp and short. "I started working on the fire detail. Her daddy got to know me and I went from being taboo to being boring. That's about when I decided dating anyone local was probably not a great idea."

Cinda had said Amos hadn't really seen anyone else local. Amos shifted and moved her into his lap as he sat back on the couch.

"When I was young and fresh out of youth camp, I learned to be careful. Some women were looking for a project. Some, like Missy, were looking for rebellion. Others would've pulled me back into a life I'd spent two years working to get out of."

Amos smoothed his hands down her back, easing the tight muscles that had her shoulders hunched together and her neck stiff as a board.

"So I went places where nobody knew me," he continued. "By the time people around here started seeing me differently, I was dating a woman in Charleston. For a while, it was a lady in Louisville. Then it was Roanoke. That ended about a year ago."

His fingers pressed under her chin, tipping her head up. "I'm here with you now, Kitten. The past is just that. It's over and done. I'll tell you anything you want to know about it because it's part of who I am, but you are the only woman who matters to me."

Katie reached up, slid her hand behind his head and pulled him down until she could kiss him. The moment his lips touched hers, all worries fled. His strong arms wrapped her body. The spicy-sweet smell of him filled her every breath.

A sob wracked her body and she broke the kiss. "I'm sorry. I'm just..." She didn't know what she was. Or where her brain was. Every thought was a fragmented mess.

"It's okay," he said. "I've got you. You can cry, or yell and scream. If you want to break things, I can find a way to do that. What do you need?"

Turning off her brain seemed like the best idea possible. And there was only one way Katie could think to do that.

"I need to forget my name," she said. "Can you do that for me?"

His fingers twitched against her and the smile that spread on his face looked soft, but there was an edge of the devil in there as well. That's what she needed right now. She needed Amos to take her to places where she didn't have to think.

"Do you want to be pampered and cuddled and made love to slowly? Or do you need to be dragged to that bed and fucked senseless?"

Someday she'd have to take him up on the idea of pampering and slow love making. Today was not that day. Amos must have read her mind. His eyes narrowed and one corner of his mouth curled up even more.

"Fucked senseless it is."

Chapter Twenty-One

Amos
November 20, Monday

Two sets of keys hung in the cabinet—the Parsons' Harvester and a Jeep Amos knew was in for an oil change. Miles clapped his shoulder, reached past and snagged the Jeep keys.

"Morning." Miles stuffed a danish in his mouth and picked up the clipboard. "Huh. Got a tow bringing in a busted radiator. And a tune-up—that can wait till tomorrow. I need to bail earlier than usual today."

Things had been pretty peaceful since the epic blow up last week. Miles had come in and quickly settled into a routine. It was only part time work, but his hourly rate at the shop was a lot more than he'd been making at the orchard, so it balanced out.

That left Amos free to work on the Harvester and he'd almost completed it. Leah had kept their dad busy checking out problems in the older cars that came in. Some days he managed the computer diagnostic systems fine, and other days they'd send him into an hour-long rant about how tools like that took all the skill out of being a mechanic.

Amos had worried about hiring his old friend, but Miles had proven to be a solid worker, like Eliza Perry had said. Maybe he really was turning his life around. *Yeah, and Drea is imagining the drug problems. Just like I imagined the way Miles and his old man looked at that trailer fire.*

"Sounds good. Let's get to it then." He wanted to get the Parsons' truck done before Thanksgiving. Thanks to the work Miles was doing, he'd actually make it. He had everything installed, now he had to get it all connected, oiled and tested before he could crank the thing up.

He pulled out several quarts of oil and a priming pump. *Time to get this old girl lubed up.* Amos popped his earbuds in, cranked up his music and got to work. He barely looked up when the tow truck pulled in and delivered a vintage Chevelle with a busted radiator. Miles was finishing up the oil change and Leah handled the tow driver. Amos dropped another quart of oil into the Harvester as Miles rolled the Chevelle into a bay.

I could get used to working like this. Three quarts down and about six more to go.

"Hey, Amos!"

Amos looked up from the truck and found Miles, hunched over the engine compartment of the old Chevy.

"This thing's shot to shit," Miles said. "Figured it was maybe just a leak. No such luck."

He disconnected the pressure tester and scribbled a note on the ticket. Amos took a look at the readings and the growing puddle under the car.

"Yeah, no patching that. Go ahead and price out a replacement. If you're comfortable estimating the job, put it all in the system. Leah or Grace will call the customer. Good work, man."

He silently kicked himself. He'd been so absorbed in his work that he hadn't spent any time talking to Miles. Which was the whole point of him being here. *Yeah, except being a chatterbox isn't gonna win Miles' trust.*

"Get that estimate in and we can grab lunch if you want. Then bug out for the day." Amos added. It was the only thing he could come up with that made sense and wouldn't raise suspicion. Miles regarded him through slitted eyes then nodded.

"Yeah. Shouldn't take too long to get that together. It's a '71 Chevelle SS 454. It'll take longer to get the damn parts." He closed the hood and smiled at the car then shook his head. "Fucking crime to let the insides look like this."

Miles had always had a soft spot for classic American muscle cars. This car looked pretty on the outside, but the engine compartment was rough. The interior wasn't much better.

"There's been some stuff done. Looks like it's a work in progress," Amos said. "A guy at the station, his wife's grandmother had one of these sittin' in her garage. Hadn't driven it for years. She wouldn't sell it, though."

Amos went back to the Harvester and worked on finding an easy stopping point so he could take an hour and grab a burger with Miles. Ideally outside the garage where they could talk.

Miles had just shut down the computer when Amos finished cleaning up. By some unspoken agreement, they walked up the road to Burger and Bun, a favorite place when they were teens.

Once their order was up, they sat at the same table they'd always chosen back in the day — the far corner, where you could see the whole dining area and the tables outside. The ideal place to people watch.

"Kinda feels good to be messing with cars again." Miles stabbed a fry into a pile of ketchup then popped it into his mouth. "How's the old man? Saw him in the yard the other day. Figured it was best to lay low."

The bite of burger in Amos' mouth turned to sawdust and he forced himself to swallow. Miles was the last person his dad wanted on the property. The explosion that would happen if the old man found out would put all the other fights that had been had to shame.

"He's being a shit," Amos replied. "Not much new there. Starting to wonder if he's losing it. His head's not on straight."

He'd only voiced those fears to his sisters, and a little to Katie. Miles knew his family. He knew the tangled relationship Amos had always had with his father. He would understand and not judge. That and Amos couldn't think of any other way to answer, and maybe the bald-faced honesty would help.

"That bites. Why're you taking the risk then?"

Too late, Amos realized the trap Miles had laid. He already knew Amos hadn't told Katie her brother was working at the garage. He had to suspect Amos' dad wouldn't be thrilled, and now he had confirmation. So why the fuck would Amos hire him?

"Everyone deserves a second chance," Amos said. "Same thing I'd tell Pops if he had a problem with you being there."

Amos put down his burger and wiped his hands then leaned back in his seat. He looked around the restaurant — surprisingly not too crowded for lunchtime. *Fuck it. Keep it simple. Keep it honest.*

"The old man is dropping the ball," Amos said as he looked back to Miles. "He's got issues, and there's more work than Leah and I can do. You'd think that's a good problem to have. Except it's not always."

He flexed his hands and tried to find the right things to say. "You get too busy, work goes downhill. Simple jobs take longer. Then you lose business. We needed help. I gathered you were looking for something.

"Being honest, you working at Perry's Orchard kinda told me you were trying to do something. Trying to make a life for yourself. And I knew that work was gonna dry up. What would you do then? There's too many guys who don't have shit off season."

He spread his hands and shrugged, hoping that gesture would convey what he couldn't with words.

"Yeah, but why me?"

This shit is definitely above my pay grade.

"Because someone who had no reason to believed in me."

The unvarnished truth seemed like the best choice. It was the only thing that could explain the unexplainable. Because he sure as shit couldn't tell Miles that the chief of police was hoping to get some dirt on him via Amos.

"Look, I did two years in the youth camp for boosting that car," Amos continued. "Coulda been worse. Hell, it should've been worse. I got out and no one wanted to touch me — Chief Lawson stood up for me. He got Bruce Talbot on board." He took a swig of soda and shook his head. "I had a choice — I could sit at home and listen to my dad bitch about my mistakes or I could do something to get myself on a different path."

Miles leaned forward. "Or you coulda gone to my dad. Why didn't you?"

That was the hard one to answer. Because asking Carl Tilman for help came at a cost. Sitting in a jail cell, the cost of involvement with the Tilman family had been clear. And it was one that Amos had no longer wanted to pay.

"Fear, I guess." That was the truth, even if Miles would interpret it differently than he meant it. "No matter how bad my old man is, I didn't want to spit in his face, y'know."

He picked up his burger and regarded his old friend. "Enough of the fucking walk down memory lane. What's got you wanting to ditch early today?"

He must've struck the right note because Miles popped another fry in his mouth and gave a sad smile.

"Memorial service for a friend."

That got Amos' attention.

"Erin Hodges?" He watched Miles for any reaction, but got nothing out of the ordinary. His smile tightened a little and he nodded. That was it.

"Yeah. We weren't like great pals or anything, but she worked at the Orchard. Least I can do is pay my respects. After that, I've got a date. Perfect thing to feel good after a downer funeral."

Amos managed a laugh, even though he wanted to choke. Would the fact that Miles and Erin were coworkers matter to Drea? Was that helpful information? "Anyone I know?"

Miles shrugged and took a bite of burger. "Maybe," he said around a mouthful of food. He chewed and swallowed. "Vicky Stewart."

Amos stilled his face and kept his hands on his burger to keep from reacting. Or reaching across the table to throttle his old friend for yet another reason.

"Micah's kid sister? Is she even eighteen yet?" She wasn't, and he knew it.

"You gonna get all self-righteous on me?" Miles wagged a fry in the air. "She's cute. Around here, most of the women our age are already taken."

That, or more likely, even if they were single, they knew Miles' history and didn't want anything to do with him.

"Besides, it's nothing serious."

Amos didn't give a shit whether it was serious or not. He was all for giving second chances, but the jury was still out on whether Miles wanted a second chance, or if he'd jumped back into the family business with both feet. That and Miles was twenty-seven and way too old to be doing anything with a high school senior.

"Just don't do anything stupid."

Miles stuffed the last bite of his burger into his mouth and rolled his eyes. They cleared the table and headed out. Miles turned away from the garage and waved.

"Catch ya 'round."

Amos waved back, stuffed his hands in his jacket pockets and walked toward the garage. He'd known about Erin's service because of Katie. She was going, of course.

Oh shit!

He pulled out his phone and was about to text Katie, then stopped. *Fuck.* He wanted to warn her that her brother would be there, but he had no reason to know that Miles was going to the service.

There was only one thing he could do. He pulled up the messages with Katie and typed.

Hey, I'm free this afternoon. Need moral support at the service later? I'll come pick you up.

He didn't bother going to the garage. Instead he headed for home. Her response came before he got his key in the door.

Yes, please. If you're okay with that. Would mean a lot to me.

He sent a thumbs-up, hurried through a shower and changed into dark pants, a turtleneck and a black jacket. If he couldn't warn Katie that her brother would be present, the least he could do was be there. Miles wasn't likely to approach Katie if Amos was there. Then again, he might. Just to watch Amos squirm.

Well, too late to back out now.

* * * *

Katie

Katie tugged the hem of her black skirt back down over her knees and Amos chuckled.

"Guess we should've taken your car," he said. He'd had to help her into his truck and her skirt had hiked up as he'd lifted her back out. "Though I can't say as I'm gonna complain about the view."

She shot him a mock glare. "This is a memorial service. Shame on you!"

Amos shrugged and winked, then offered his arm. Katie slipped her hand into the bend of his elbow as they made their way across the cracked pavement to the small church.

"My mom did church on the regular," he said. "The old man, not so much. Never was my thing. You?"

Katie shook her head. "My parents? You kidding?"

They stepped into the stifling heat of the entry and Katie stopped in her tracks. Miles sat in a pew about halfway into the sanctuary, his dark hair shining like he'd just washed it.

Amos tugged her hand then looked down at her when she didn't move.

"You okay?"

Katie tipped her head toward her brother and Amos' gaze followed. His eyes narrowed and he took a slow breath.

"Why is he here?" The thought of leaving was tempting. They could slip out, unseen.

"Looks like he's with the staff from Perry's Orchard. Erin worked there." He squeezed her hand. "If you don't wanna…"

"No. It's fine. I'll be fine. I need to be able to do this." She gripped Amos' hand and led the way to a spot near the back, on the opposite side of the aisle, as far from her brother as she could get.

Katie barely paid attention to the service. She had her eyes glued to Miles the whole time. At one point, he turned and glanced their direction. Katie shrank behind Amos, hoping her brother hadn't seen her.

Amos sat bolt upright, his eyes fixed front, never glancing at his former best friend. Maybe the bad blood between them ran deeper than she imagined. At the end of the service, the family invited everyone to stay for refreshments.

Amos leaned in to Katie. "Do you need to speak to her parents? Or anyone?"

His tone implied he'd like to get the hell out of there as soon as possible and she couldn't agree more. She shook her head and stood.

"Let's go."

Most of the guests were moving forward to the side doors that led to the fellowship hall, while she and Amos went against the tide, aiming for the exit door.

"Fancy seein' y'all here."

Katie stopped at the familiar voice. Amos hissed in a breath and they both turned. Miles leaned against the sanctuary entrance and smiled.

"Heard y'all were a thing. Who'da guessed," he said, then nodded to Katie. "Figured I'd see you here. You being the kids' teacher and all."

Miles' gaze shifted from Katie to Amos and he chuckled, then brought his attention back to Katie.

"You look like a scared rabbit, sis. I ain't gonna bite."

He sketched a salute and sauntered back into the sanctuary, his laughter carrying and drawing attention their way. Amos' jaw clenched and his fingers tightened on Katie's hand. He muttered something under his breath, then shook his head and hurried her out the door ahead of him.

Amos didn't speak as they crossed the lot. At his truck, he didn't wait for her to ask for help. He grabbed her waist and lifted her in, then quickly closed her door and hurried around to his side. He had the truck in gear and was pulling out of the lot before she had her seatbelt fastened.

This was not a side of Amos she'd seen. The tight jaw and furrowed brow made him look angry and a little dangerous. His fingers gripped the wheel so hard his knuckles were pale. When he finally pulled to a stop, Katie glanced out the window at a row of single-story cottages.

"Your place?"

"Yeah." Amos closed his eyes and she could almost hear him counting as he took a deep breath in.

"I'm sorry," he said. "I let Miles rattle me, and I shouldn't have. I was there to be a support for you and I fucked up."

Katie reached over and placed a hand on Amos' arm. "If I'd known he was going to be there, I wouldn't have gone, and I wouldn't have had you with me if for some reason I did decide to go. You've got just as much reason to hate him as I do."

Amos opened his eyes and turned to her. The pain in his gorgeous blue eyes was almost too much to bear. Then he smiled and something soft and wonderful replaced the anguish she'd just seen.

"You needed me with you." He stroked a finger down her cheek, then cupped her chin and held her gaze. "Yeah, I wasn't thrilled to see Miles, but I would never expect you to deal with that alone. You've got me around." He nodded at the bright red cottage in front of them. "I autopiloted here. It's not much, but it's home. Or we can go to your place. Or I can drop you there. What do you need?"

Katie raised her hands and cradled his face between her palms.

"Never mind me. What do you need?"

His eyes closed for a few seconds and his lips pressed into a thin line. When he opened his eyes again, he seemed back to his normal self. Smiling, self-assured and a little bit cocky.

"I need time with my girl," he said. "Not sure what I've got in the place to eat, but I guarantee we can figure out something that's gonna be better than funeral food."

He hopped out of the truck and came to get her. Instead of putting her down when he lifted her out, he swung her into his arms and carried her to the cottage door. Katie worried he'd drop her as he tried to turn the knob, but somehow he managed it.

She wasn't sure what she expected the inside of Amos' place to look like, but it wasn't this. The door opened into a small room with an overstuffed chair and ottoman, a small television, and floor to ceiling bookshelves that were overflowing with books. Amos deposited her in the chair and straightened.

"Feel free to look around. Bedroom and bathroom through there." He pointed to a door on the wall opposite the entrance. "I'll figure out food." He leaned down and kissed her, then disappeared through a side door.

Katie stood and perused Amos' book collection. One shelf was filled with fire science books. Another on emergency management and a bunch of technical looking manuals. She imagined those were part of him trying to get funding for a paid fire department. One shelf was filled with history books — the United States, Europe, several other countries, global maritime history, a few books on the coal mines and several on the history and impact of colonialism.

"Huh. Unexpected." The next several shelves looked like fiction.

"Grilled cheese okay with you?" Amos popped his head through the doorway. He didn't seem bothered by the sight of her staring at his library.

"Yeah," she replied. "Sounds great."

She ran her finger along the shelves. Alphabetical by author. *Who knew Amos had a little organizational streak?* If he'd read everything on his shelves, he had broad tastes. Horror, science fiction, fantasy, spy novels and thrillers, a few mysteries, and even a couple of romance novels all nestled together.

"Food's ready."

Katie stepped through the side door into a galley kitchen with a small dining area tucked under a window. Amos had already laid sandwiches and bowls of tomato soup on the table. He handed her a spoon and joined her.

"Thanks. I hadn't realized how hungry I was. That's quite a collection of books. I didn't even finish going through it all."

Amos paused as he was about to dip his sandwich in the soup. "Youth camp—you're either working, taking classes, working out, or reading. No television. No games. Hell, no electronics, really. Discovered I loved reading."

He never talked much about the two years he'd spent in a youth detention center. What he did share tended to be vague and he'd quickly change the subject. She supposed she couldn't blame him.

"What's on the rest of the shelves?"

Amos chuckled and sat back. His gaze turned up to the ceiling as if he could see the wall of books up there.

"Couple of boxed sets and some hard-cover classics I picked up used. Down on the bottom, a bunch of stuff on auto mechanics—I get most of that online these days, but some companies still do printed manuals. A shelf of manga. And some erotica and a lot of poetry."

The bite of sandwich Katie had just swallowed threatened to stick in her throat. She took a quick drink and managed to choke it down without coughing. The erotica didn't surprise her, all things considered, but the poetry did. She took another sip of water and smiled.

"Eclectic tastes," she said. "I imagine it causes a few raised eyebrows."

"I always have a book with me at the station," he replied. "Lots of the guys do. But this?" He waved his hand in the direction of the living room. "You're the third person I've had over. The other two are my sisters."

Something about that seemed odd. Amos was friendly and social all the time.

"Why so private? You don't seem the type."

He sat his spoon down, wiped his mouth on a napkin and steepled his fingers in front of his chin.

"My life got picked apart when I got arrested," he said, finally. "When I came back, well…ah… You know how gossip is. And folks figured it was fair to ask a bunch of personal questions. I mean, I was a kid. It makes sense to me now, but at the time it was a bit annoying."

His words were simple, said without rancor, but his eyes spoke of the pain he'd gone through. Hadn't she felt some of that herself? She'd come back knowing her life would be on display because she was a Tilman. She could only imagine how much worse it must have been for Amos.

"Didn't take long for me to realize that was the way it was gonna be," he continued. "First, I lived at my folks' place. Apartment over the garage. I didn't have people over because my old man would scrutinize everyone. He'd ask questions. Grill me. Grill them if he had a chance."

He gave a short, bitter sounding chuckle. "Funny thing was, I got used to it. And I got used to my space being mine. Private. Sort of a haven where I didn't have to live up to anyone's expectations or answer any questions. I could just be me. Guess the habit stuck."

Katie reached across the small table and tugged at his sleeve. "How about we finish lunch then you give me a tour of the bedroom?"

A slow grin curled his lips, then his eyes crinkled at the corners. He lifted his eyebrows and cocked his head to the side.

"Want something?"

Chapter Twenty-Two

"You and Amos got plans for turkey day?" Cinda Gable dropped into a seat next to Katie in the teacher's lounge. She poked at the tray of food — a bunch of traditional early American dishes the fifth and sixth grade classes had put together. "I dunno why I braved this stuff."

Katie chuckled and pulled out her packed lunch. "I did warn you. I am so glad I'm not on lunch duty this week. And no. He's at the fire department. His family doesn't do much, so he tries to make sure the other crew can take the time off to be with family. It's sweet."

As someone who hadn't grown up doing a family dinner or anything, Katie didn't much care. They'd spent time together Monday and Tuesday, and had plans for Friday night. This was life when you were dating a firefighter.

"Well, I know it's last-minute and all, and I kept meaning to ask, but we'd love to have you over," Cinda said. "We call it Friendsgiving. Larry comes from a huge family and they do a great big thing out at his grandparents' place. Anyone who doesn't have family, or who doesn't get along with their family, is welcome."

She pulled out her phone and tapped the screen, then slid it over to Katie. "That's last year. It's fun. Seriously. You should come out."

Katie swiped through the pictures, expecting to see harvest-themed decor, but instead there were rainbows everywhere. It looked like a hundred people in what had to be an old barn.

"That looks like fun," she replied, and actually meant it. "Yeah. If you're sure. I'd love to come."

"Great!" Cinda pocketed her phone. "I'll text you the details, but doors open at two."

She stopped as the school resource officer came over to their table. "Hey, we're shutting the playground down and bringing all the older students into the cafeteria and auditorium. It will be easier to take the kindergarten and first grade students to the library, if you two can head there, I'll have staff bring them over."

Cinda scowled, but nodded. Around the room, several other teachers rose and hurried through cleaning up their lunch before leaving.

"What's going on?" Katie had been through school lockdowns before. This didn't feel quite like that, but it was still something unusual.

The resource officer bit his lip and Katie didn't think he was going to answer. Then he scratched his chin and leaned down. "We had a group of high school students loitering near the playground. Just outside the fence. One of the playground monitors saw a gun. We've called police and are acting out of abundance of caution. We've also called parents, pickup for the half day students is going to be delayed."

Cinda looked stricken. Her eyes went wide and her mouth hung open. Katie thanked the resource officer, then stuffed her lunch back into her bag. She'd eat later. She grabbed Cinda's tray.

"Come on, let's get to the library." Katie tugged Cinda's arm. "We can let the students finish lunch then do story time in the reading corner. Dim all the lights and make it like a camp-out. They'll like that."

Cinda shook herself and stood. "Yeah, okay. That sounds like a plan."

They hurried to the library and Katie scanned the room. There was one door at the front and a fire door at the back. They couldn't do much about the big windows that overlooked the walkway outside. There weren't even drapes or blinds to cover them. She palmed the bank of light switches, casting the front of the library into darkness. Luckily, the reading corner was in the back of the room, tucked behind rows of shelves.

"Cinda, can you switch on the wall lights in the reading corner? I'm gonna turn off all the overheads." She flicked the last line of switches and looked around again. Hopefully, the soft glow of the wall lights wouldn't be visible from outside the room.

A parade of students came around the corner, led by one playground monitor, with another bringing up the rear. Katie opened the library door and ushered everyone inside, doing a quick headcount as they went past.

"We're going to go back to the reading corner and have a picnic!" Katie forced her voice to stay stable and happy sounding. This was probably nothing. An abundance of caution, like the resource officer had said. If all went well, it would be cleared up within an hour.

I hope.

As soon as everyone was settled and eating, Katie sent a note to Amos, letting him know what was going on. Then she scanned the books, looking for something that would hold the attention of a group of anxious five-to-seven year olds.

Two hours later, half of the kindergartners were dozing on the carpet while the rest of the students watched a movie on a laptop.

She took the moment of down time to text Amos again. He'd sent a flurry of texts earlier and she'd been so busy she couldn't respond. She needed to let him know she was okay. No sooner had she hit send then her phone buzzed with an incoming group text.

"That's the all clear," Katie whispered to Cinda. "They're asking everyone to stay put for now." Within minutes, the resource officer and Principal Dubois came in.

"We've got some parents here for pickup already," the principal said. "They'll be brought onto campus in small groups. Before we do that, any children who bus home, and whose parents haven't contacted the school, will be escorted to their classrooms to collect their belongings, and then to their busses."

None of Katie's students took the bus, but several of Cinda's did. There was a bit of a scramble as they figured out which students were going. It took another hour to get through all the students who were waiting for pickup.

Katie and Cinda had just started cleaning up when the principal called them to the auditorium. They filed in with the rest of the teachers and staff and quickly settled into seats. Drea Parsons stood at the front of the room and as soon as the doors were shut, she stepped forward and everyone went silent.

"First, I want to thank all of you for handling a difficult situation with grace. This is not something we're used to in Orchard Creek." The chief of police took a moment and looked around the room. Then she let out a slow breath.

"I am going to be as transparent as I can be about today. No arrests were made, however, we do have a couple of persons of interest. As many of you know, we've had a rising drug problem in the area for some time now."

She pulled a whiteboard over and jotted down an email. "If you send a request here, we will forward you an information packet. I've also made that same packet available to all school administrators.

"I can't tell you much about the events of today as this is an ongoing investigation," she continued. "What I can tell you is a small group of minors was gathered near the playground at lunch time. The middle school and elementary school share a fence line in that area and it is likely this was a drug transaction."

A few gasps echoed in the room, followed by whispered chatter. No one wanted to imagine middle school children buying drugs. Or high school children selling them. Maybe that happened in big cities, but not in this small town.

"A male appearing to be around thirty, average height, thin, with dark hair showed up and there were some heated words. That's when a witness says they saw a gun and made the call to police. We were on scene within minutes, but by then, the adult male had left, and the teenagers claimed they were on their lunch break and taking a shortcut back from getting burgers."

The fact that the description of the adult male matched her brother didn't escape Katie. *What the fuck was Miles doing around the school and was he the one with a gun?*

"School administrators made the decision to go into partial lockdown," Drea said. "We have no reason to believe an armed person ever entered school property. Nor do we believe there was any danger to students or staff on campus. We have drafted a community notice informing parents what we found, and praising the school for swift action. If you have any questions, please email. I know it's been a long day. Thank you."

Drea turned and left without another word and the room erupted into loud chatter until Principal Dubois called everyone to order.

"I appreciate the desire to chat about this, but we still have work to do before we can shut the school down for the holiday weekend. We will have a staff meeting next week for any further discussion."

Katie hurried to her class and called Amos the moment the door closed behind her. He picked up on the first ring.

"Are you okay?"

Katie summarized what had happened, including Drea's description of the man. The phone went so silent Katie thought they'd been disconnected.

"Huh." That single syllable sounded distracted. "What time was that?"

She tucked another chair under the table then shoved the craft bins back in place. "Drea said just before lunch, but we were sitting down to eat when they called for a lockdown. I guess around noon. Why?"

He muttered something she didn't catch. "Amos, why? What's going on?"

"Ah, it's nothing," he replied. "I was tied up with the Parsons' truck. Danny came to pick it up today, but there was some chatter on the radio. You know how tight fire and police are. I'm glad you're okay. You decided what you're doing tomorrow? You could always come by the station."

That was the first time he'd invited her to visit him at work. The idea brought a smile to her face. Maybe she'd do just that. After whatever happened at the Gable's.

"Cinda asked me to their Friendsgiving," she said. "But I could swing by after. I mean, I'd like that."

"Aw, score on that invite!" Amos' chuckle carried over the phone line and in an instant, the stress of her day faded. His presence, even over the phone, was a balm to her soul. "Been to that a time or two. You'll enjoy it. Really relaxed and a good time. Speaking of good times..."

The drop in his voice sent shivers of pleasure up her spine.

"Friday night," he continued. "I'm thinking an early dinner out, then a long and not so quiet night in. I want to hear you begging me to make you come."

The shivers turned into a raging torrent of desire. She'd have to make sure her vibrator was fully charged. She was going to need it to get through the next two nights.

"I can hear your brain churning," he said. "What if I said no playing with yourself until then? I want you aching for me."

A moan slipped from Katie's lips. "Are you serious?"

She knew he was. What's more, she knew she would do exactly as he asked. And by Friday night, she'd be ready to beg for anything. Which was exactly what he wanted.

"Never mind," she said. "Don't answer that."

"So, yes or no, Kitten?"

Katie closed her eyes. Every time with Amos had been something remarkable. It was like he knew exactly what she needed and how to coax her to the highest peaks of pleasure.

"Yes."

"Good girl."

Chapter Twenty-Three

Amos
November 24, Friday

The throaty roar of the Chevelle's engine greeted Amos as he stepped onto the lot. Leah knocked her knuckles on the muscle car's hood then waved as the owner drove off.

"I'm not too proud to say it. Miles does good work." She hooked her thumb toward the side garage. "He's in there now, plugging away on a rebalance. But that beast? The parts didn't come in till late Wednesday. He knows he doesn't have to work holidays, right?"

Amos shrugged. It was good to see Leah smiling and happy. They'd gotten lucky so far. The old man worked when he could and stayed out of the side garage. So long as there was work to be had and everything was going smoothly, he seemed happy.

As for Amos, he was running on almost no sleep after a day full of turkey deep fryer fires turned into a night of car accidents and a chimney fire. But he had work at the garage to get done and Katie to see tonight. Somewhere in there he needed to keep working on getting back into Miles' confidence. Drea had made that clear after the incident at the elementary school.

Classic rock blared from the speakers and Miles waved as Amos came in and checked his tickets for the day. Just one. A tune up on a Cherokee that was already sitting in his bay.

He gathered his supplies and got to work. Whatever Miles was otherwise, he was a damn fine coworker. Not a lot of idle talk. Decent music. Solid work ethic. *Maybe Drea's wrong about him. Maybe Katie's wrong, too. Maybe Miles has changed.*

The trailer fire on Halloween said otherwise. Amos had to remember that, plus he had a promise to keep to Drea. Whether Katie was right or wrong about her brother didn't matter. He'd hurt her, and that, Amos couldn't forgive. She meant too much to him for that.

They knocked off for lunch and Amos figured Miles would take off for the day, but instead, he came back and cleaned the garage bays while Amos finished the tune up.

"Hey, why don't we go grab a beer or something," Miles said as Amos hung the car's key up and closed out the computer for the day.

Amos froze. It was the first time Miles had suggested something social. Maybe this was the in he'd been waiting for. He could grab a beer with Miles and still be back in time for dinner with Katie.

"Yeah, man, sounds good," Amos replied. "Lemme give Leah a heads up we're closing down over here."

They wound up at a shabby bar north of town. Miles was clearly a regular. The bartender greeted him as they walked in, and they immediately joined a small group gathered around the pool tables.

A beer turned to two, then three and a game of pool as the group grew. Amos was pretty sure there were a few high school kids in the bunch, and an inordinately high number of young women who all seemed to fawn over Miles and clamor for his attention.

Aside from those things, it wasn't any different than what went on in any bar around the county. Just folks letting off steam after a long work week. Someone handed Amos another beer and he took a swig without thinking about it.

He leaned back and watched his old friend work the pool table. The crowd had shifted, new faces came and went. Miles shook hands with a burly blond man, then pocketed something. A few minutes later, he was kissing a pretty redhead on the cheek and she walked away stuffing something into her bra.

Amos was pretty sure he'd just seen two drug deals. What he wasn't sure of was whether it mattered. Those kinds of things might not be big enough for Drea. Either of them coulda been nothing. He wasn't cut out for this shit.

"Hey, man, another game?" Miles dropped onto the stool next to him and clapped him on the shoulder.

Amos tipped his head back. Four beers was more than his limit if he was gonna drive and he had an early dinner with Katie to get to. *Shit!*

"Nah, I gotta bug out," he replied. "Got plans."

Miles tapped the neck of his beer bottle against Amos'. "Cmon. One last game then we'll get you outta here. You need a bit before you drive anyway, right?"

He raised an eyebrow at the empty beer in Amos' hand. "You want a coffee or something?"

When did Miles get so accommodating?

"Just a soda, thanks. And yeah, fine. You're right. I'm not ready to drive. I do need to send a text."

He pulled out his phone and typed a note to Katie, letting her know he'd gotten tied up and might be a little late. By the time he hit send, someone had handed him a tall glass of soda and he downed half of it gratefully.

He must've needed the caffeine because a few minutes later, he was bouncing on his toes as he surveyed the pool table for his next shot.

"Too bad you've got a date," Miles said as Amos bent over the table. "We've got an awesome party going tonight. You should hang around."

Fuck. There was the opportunity he'd been hoping for. A way to see Miles in his element and have something to give to Drea. He couldn't cancel on Katie. He needed to finish this game and leave. He reached for his drink and found it empty.

"Hang on. I got ya!" The pretty girl was gone before Amos could say he wanted a soda. She was back before his next turn, handing him a brimming glass. He took a big swallow before he realized it was a draft beer. *Fuck it.* He shrugged and stepped back to the pool table.

It had been too long since he'd been able to relax and have fun. Even social events with the fire crew were filled with politics and shop talk.

"Where is this party?" He chalked his cue and called his shot. "I can be a little late." He took the shot and sank the ball. He was having too much fun to leave.

"Right here, man," Miles replied. "And right now. Band's settin' up already." He nodded to the end of the room where a handful of musicians were plugging cords into speakers. The group gathered around the pool tables had grown to a crowd and if he'd thought Miles was surrounded by women before, that was nothing.

The atmosphere was fun—party central. Amos had his phone out again and the text thread with Katie pulled up. *What do I tell her? I can't lie.*

A tipsy girl tumbled into his lap and Amos caught her before she fell to the floor. She was definitely too young to be in a bar. She looked like she might be seventeen. Her pupils were huge, even for in the dim light, and she giggled as Amos set her back on her feet.

"Thanks!" She laid her hand on his chest and stepped closer. "Hey, I'm Vicky. You should do one of those firefighter calendars. You're built for it."

Her fingers slid to his shoulder and squeezed, then she gave him a bright smile. Something clicked as he put her name and face together. *Shit. Micah's kid sister. Fuck me.* That was a dash of cold water. *What the fuck am I doing here?*

He stood, apologizing to Vicky, explaining he had to go. Across the pool table, Miles held a lighter to a pipe for one of the women. Amos was pretty damn sure it wasn't tobacco or even pot. Maybe he could get a picture for Drea. He reached for his phone but his pocket was empty.

*Where the fuck…*Oh yeah, he'd been about to text Katie when he'd been landed on. He scanned the floor. Nothing. He checked the seats. The bar. He even went to the bathroom and looked around. Eventually he found it under the pool table. The screen was cracked. No, not cracked. Shattered.

Fuck.

He stuffed his busted phone into his pocket and tried to get Miles' attention to let him know he was leaving. Except Miles was nowhere to be found. He and the handful of women who'd been hanging on him were gone. The rest of the crowd pulsed to the music.

When did the band start up?

Amos checked his pockets for his keys. *Good. Still got those.* He eyed the two empty beer glasses near his stool and crossed his fingers. He didn't recall having a second glass after the soda, but he didn't feel buzzed. In fact, he felt on top of the world. Wide awake and ready to go.

He didn't bother going home. He went straight to Katie's, hoping she'd forgive him for being late, and a little drunk, and for not texting her that his might be a little late had turned into being very late. At least he had a broken phone to show her he couldn't text.

He took her stairs two at a time and pounded on her door. It flew open and two thoughts hit him at the same time—she was absolutely gorgeous and she was absolutely pissed off.

"I'm sorry," he said, but he stopped when Katie held up her phone. It was a blurry picture of him and the tipsy girl who'd fallen in his lap. He had his hands around her waist. He knew exactly what was happening in that moment and even to him it looked bad, but who'd taken the picture?

Fucking Miles.

"You're drunk. You missed our date for this. And for some unknown fucking reason, you figured it was a good idea to send me this picture. Go home."

She stepped back and slammed the door. The sound of her locks turning was the loudest thing he'd ever heard.

Amos climbed back into his truck and slammed his hand against the steering wheel. He couldn't even call or text Drea to let her know what happened. *Fuck it.* He'd get home and sleep then deal with the fallout in the morning.

He jammed the truck into gear and tried not to think as he drove home. He pulled up to the cottage and swore.

The front windows were busted in and his door gaped open, hanging crooked on its hinges. He climbed out of the truck and approached the ruined front door. Inside was even worse. His books were strewn around the room and torn pages fluttered in the breeze coming from the broken windows. The television was smashed and it looked like someone had taken a baseball bat to every available surface.

He reached for his phone on reflex, then cursed when his fingers grazed the fractured screen. He'd go to the garage. He could call the police from there.

Amos stepped back outside and stopped in his tracks as red and blue lights flashed and a police cruiser screeched to a halt in his drive.

Please let it be Drea.

Chapter Twenty-Four

Katie
November 25, Saturday

The photo stared up at Katie, a stark reminder that she'd gone and done it again. She'd fallen for the wrong guy. She'd been right to question the love bombing. It was all bullshit.

She stabbed the phone to delete the picture, then thought better of it. No. She'd keep this as a reminder.

She'd cried herself to sleep the night before and she'd probably do the same thing tonight. She couldn't imagine facing everyone. She didn't want to talk about Amos. She didn't even want to think about him.

Except he was all she could think about. Her phone rang and she hit the ignore button then flipped the ringer off. She didn't care who it was. She was not available today. For anything.

She sat curled on her couch, alternating between staring at the blurry photo and trying to figure out how she was going to sleep in her bed again when all she could picture every time she looked at it was all the things Amos had done to her between those sheets. And how much she'd enjoyed it all.

Someone banged on her door around noon and Katie ignored that as well. She went hunting for her earbuds when the banging continued. *They have to be around here somewhere.*

"Katie! It's Drea!"

Why was the chief of police banging on her door on a Saturday?

She unbolted the door and stared at the woman. The small swell of a belly under the uniform shirt surprised her. She hadn't realized Drea was pregnant. Katie shook her head. What difference did it make?

"What can I do for you?" She saw no reason to be polite. She had no business with the police.

"You can invite me in," Drea said. "There are things I think you need to know that I'd rather you hear from me, and some questions I have for you."

Something in her tone made Katie step back and throw the door wide. Drea moved into the room and gently took the door from Katie, then closed it.

"You might want to sit," Drea said.

Katie didn't like the sound of that. Not one bit. She dropped to the loveseat and stared at the chief of police.

"I don't know what to say first." Drea ran a hand through her hair, then pulled a kitchen chair over and sat down facing Katie.

"Amos was arrested last night," Drea said. Despite everything, it felt like a punch to the gut. Katie hugged a pillow to her chest and nodded for Drea to go on.

"There's a whole big mess here and I'm not sure what the truth is," Drea continued. "Someone reported seeing him with an underage girl at a bar. Then we got a call about a disturbance by the old coal company cottages where he lives. I wasn't on duty last night. When the officer got there, Amos' place was, well, a shambles. He was also drunk and possibly high."

Katie didn't want to hear more. She needed to hear more. This wasn't the Amos she knew. But she'd been wrong about men before. Too many times to count.

"Long story short," Drea continued, "Amos was over the legal limit to drive, but that's the least of the worries. He also tested positive for methamphetamines and drugs and paraphernalia were found in his cottage."

That got Katie's attention. "Wait. He what? Amos doesn't...no. He's not... I've never seen any signs of that."

Drea held up her hand and shook her head. "We have leads that tie him to a meth lab that exploded on Halloween. We have meth in his system last night and in his home. Witnesses place him at a bar that's a known party spot and say they saw him providing drugs to a minor."

A sick feeling curled into Katie's stomach. How could she have been so wrong about him?

"I don't like any of this, and I don't believe it," Drea said. "But I have to follow the evidence, no matter what my personal feelings are. Normally, I wouldn't tell anyone these details, but..."

She leaned forward, her elbows on her knees. "I had reason to believe that your brother, Miles, was involved with the increase of drug sales we've seen. And I had asked Amos to see if Miles would talk to him."

Ice water dumped into Katie's veins. "He was talking to my brother?"

"Yeah," Drea responded. "And that was one of my questions. I take it he didn't tell you anything?"

Katie shook her head. "We saw Miles at Erin's memorial. Amos acted weird, but... I mean, there's a lot of water under that bridge."

"Miles was working at the garage," Drea said. "Leah Kimmel knew what it was about. I'm surprised Amos didn't tell you."

So was Katie. The fact that he didn't hurt as much as seeing the picture of him with another woman. Well, girl.

"So, you said you had questions." Katie wanted to get this conversation done and over with. Whatever Amos was up to, even if he was talking to Miles to help the chief, he had lied to Katie. Repeatedly.

"Did he text you at all last night?"

"What difference does it make?" She'd gotten two texts from Amos. One saying he was running late and the picture with the girl.

"I'm playing that one close to my chest," Drea replied. "Let's just say, I have a theory."

Katie sighed and thumbed her phone on, flipped to the last messages from Amos and handed the phone to Drea. The chief looked at the screen and nodded.

"Would you mind screenshotting this and sending it to me?" Drea handed the phone back. "Any clue why Amos would send you that picture? I mean, it seems... odd, don't you think?"

It seemed very odd. Then again, everything about the night before seemed odd. Amos always gave a reason if he was going to be late. Last night, he'd just said he'd gotten tied up. Then the picture had come through with no text at all. Katie tapped the image to enlarge it and forced herself to look at it again.

"It's not a selfie," she said and held the phone up for Drea to see. "His hands are on her waist, and hers are on his shoulders. Someone else took the picture."

Katie sat back on the couch and stared at the woman in front of her. "You think something weird is going on."

Drea's expression said that was exactly what she thought, but she waggled a hand back and forth in a 'so-so' gesture. "I think a man I respect is in a world of trouble, and my job is to get to the bottom of it. Find out the truth."

"The drug problems in town aren't new," Katie said. "But they've changed. Right?" She watched Drea for some sign she was on the right track, but the chief's face stayed impassive.

"It's a younger crowd now, isn't it? More teenagers. Young adults. Like before, when Amos got in trouble the first time. Someone's targeting the kids. That's why you thought Miles had something to do with it."

Drea stood and brushed non-existent wrinkles from her pants. "You ever consider a career in law enforcement? Look, I'm sorry to barge in on you with this. I'm sorry I can't give you more information, or happier news. But I thought you deserved to hear as much of the facts as I can give you right now."

She took a deep breath and blew it out slowly. "It's none of my business, but if you care for him at all, wait till all this is over before you make up your mind on anything."

Katie laughed. She couldn't stop it if she tried. The laughter bubbled out, bordering on hysterics. "I don't know what to make of any of this. What's more, I don't want to. I almost didn't come back here because I knew the weight of being a Tilman. I knew what people would think of me because of my dad, and to a lesser extent, my brother. But Orchard Creek is home, and here I am. For all the fucking good it's done me."

The chief offered her hand and Katie stared at it a moment before shaking.

"It's my belief that all of this will work out," Drea said. "If I'm right, I hope you can find it in you to understand. I'll show myself out."

Katie held it together until the door clicked shut behind the chief. Then the tears came again. Great wracking sobs that shook her body.

Amos had told her he had no desire to rekindle a friendship with Miles. But he'd given his old friend a job. He'd been hanging out with him, and lying to Katie about it. Maybe it was to help the chief of police, but why wouldn't he tell Katie that?

She stood in a rush and packed a bag. She couldn't sleep here tonight. She wouldn't crawl into the bed she and Amos had shared so many times over the past few weeks.

Has it really only been a few weeks?

It felt like Amos had always been there. He was a part of her, and she of him. Now that part had been ripped away and Katie was left bleeding. She sank to the floor, clutching the overnight bag.

She had classes to teach on Monday. She could go away. Go to Charleston for the night. But she'd still have to come back here and face the pillow that smelled like Amos. See his toothbrush in the bathroom. Or his work schedule on her wall calendar.

She picked up her phone and pulled up Cinda Gable's number. Cinda was the closest thing Katie had to a friend here. Aside from Amos. Her finger hovered over the call button. Years of hiding from her family's drama made her hesitate.

Time to break those molds.

She hit the button and pulled in a deep breath, crossing her fingers that Cinda was free.

"Katie? Is everything okay?"

* * * *

Amos

Amos rolled his sleeve back down and watched the tech label all the vials of blood.

Leah had visited in the morning with a change of clothes and new cell phone that she'd had to leave with Drea. His sister had already contacted an attorney and Amos had a short call with their office. They advised him to refuse any further testing until the lawyer could make it down on Monday. When Drea had shown up and told him she wanted more extensive tests to send to a friend from the ATF, Amos had agreed. Lawyer be damned, he trusted his friends and figured it couldn't hurt.

He had an idea how meth had gotten into his system — all the beers with Miles and his crowd. Amos had never opened a bottle himself and hadn't taken the glasses of soda or draft beers directly from the bartender. A mistake most women would know better than to make.

He'd been an idiot.

"What's all this for?" Amos nodded at the pile of samples. Blood. Urine. Hair. Who knew what all else.

The tech shook their head. "Dunno, man, I just collect the specimens. This stuff is going straight to some private lab in Charleston. That's all I know."

Well, that tracked with what Drea had said.

The lab tech left and Amos sat staring at the holding cell wall. By now, the gossip mill would be in full swing. So much for rebuilding his life. Ten years down the drain. Once again thanks to Miles Tilman.

"Hey, I talked the judge into releasing you on your own recognizance." Drea unlocked the cell door and stood aside.

For half a minute, he'd been angry at her. If she hadn't asked for his help, he would have happily avoided Miles and he wouldn't be in this shit situation. The more he thought about it, the more he realized she was just doing her job.

The entire steaming pile of trouble was on Amos' head. He should have talked to Katie. He should have been more cautious around Miles and his friends. *Coulda, woulda, shoulda.*

He followed Drea out of the holding area and to her office. She pointed at two chairs in front of her desk. Once Amos was seated, she didn't go around the desk, but instead took the chair next to him.

"I'm sorry," Drea said. "I put a lot on you and whatever the truth of the matter is, you're here in part because of me. I've got a former colleague running your samples and he's a fucking lab genius. It'll still take a day to get full results."

Amos shook his head. "Don't know what good that'll do. The shit's in my system. No amount of me saying I didn't take anything is gonna change that."

"No, but a basic test just screens for the presence of substances. More advanced testing may be able to give us more. I, uh…even included stomach contents."

Amos groaned, then laughed. Drea had shown up at the station shortly after he'd been booked. By then, Amos had been shaking and nauseous. She'd managed to grab an empty trash basket before he'd hurled all over the floor.

"You bagged puke?" He shook his head. Leave it to Drea to think of things like that.

"Bagged, tagged, and logged as evidence," she said. "Not sure the other staff were thrilled with finding that in the fridge this morning, but whatever." She shifted in the seat and leaned forward. "Point is, I've got Peter Adams on the labs. If half of what he says he can do is true, by this time tomorrow, we'll know if the meth was ingested. How much. If you'd used before. And a whole bunch of other shit that baffles even me."

That was the first bit of relief Amos felt. He knew he hadn't done anything before. He sure as shit hadn't snorted or shot up. All of that solved one of his problems.

"What about the girl? That was Vicky Stewart. I know her brother."

Drea spread her hands. "We're working on that. On the plus side, she's seventeen so she's over the age of consent. She's just not old enough to be drinking in a bar. We're also working on who trashed your place. And digging into the meth lab. If all goes well, this will be nothing more than a little blip and you'll be in the clear by Monday."

"Thank you," he said. "You don't have to be doing this, and I appreciate it."

Drea rose and laid a hand on his shoulder. "Yeah, I do have to. Because I believe you. Plus, the whole goal here is to get the bad guy, and that's not you."

Just hearing her say it eased some of his tension. With luck, she wasn't the only person who'd feel that way. Maybe his hard-won reputation would survive.

"Amos, we'll figure it out. I promise. Meanwhile, you got a place to stay?"

The laugh that came out of his mouth sounded as bitter as he felt.

"My old man isn't gonna let me anywhere near his place," he said. "And I don't imagine Katie wants anything to do with me. I'll call Shawn, see how things are at the station. If I can't stay there, I'll figure something out."

"I already called him," she replied. "I think your crew will surprise you. If that doesn't work out, or you're not comfortable, give me a call. We've got cottages at Parsons Acres. You can stay there till this is sorted."

She picked up a thick package from her desk and handed it to him. "Wallet, keys, broken phone, the works. If it was on you when you were picked up, it's in there. The new phone Leah brought as well. And your truck is out back."

Amos took the bundle and stood. He shook Drea's hand and turned to the door. All he wanted to do was get out of here and get someplace he could rage and scream at the world. His dad being disappointed in him, again, was no big deal. The prospect of losing the respect he'd worked the last ten years to build hurt, but he could get past that. Even if it meant moving, he'd manage.

The thing tearing at his soul was Katie. He'd fucked up. There was no avoiding that. It didn't matter that he thought he was protecting her. It didn't matter why he didn't talk to her. The fact was — his choices had led to her being hurt and he knew damn good and well how she'd take it all. She'd see that he didn't trust her. She'd see that he lied to her. His reasons were irrelevant.

It took nearly everything he had in him to not climb in his truck, chase down Miles, and pound him into the ground. The problem was, doing that wouldn't solve anything. Nor would it make him feel any better.

Instead, he went to his cottage to get a better look at how bad it was and see if he could salvage anything. Drea said some of the fire crew had come by and boarded up the busted windows. They'd even rehung the door.

Inside was worse than he recalled. Then again, the police had probably added to the mess in their search. His closet and dresser had both been tossed through, but somehow the clothes in the dryer had escaped notice. Amos packed everything he could into a bag.

In the living room, he sorted through the books, hoping to find a few still intact. Miraculously, only a few were badly damaged. The rest had been strewn about.

What the fuck is the message here?

It had to have been Miles. Or someone working for him. He might have figured out why Amos was talking to him. Or it was Miles being an asshole. Anything was possible.

"Whoa. This place is trashed."

Amos gritted his teeth and counted to ten. In daylight, with no makeup on, Vicky Stewart looked even younger than she had last night.

"Do me a favor and stay outside. In fact, go away. The last thing I need is someone seeing you here."

She rolled her eyes, crossed her arms over her chest and propped herself in the doorway.

"There's a party tonight…"

Amos stood and glared. The girl shut her mouth and shrank from him, her eyes wide. *Fuck.* He put his hands out and sat back down on the floor.

"I'm not gonna hurt you. I just want you to go. What the fuck are you doing with that crowd?"

Vicky huffed. "What do you care? I'm trying to help you, asshole. There's a party at the trailer park. Bet your ass Miles will be there."

Amos nodded and tossed another book into the trash pile. "And you're telling me this why?"

That earned him another eye roll. "Fucker ditched me last night after promising I could party with him. Then I heard folks talking about you and somebody had this picture and I figured he was just using me to fuck you over. Figured you'd be looking for payback."

She straightened, tossed her hair over her shoulder and scanned the room. "What the fuck did you do to piss him off?"

Either the girl was telling the truth and there really was a party, or she was feeding him a line of bullshit to see if he'd go to the cops. Yesterday, he might have debated what to do. Today, he didn't hesitate. As soon as Vicky left, he fished out his phone and texted Drea.

He tossed another book and stood. *Fuck this.* Amos grabbed his clothes and some personal items, pulled the door shut behind him and locked it, then drove to the station. He parked in the back and texted Shawn Dubois, his second in command. The response was immediate.

Get your ass in here. What the fuck mess did you stick your dick into?

Another weight lifted from Amos' shoulders. He couldn't handle losing Katie and the fire department. That would've been too much. He grabbed his things and went inside, not knowing what to expect.

"Sit your ass down and eat." Shawn shoved Amos toward the big table near the kitchen. "Then start explaining what the fuck is going on."

It all tumbled out as he shoveled searing hot chili into his mouth. He'd barely eaten all day and whatever little he'd had last night had come up in the police station. He told Shawn everything—from the first time Miles had come into the garage to Vicky showing up at his cottage before he came to the station.

"That is some of the most fucked-up shit I've ever heard," Shawn said when Amos finished talking.

"If we can't get this cleared up fast, I'll step down," Amos said. "You'll need to take over. The vote is just over two weeks away and I won't risk the council going against it because of me."

Shawn swore under his breath. "This department exists the way it does because of you. This shit will get fixed. One way or another."

Like a lot of the crew, Shawn wasn't all sunshine and rainbows. He was a brawler and all it would take would be for Amos to say the word and half the crew would make sure Miles Tilman thought twice before doing anything so colossally stupid again.

Folks who grew up on the mountain had their own idea of justice and it wasn't always pretty. Amos' phone buzzed. Drea's name popped up.

"Chief texting you? Think she's being straight or she blowing smoke?"

Amos let out a short laugh. "Andrea Hidalgo? 'Scuse me, Parsons now. You think she could be anything but straight up?"

"I mean, who knows?" Shawn shrugged. "She didn't fuck around with all those fires and Robert

Moore and CeeCee Cobb. But she did get the feds involved. So, jury's out."

That would forever hang over Drea's head, no matter how good the new chief of police was. She had brought a federal investigation into Orchard Creek. Never mind that it made sense. Or that she'd caught a murderer.

Amos thumbed open the text from Drea.

I'll pick you up at eight. You can identify people who were at the bar last night.

Amos read the text twice then sent a thumbs-up. No reason not to at this point — it couldn't cause any more damage than was already done. He rinsed his dishes, stuck them in the dishwasher and went to shower. Maybe he could salvage more from this mess than he thought.

Just not the most important part — Katie.

Chapter Twenty-Five

Katie
November 26, Sunday

Katie picked up her coffee and retreated to the far corner of the shop. She didn't feel like being around people, but she didn't want to sit home and mope either. Every eye had been on her when she walked in, and she could feel the stares even now.

What the hell had possessed her to return to this fucking town? It was time to give up her little fantasy of being a school teacher in a beautiful mountain setting. She wasn't going to get that here.

She was a Tilman. Doomed to bring trouble. And Amos? Well, he was her toxic brother's best friend. Always had been and always would be.

Someone dropped into the seat opposite her and Katie looked up to see Micah Stewart chewing on his lip, looking like he had something big to get off his chest.

"Whatever you're about to say, I don't want to hear it." Katie grabbed the coffee she'd barely touched and slid to get out of the bench seat. Micah's hand landed on hers. His trembling fingers said he was more nervous than she'd thought.

"Please, I think you want to hear this." He pulled his hand away, but his worried puppy dog eyes convinced her to settle back in her seat. She folded her hands around her coffee cup and raised her eyebrows at him.

"My kid sister was arrested last night. She was at a party in West Creek."

The name sent a boulder of ice into Katie's stomach. She didn't know the Stewart family well, and she'd really only seen Micah around fire department events, but she knew him to be a nice and responsible young man. His heart had to be breaking over his sister. He held up his phone with a picture of a pretty blond who looked vaguely familiar. Katie leaned closer.

"That's..." Her hand flew to her mouth and she stared between the picture on the phone and the sad-eyed young man in front of her, terrified of what he was about to say.

"It was a set-up," Micah said. "Everything Friday night was a set-up. Vicky says Miles arranged everything. She owed Miles for her habit and he convinced her to do a favor—in exchange, she could party with him."

While that was interesting news, it didn't change the fact that Amos had lied to her. Repeatedly.

"Was that it?" She didn't like being so cold, but if Micah thought she'd let it all go because her brother had decided to be an asshole, he had another think coming. Miles was always an asshole and always manipulative. And Amos should have known that.

"I know you're pissed, but please, just hear me out," Micah replied. "Vicky told Amos about the party, figuring he'd come and beat Miles up or something." He let out a bitter laugh. "She's a little bit of a drama queen. I guess she didn't figure he'd tell the cops instead. Trouble was, Miles wasn't there. Dwight Phelps was."

Katie's brain tried to wrap itself around what Micah was saying. "Wait. Can you maybe just give me the basics here?"

Micah shrugged. "I don't know everything. What I do know is Amos wasn't part of Miles' usual crowd. Vicky made that clear. She saw someone slip drugs into Amos' drink and Miles told her to come on to Amos. In some teenage girl snit, she told Amos about the party last night, and boom, the cops show up. Everybody got arrested. Except Miles and your dad, of course, because they were nowhere to be found."

That made things about as clear as mud as far as Katie was concerned. It sure as shit didn't explain what Amos was doing at the bar in the first place.

"You said Dwight Phelps?"

"Yeah," Micah replied. "He was in the holding cell when we went to get Vicky. We don't have a juvie around here, so minors are held in a different cell until transport can be arranged to the county. But they let her go with our parents."

"I hope everything works out with your sister," Katie replied. She meant it. She'd seen first-hand the damage drugs could do in someone's life. "And thank you for telling me this. I've uh... I've gotta go."

She fumbled out of the booth seat and tossed her coffee even though it was still almost full. She made it to her car and drove out of the lot with no real destination in mind.

Whatever Amos had been doing, whatever his reasons, he hadn't shared them with Katie. Yeah, okay, it was good to know he hadn't been making out with some teenage girl. The thought of that brought bile to her throat. It was possible he hadn't been using and the drugs in his system were from someone spiking his drink that night.

Maybe there were a lot of excuses and reasons and justifications. None of it changed the fact that he hadn't trusted her. That he had lied to her.

She stopped at an intersection and looked around. The bright Kimmel and Sons sign caught her attention and she whipped her car into the lot. Leah Kimmel came out of the garage, wiping her hands on a towel and an uncertain smile on her face.

"Amos isn't here," she said, then she cocked her head to the side in a move so like her younger brother's Katie figured it had to be a family trait. "You're not looking for him, are you?"

Katie shook her head. She didn't know what she was looking for or why she was here. She just knew it felt right somehow.

"Come on in. I'll make coffee."

Katie got out and followed Leah across the lot to a flight of stairs behind the garage.

"My apartment is up here. Dad's not doing so hot these days and hearing about Amos can set him off. That and, well…no offense, but he's none too fond of your brother, or your daddy."

Katie tried not to laugh, but failed. That was old news and nothing she wasn't used to. She could change her name. She could find some other small town where nobody recognized her. Yeah, that sounded like a good plan. She could have her small-town life, just not here. And not as Katie Tilman.

Leah opened the door to a small, airy space with big windows and comfortable-looking furniture. She pointed Katie to an overstuffed chair then turned to the tiny kitchen off to one side.

"I do most of my cooking in the house," Leah said. "But coffee? That I can do. Not to be rude, but why are you here? Or do you even know?"

The laughter threatened to bubble up again, making Katie feel like she might be on the verge of hysterics. She swallowed it down and spread her hands. "I don't know. I got in the car and drove. And here I am."

Leah stared at her for a long moment then shook her head and poured coffees. She handed Katie a cup then sat on the sofa, cradling her own drink.

"The chief of police pulled some strings, called in a favor, I don't know what, but she had them run all sorts of tests on my brother." She pulled her phone out and tapped the screen then turned it to Katie. She couldn't make sense of the string of words and numbers. She arched an eyebrow at Leah.

"Apparently, they can tell all sorts of things with the more detailed tests." Leah pulled up another image – a screenshot of a text conversation between Drea and someone at the ATF. "This is the guy who did the testing. He said it showed Amos wasn't a habitual user and the drugs were ingested. Which fits with what Amos said, and what Vicky told the police."

Katie resisted the urge to find a wall and beat her head into it. "That's great, and I'm happy for him, but it doesn't change the rest of it. All he had to do was talk to me. That's it. Instead, he lied." She looked down at the cup in her hands and laughed. "Sure, Miles is an asshole. Sure, Amos getting into trouble is my brother's fault. But Amos made his own choices here. And maybe he thought he was protecting me or something, but that's not his decision to make."

She didn't know why she was telling Leah this. It wouldn't make any difference.

"Do you know why Amos spent two years in the youth detention facility?"

Katie shrugged. "I gather he stole a car."

Leah nodded and a sad smile curled her lips. "He and Miles stole a car," she said.

There was more to the story, Katie could feel it. Some heavy weight that would either drive her down even more, or set her free. She wasn't sure she wanted to know everything. She was sure she had to know it.

"Neither of them ever told me that," she said.

"Of course not. Your brother would never admit it and Amos, well…" Leah shifted in her seat and took a sip of coffee. She sat the cup on the table next to her and leaned forward.

"Miles and Amos were up to their eyeballs with Carl Tilman and Dwight Phelps. Petty stuff mostly — a delivery or a pickup. Collect a payment or two. They were minors. If they were caught, the charges would be minimal."

All the spit dried up in Katie's mouth. She'd known Miles had been into some shady shit when he was younger, but not this deep.

"For some stupid reason, those two idiots decided to steal a car. They went joyriding around. Amos claimed it was on orders from Carl Tilman — a little payback for someone who tried to fuck him over. They torched the car and abandoned it near an old mining town. Trouble was, they were drunk as fuck and Amos took a tumble. Passed out. Miles left him."

Leah picked up her coffee, took a sip and gave a sad smile. "Bigger trouble was, they were in the county. Outside of Chief Lawson's jurisdiction. And they'd crossed multiple counties that night. A little thing became a big thing."

She bit her lip and closed her eyes. "Miles claimed he wasn't there, and your mama backed him up. Said he was with her the whole time. Our dad told Amos he could keep his ass in jail. Your daddy came along and offered to take care of Amos if he'd take his lumps and keep quiet."

Katie remembered her mother frantically packing their bags, insisting they weren't going to do this anymore. The yelling and screaming that happened that night as her mother shoved belongings into the car.

"I dunno why, but Chief Lawson got involved. Convinced the District Attorney to reduce the charges if Amos would tell the whole truth. I guess they were hoping he'd have enough to go after Carl or Dwight," Leah continued. "Except he didn't. Those two played everything so close, there was no way those two boys would know anything real. Maybe Miles did, but not Amos. And I think you know the rest."

Jan Tilman had packed her two children into a car brimming with all the clothes and basic belongings she could manage on short notice and they had fled. It was supposed to be a fresh start for all of them. Except Miles had never stopped being a troublemaker. And their mother had never stopped hitting the bottle or bouncing from one dead-end job to the next. It was a cycle Katie had vowed she would break.

She shook her head and brought her mind back to the present.

"All the more reason for Amos to know better," Katie said. "And for him to tell me what was going on."

She stood, set her half empty coffee on the kitchen counter and faced Amos' big sister.

"This just proves I made a mistake coming here. Some shit runs too deep. Thanks for the coffee and for talking to me. I'm sorry it doesn't change how I feel."

Katie let herself out and hurried to her car. It was all too much. She'd figured she could come back to Orchard Creek and avoid her dad, and eventually people would forget she was a Tilman. When she and Amos started hanging out it was like all her childish teenage dreams were coming true.

Then Miles showed back up and in no time, her wonderful world came crumbling down like a castle made of sand. She should have stuck to her plan of swearing off men and kept Amos at a distance.

Well, she could suck it up and deal for the rest of the school year. Just show up, do her job, and go home. Contract renewals were coming up. Maybe the school wouldn't even offer to renew hers. If they did, she'd decline. Come spring, she'd start looking for someplace new. Move over summer.

Someplace where she didn't know anybody.

Chapter Twenty-Six

Amos
December 11, Monday

Leah and Grace sat across the table from Amos, both of them staring at him like he'd just grown a second head or something. He spread his hands on the table and tried again.

"Look, this isn't out of the blue," he said. "I've had a lot of time to think over the past couple weeks, and I know it's the right choice."

They sat at the worn kitchen table where they'd all grown up, eating cereal together on weekend mornings. Doing homework on school nights. Leah had finally convinced the old man to see his doctor, and Amos knew this was his one chance to talk to his sisters while their dad was out. The old man would be home soon and whether his sisters liked it or not, this was something Amos had to do.

"The town council vote is this afternoon," Amos said. "If they fund the fire department, great. If they don't, I'm gonna apply at the county."

He reached across the table and took Grace's hand because she looked like she was about to cry.

"Y'know what. You're right." Leah's agreement surprised him and he snapped his head around to look at his older sibling. "Dad's been off his game more than usual. Having Miles here even for that brief time was a wonder. We got so much more done with so much less stress. It's time. He needs to make a decision to let me manage the garage the way it should be, or he can close it."

She grabbed Grace's other hand. "And you, kiddo. You need to be able to go to college. I know you want his approval, but you may never get it. You have to do what's right for you. Follow your heart, even if it takes you far away from home."

A single tear spilled down Grace's cheek and she sniffed. Amos let go of her fingers and tossed her the box of tissues that always sat on the shelf near the table.

"We've all three put our lives on hold. Waiting," Amos said. "It's time to stop waiting and move forward."

"Lemme guess, y'all are fussin' about the business again?" The old man stood in the kitchen doorway, glaring at his three children. He made his way to the coffee pot, poured a cup, then sat down at the head of the table.

"You don't get a say in the garage." He pointed at Amos. "You know damn good and well the council's gonna vote yes. They're not gonna say no when they've got Drea Parsons shillin' the idea."

His gaze roamed over the three of them again. His eyes were red and tired looking and his face had lost what little color he normally had. He looked old and worn out but he smiled at his children.

"Dad, I think you should hear Amos out." Leah folded her hands on the table, a sure sign she was biting her tongue and choosing what words she did say very carefully.

Amos took a deep breath and figured he'd start with the easiest part of the conversation. "You're right. I'm reasonably sure the council will approve funding the department. There's a slim chance they won't."

The old man nodded. "And you've decided to move on if that's the case."

There was no rancor in his tone. It was just a factual statement.

"Yeah. It's time." Amos crossed his fingers the next part went as smoothly. "Grace found a program at West Virginia University."

He eyed his younger sister, willing her to not give in.

"I put in the application, Daddy." Grace's eyes were wide and she looked a little like a deer in headlights, but her mouth was set. "I can start in spring as a transfer student. Pick up some core classes."

The old man's fingers tapped on the table. A rapid rhythm. Index finger, middle finger, ring finger, pinkie. Then backward. A pause, then he'd repeat it.

"Morgantown's almost four hours away," he said. "Still, WVU is where your mama went."

The coy smile on Grace's face was a dead giveaway that she'd not only known that, and had counted on it making a difference. She could have chosen University of Charleston to be closer, but she wanted to pursue criminal justice and forensics. Charleston would have been a steppingstone. The other universities offering similar courses were out of state. By comparison, WVU looked good.

"I s'pose the next topic is the business?" The old man glared at Amos as if his son were the cause of all his woes. *Hell, for all I know, maybe I am.*

"The garage can't continue running as it has been," Leah said. "The little bit of time we had help, business was smoother and turnaround times better. Once Amos leaves, we lose a full-time mechanic. When Grace goes off to school, we lose our office person. Who's gonna pick up that slack?"

The old man laid his palms on the table and pushed himself upright in his seat. His mouth pressed into a thin line and he scowled at his two girls before turning to Amos.

"If this one hadn't gone and brought that good for nothing friend of his on and fucked up—again, I might add—things would be different."

He crossed his arms and nodded as if that was the way of things. In the past, no one in the family would argue once Roy Kimmel reached this point. Amos was done living in the past.

"Yeah, I've made some mistakes, but you are wrong on one big count there," Amos said. "Things would not be different."

Their dad's eyes popped open as if his son had slapped him, but Amos was determined to say what needed to be said.

"Nothing changes the fact that I'll be shifting to full time at the fire department. Nor does it change the fact that Grace wants to go to college—not stay here doing office work."

He took in a slow breath and braced himself for what he had to say next.

"And whether you like it or not, nothing changes the fact that you are not able to carry the workload that you could when you were younger. There's nothing wrong with that. It just is what it is."

Amos glanced to his sisters. Leah inclined her head once and Grace mouthed "say it" at him. It was the mixture of fierce determination and abject pain in his kid sister's eyes that gave Amos the courage to continue.

"You said you'd close the business before letting Leah take it over," Amos said. "Well, then. Do it. In your words, shit or get off the pot. Things can't keep going the way they are, and there is no successful path forward that doesn't involve Leah stepping up and doing what she's so damn good at."

"And that I love," Leah chimed in. "Daddy, our family built this business and it means something to me. To all of us. I want to keep it that way. Please, let me."

The old man's scowl deepened and he passed a hand over his face. Amos reached and took his sisters' hands in his and the three siblings waited as their father processed everything they'd said.

The hair on the back of Amos' neck stood up at the current of tension hanging in the air. He didn't know for sure what would happen if their dad didn't agree, but he had a feeling it would shatter the family. It might break Grace's heart, but she'd go to college anyway. Amos knew where he belonged, and it wasn't here. Leah was the only one he wasn't sure of. Like as not, she'd stay for a bit, then eventually she too would leave.

"Your mama and I put aside some money for things like school, or weddings, grandkids." The old man swiped at his face again, only this time, Amos saw the tears on his cheeks. "Grace, you go on to college. You chase your dreams. I wouldn't be much of a father if I didn't support my baby girl in that."

He swallowed hard and glared at Amos. "You've always been a headstrong, stubborn, pain in my ass. Guess some things never change. And I guess you gotta go where you feel called."

That was about as close to a blessing as Amos figured he'd ever get from his father. All things considered, he'd take it.

The old man turned to his eldest. Leah squared her shoulders and tossed her head back. Whatever was about to come out of their dad's mouth, that look said she would not flinch or shy from it.

"Doc convinced me today that I need to take it a bit easier. I don't like not being in control." He drummed his fingers on the table then nodded. "Show me a business plan that doesn't involve a loan. I'll listen this time. There's a bit in savings we could invest in the garage. Convince me."

The sigh of relief that came out of Leah's mouth made all of them smile, then Grace giggled and the rest of them dissolved into laughter.

Leah got herself under control first. "Why don't I make lunch?"

And just like that, the heavy cloud that had hung over every family interaction since their mother passed began to dissipate. Amos smiled at his sisters. He could handle his dad being pissed off at him. Better him than the other two. Amos could roll with it in ways they couldn't. And the old man would eventually get over it. A least a little bit.

After lunch, he changed clothes and drove himself into town. Drea met him outside the library where the town council was meeting.

"You ready for this?" She tugged her uniform shirt down over her growing baby bump. For the first time, he really thought about the future of the family business. There hadn't been an 'and Sons' at the garage for a long time. Their dad was the only boy in the family. Same as his father. Maybe they wanted to continue the business, or they might have felt they had no other choice.

"I guess," he replied. They walked inside and took seats in the nearly full meeting space. Amos didn't pay a bit of attention to the opening remarks, or any of the reports from the council officers.

Leah wasn't married and as far as he knew, she'd only ever dated Jake Parsons. Hell, he didn't even know if she liked men. Or if she wasn't into love and romance. Or what. If Grace moved away for college, she wasn't too likely to come back. And Amos...

He'd never thought much about getting married or having kids. He'd been too busy getting his life straightened out. He'd liked dating casually. Until Katie. She was the first woman who made him think forever, and he'd gone and fucked that up.

An elbow in his ribs brought his mind back to the council meeting. Retired Chief Mack Lawson stood, stuck his reading glasses on his nose and glanced at the piece of paper in his hand.

"We currently have an all-volunteer fire department, ably commanded by Amos Kimmel." Lawson paused as there was a smattering of applause in the room. "The council has discussed the matter in private meetings and will not be putting the matter to a vote tonight."

He paused as a rumble went through the attendees. The whispers rose until Lawson called out for folks to settle down. It took him a few tries and when the chatter stopped, the retired chief cleared his throat and glared over his glasses at the crowd.

"According to town bylaws, the council has authority to make these decisions without a public vote." He stopped and pointed a finger toward a group in the back. "Hold your comments until I'm finished, please. The council has prepared a statement, which I will read tonight."

Drea's brows furrowed and she glanced from the former chief to Amos. Lawson cleared his throat again as a small murmur rose in the room.

"Settle down." His voice boomed out and everyone quieted. He tossed the paper to the table and braced his hands on the podium. "I don't need to read a buncha official blah-blah here. You want to read it all, I'm sure it'll be on the website. Let's just cut to the chase."

He glanced at his fellow council members then his eyes settled on Amos. "The Orchard Creek Town Council, by unanimous decision, has elected to fund a fully staffed fire department."

The room erupted in cheers. Drea clapped and whistled. Amos' chest tightened as everything he'd been working for clicked into place.

"Amos, would you please stand so folks can get a look at you," Lawson continued. "Not like you're a stranger to any of us."

Amos shook himself and stood, aware of every set of eyes in the room turning to him. Just a couple weeks before, he'd sat in the town's holding cell, accused of everything from manufacturing drugs to corruption of a minor. Thanks to a lot of hard work from Drea Parsons, all the charges had been dropped.

"Also by unanimous decision, the council appointed Amos Kimmel as Fire Chief. That is, assuming he agrees to serve."

In an instant, Amos was surrounded by his crew. Shawn Dubois and Micah Stewart clapped Amos on the shoulder. Drea stood and hugged him. Amos faced the council.

"Thank you," he raised his voice to be heard over the commotion in the room. "And you know I'll take it. Gladly!"

Later, he set up a meeting with the council to get the budget and the plans for the department. He thanked Drea, again. She'd been a driving force behind getting this done. Then he met his crew at Oak Bridge for beers and a round of darts.

Later still, home alone and looking at the new windows and the wall that still needed repainting, and the half empty bookshelves, he should have been happy. He had everything he'd wanted — his dad had at least sort of agreed to let Leah take on the business and encouraged Grace to go to college. The council not only approved the fire department but in a surprise move, made Amos chief.

Even the recent blunder with Miles hadn't erased the past ten years of hard work and dedication. For that, he was grateful.

Still, it all felt empty without Katie.

Chapter Twenty-Seven

Katie
December 20, Wednesday

Katie cradled a cup of tea and stared at the stack of paper on the little table in front of her. The last day before winter break and she'd been called into the school office to pick up her contract for next year. She hadn't opened the envelope until she was safely home.

The deadline for response was a little over a month away — the last day of January. She had time to make her decision.

She set her tea down and grabbed her laptop. She'd already applied for two jobs. One in Charleston and one near Morgantown. She wasn't ready to look outside the state yet. She supposed she could go back to Pennsylvania. It wouldn't take much to renew her credentials there.

She opened her email. The Charleston job declined, saying they'd already hired someone. *That was fast.* She didn't expect to hear on the Morgantown job before the holidays. Part of her wanted to leave. Not even finish out the year. But she couldn't do that and have any hope of getting a decent job after.

No, she'd have to stick it out. The question was whether Orchard Creek was the right place for her to settle down. As much as she'd hated parts of it growing up, it was all she'd known. And when they'd moved away, it was all she craved.

But she could get the mountains and the trees anywhere. She could find a small town where everyone knew everyone somewhere they didn't know her. Yet.

She'd swear off men again. Maybe she was meant to be single for the rest of her life. She could do that. Morgantown was a college town. It would be perfect. If she landed that job, she could find a little place and make that home.

She picked up her tea. Tepid. *Ew.* Did she really want to spend the first afternoon of winter break, still in her work clothes, poring over job boards and making imaginary plans for a teaching position she hadn't yet landed?

Nope.

What she wanted was to be curled up with Amos, snug under the covers. Or enjoying a winter hike. Or going to Charleston, or even drive over to Lexington or Cincinnati for the weekend if he was free.

She set her computer and tea aside and stood in a rush. Katie didn't stop to think. She grabbed her purse and keys, threw on a coat and hurried out the door. If she sat around her apartment one more day mooning over Amos, she'd scream.

A fritter sounds good.

With a plan in mind, Katie put her car in gear and headed for her favorite coffee shop. Guaranteed they'd have some seasonal baked goods. She'd enjoy half with her coffee at the shop and have the second half for breakfast tomorrow.

The place was more crowded than usual on a weekday afternoon, but then she remembered school was out. She took her order and looked around for an open seat. A couple got up from a small two-top in the back and gestured to Katie. She slid into the seat with a smile of thanks before they turned and left.

Sure that everyone was staring at her and wondering what had happened with her and Amos, Katie focused on cutting her fritter in half. She hadn't even asked what was in it. She'd just ordered the seasonal special, but it looked like apple. She broke off a piece and popped it in her mouth.

An explosion of flavor had he closing her eyes in bliss. Maple syrup and something spicy and the fruit was almost buttery and very soft and smooth.

"The maple-pear fritters here are a treat." Amos' rich voice poured over her and soothed her aching soul. One simple sentence. A handful of words and she was ready to melt. She opened her eyes and found him standing next to the table, his eyes full of doubt and questions.

"May I sit?" He laid a hand on the empty seat across from her. She tried not to think about the feel of his fingers on her skin, or tangled in her hair. She should get up. Leave. Tell him to fuck off.

Instead, she nodded and watched in a torturous mix of desire and anger as he shed his coat and settled his long body into the tiny bistro chair.

"I fucked up," he said. "No apology can ever change that or make up for it. I tried to think about what I could do to win you back. Then I realized it didn't matter. I could give you the sun and the moon and the stars, and it would ring false. Just another gesture full of empty promises."

He wasn't wrong. She'd spent the last few weeks agonizing over how she'd repeated her own stupid history — falling for a guy and his pretty words. The fact that he acknowledged it had her curious.

"Town approved the fire department," he said.

"Yeah, I heard. Congratulations." She could at least be nice. There was no reason to be a jerk just because he'd ripped her heart out.

"I'd like, if you're open to the idea, to tell you everything," he said. "I know you've probably heard a lot, but not the whole story. I don't know if hearing it will make any difference, and I'm not excusing the fact that I wasn't honest with you."

There was another surprise. No excuses. No shifting the blame to her. No expectations of absolution based on whatever cock and bull story he'd probably cooked up.

"Sure," she replied. "If you need to get it off your chest. Go for it. Right here. Right now. This is your one and only chance to do that."

There would be no going someplace more private. If they did that, her body would betray her mind. She was already struggling with the desire to reach out and touch him. To tell him how much she'd missed his kisses.

Amos chuckled then shrugged. "At this point, I've got nothing to hide and no pride about it."

He told her about the night of the trailer park fire. She'd heard it from him before, but this time, he included talking to Drea and her asking for his help. He told her about Miles' visit to the garage, and all the troubles they were having staying on top of the work. How that had been the start of a plan to get Miles to talk to him again.

She finished her coffee and Amos went to get her a refill. He came back with a fresh coffee for her and one for himself as well. He sat and continued talking, telling her about talking to his sister, and setting it up for Miles to come to work at the garage and how he'd been surprised at how good Miles could be sometimes.

"Not gonna lie," Amos said. "There were times I wondered if he really had changed. I never got anything out of him. Nothing helpful anyway. Then...well...we finished up early and Miles suggested we grab a beer. I figured that was my chance."

When he told her how that unfolded, first she cringed, then she got angry for him. She'd grown to adulthood seeing how manipulative Miles could be. She knew his tricks and how nasty he'd turn if he felt someone crossed him. Amos had only known the teenage Miles. She couldn't blame Amos for getting sucked into her brother's tangled mess. The more he talked about that night and the aftermath, the angrier she got.

Still, he should have told her something.

"I got lucky," Amos said. "Drea believed in me. The town believed in me."

He cleared his throat and took a sip of coffee. "After that, I made a decision. My sisters and I talked to our dad. He's not happy about all of it, but Grace will be transferring to the university in the spring and Leah's taking over the garage. And I've got the fire department."

Amos swallowed hard. His fingers clenched on his coffee cup. "Family's good. We've got a paid fire department starting in January. My stuff can be replaced. Dwight Phelps is gonna go to jail, and maybe he'll point a finger at Carl Tilman."

He stopped and gave her a sad smile. "I'd say I'm sorry about your daddy, but I know better. Even if he doesn't go down this time, I have to believe he and Miles will fuck up eventually."

If only the world worked that way. In Katie's experience, it didn't.

"I'm happy for you," she said. "You got everything you wanted." The hell of it was, it was true. She might be mad as hell at Amos, but she still wanted the best for him. If she was being honest with herself, she still loved him. But that kind of thinking could lead to stupid choices.

"Not everything," he whispered. "I fucked up the one thing that meant the most to me. I lost you."

Katie willed herself not to respond. His words tugged at her heart, begging forgiveness and understanding. And everything in her jumped for joy at the thought of having him back.

"No apology will ever be enough," he continued, "but I am sorry. I made some idiotic decisions and I hurt you — the person who means everything to me."

His words sent her heart soaring and her brain was running out of reasons to deny her heart what it craved. Amos reached across the table and took her hand in his.

"I love you more than I could ever hope to say in words. You are my world. My everything." His fingers twined around hers and squeezed gently. "I have no expectations here, but I promise I will never keep secrets from you again. I would like the chance to win back your trust."

If someone were animating the internal war Katie was going through, right now, her heart would be gleefully beating her brain into submission.

"Someone I care deeply about once told me a very personal story about second chances," she said. She slid the untouched half of her fritter across the table. "I'll share so long as you buy another on the way out."

Amos' eyebrows raised and his lips curled into a smile. "There are so many ways I could interpret that."

She'd missed their banter. And his easy smile that looked boyish and devilish at the same time. Most of all, she'd missed his company.

Sure, he'd made mistakes, but he was right—everyone deserved a second chance.

"Your first inclination is probably accurate," she said and crossed her fingers that she was right on both counts—that Amos was being genuine and that his first thought about her suggestion was that they share the second fritter tomorrow morning after waking up together in her bed.

His smile turned more devilish and she knew. He leaned forward and his fingers tightened on hers. "You expect me to sit here after that?"

"Yep," she replied. "I'm going to finish my half and enjoy my second coffee. I needed to get out a bit and I'm going to relish it."

He settled back in his chair and tore off a bite of his half of the fritter. Watching the pleasure on his face as he popped it in his mouth was almost as good as having a bite herself. It also sent her brain careening down the path of remembering the look of bliss on his face during sex.

"Oh, that thought had to be delicious," he said, his voice dropping into a dangerous rumble.

Katie cleared her throat and arched an eyebrow at him.

"I've got until the end of January to decide if I'm going to accept the contract I was offered for next year," she said. "If I take it, I stay here. If I don't, I'll find something somewhere else."

"So I've got just over a month to convince you to stay," he replied. "And you want to start in bed?"

Heat crept up her cheeks and she imagined she was flushed bright pink. She mustered every bit of bravado she could find. "Are you saying you don't?"

Amos stood and went to the counter. Within minutes, he was back with a second fritter in a bag. He wrapped the rest of his half, then reached across the table and did the same to hers. He slipped both pieces into the bag. Then he stood and pulled her up next to him.

His strong arms circled her waist and Katie knew the bliss of being right where she longed to be.

"Kitten," he growled the pet name in her ear. "I want you in my life always and in all ways. But yes, I want you sprawled naked in bed with my name on your lips as I make you come, over and over again."

Katie lifted her arms to rest on his shoulders, then slid her fingers into his hair. "I love you, too. Now take me home, please."

The hoots and hollers that erupted when Amos kissed her didn't matter. Katie didn't care if they were feeding the gossip beast and everyone would be talking about their very public make up.

Amos lifted his head and smiled. "You've got about five seconds to collect your coat before I go all caveman and throw you over my shoulder. Let's get out of here."

They scrambled into their coats and hurried outside. "We'll have to take your car. I'm on the bike and don't have a second helmet." Amos picked her up and carried her to her car. Katie hit the key fob to unlock the doors and Amos deposited her in the driver's seat.

"We could just take…" Katie stopped as Amos laid a finger over her lips.

"We've been apart too long. I don't want to spend another second away from you. We can come back and get my bike tomorrow."

He kissed her again and the heat spread. She didn't just want him. She needed him.

"I love you," she whispered against his mouth. Amos pulled back and gave her the cocky smile she loved so much.

"My Kitten," he said as he cupped her cheek. "My everything."

Epilogue

Fall Festival — the following year

The cherry red Harvester emblazoned with the Parsons Acres logo sat next to a small corral where smiling children took rides on a handful of beautiful ponies. Danny Parsons sat on the tailgate, rocking a baby.

"That's new." Amos nodded to the pony ride just as Kyle Elkins scrambled off the corral rails and came running.

"Miss Katie!" He threw his arms around Katie's legs then practically launched himself at Amos, who swooped the little boy into the air and airplaned him in a circle before setting him back on his feet.

"Have you done a pony ride yet?"

Kyle had started second grade this year, and since his mother was the ranch manager at Parsons Acres, Katie imagined a sedate walk in a tiny corral might bore the adventurous boy.

"Nah," Kyle said, confirming her suspicions. "I'm helping! Mama says next year I can do the gymkhana!"

Lily Elkins perched on the top rail, keeping her eye on everything around her while her sister Penny led a new group around the ride.

"How y'all like the new addition to the Fall Festival?" Danny stood next to them, the baby curled in the crook of his arm. Paul Parsons had a shock of almost black hair, just like his mother, and his father's bright blue eyes.

An unexpected tug to hold the baby pulled at Katie. She'd never thought about having children. Not really.

"I love it," she answered Danny's question, if for no other reason than to get her mind off what Cinda Gable called 'baby fever'.

"Eliza mentioned it when we were talking about set-up and safety," Amos said. "Surprised no one had thought of it before."

Danny shrugged and shifted baby Paul to the other arm. The baby waved his hands in the air and fussed a moment before quieting back down. "Well, we weren't set up for it before. Not too many folks who run these things wanna come all the way out here for something this small. Glad we could finally do it."

Paul fussed again and Danny scooped the baby into one hand then passed him to Amos. Seeing her boyfriend cradling a five month old in his giant hands did not do anything to calm the sudden 'I want one' urge.

Amos was good with children. He talked to them on their level. Back when she'd first seen him again, Cinda Gable had said Amos was a big kid himself, and in many ways, it was true. He held on to a joy for life that most people lost somewhere between graduating school and figuring out they had bills to pay.

"Oh good, you're here." Drea Parsons walked up with a tall, sandy-haired man who practically screamed federal agent even though he was in jeans and a sweater.

"This lovely lady is Katie Tilman." The man shook hands with Katie, then Drea pointed at Amos.

"And this is her boyfriend, Amos Kimmel. Amos, I'd like you to meet your savior. This is Peter Adams."

The man rolled his eyes and stuck out his hand. "Good to finally meet you. I know your sister, Grace. She applied for an internship with us this fall. Wicked smart."

Amos handed the baby to Katie before he took the man's hand. Katie stared down at the little bundle that was Paul Parsons. He smelled of baby powder and something fresh and clean. The little tug grew.

Nope. Not even thinking about that. Hell no.

Except she was thinking about it. Even as she tried to focus on the animated conversation happening between Amos, Drea and Peter. She barely noticed when Grace Kimmel joined the group, then Danny tapped Katie's shoulder and she handed the baby off to him. He grabbed his wife's hand and they took off. Katie tuned back into the conversation.

"It's all set," Grace said to her big brother, then turned to Peter without waiting for Amos to say anything. "Drea told me she had a guest here who's never had a West Virginia Chili Dog. Is that true?"

Katie turned to Amos, whose gaze was glued on his sister. "What's all set? What's Grace up to?"

When Amos looked back at her, the mischief in his eyes was clear. "So, what d'ya think? Would you call the last Fall Festival our first date?"

He laced his fingers into hers and they set off toward the corn maze.

"I don't know," Katie replied. "You didn't ask me out till over a week later. I think Charleston was our first date."

They'd had this discussion before. Just like they'd tried to decide when they first started officially dating. Amos maintained it was the night they went to dinner in Charleston while Katie insisted it was the Halloween Carnival, or possibly the first time they had sex. Or it could have been when she asked him to define what they were. Or it was the week before that when he'd first claimed her as his?

They entered the corn maze and Amos led the way. After a few turns, Katie started to wonder if they were all alone in the twisting rows. It was late in the afternoon, too late for lunch and it seemed oddly quiet. They ran into a few dead ends and had to backtrack and take a new path. Then Amos rounded another corner and pulled her to a stop.

He wrapped his arms around her waist and kissed her slowly. Katie's toes curled as the familiar heat spread. The last nine months had been a whirlwind as Amos had worked to fully staff the new fire department and Katie had accepted the contract to continue teaching. They'd taken a week's vacation together at the start of summer and when they'd come back, Amos had suggested they move in together.

The idea made sense, so Katie had agreed. She'd never known that kind of joy and contentment before. She never wanted it to end.

"I should have done that last year," Amos said. "Kissed you in the corn maze. I think I knew then, but definitely the night we went to Charleston. That's when I knew for sure."

She laid her head on his chest, listening to the strong thudding of his heartbeat. "Knew what?"

Amos took her hand and smiled at her. "Close your eyes, Kitten."

Katie didn't question. She trusted Amos with everything — body, mind, heart and soul. He guided her as they went around another turn before he stopped again.

"Move forward two steps," he whispered in her ear. Katie took two steps. "Count to ten then open your eyes."

Amos moved away from her as she started counting. When she got to ten, she opened her eyes.

The center of the maze was filled with glowing jack-o-lanterns, the same as last year. But last year, Amos wasn't down on one knee holding a giant bouquet of flowers that were so deep red they were almost black. He set the flowers down and took both her hands in his.

"I told you before that you are my everything," Amos said. "But that isn't quite true. Yet."

The world came to a complete stop as she gazed into Amos' gorgeous blue eyes.

"What do you mean that's not quite true?"

His smile was pure devil. "I love you more than I ever imagined it was possible to love. I am yours, completely, and I know you are mine. There's one thing missing. Katie, will you marry me? Do me the honor of becoming my wife."

Katie couldn't find her voice if she tried. She managed to nod and Amos pulled her down until she sat on his knee and he wrapped an arm around her waist and kissed her. His other hand threaded into her hair and he held her tight as his tongue slid into her mouth in a searing kiss.

He lifted his head and smiled. "What did you think I meant? You had a look on your face."

One hand stroked down her back and Katie arched in pleasure at his touch. The hand in her hair tightened. She knew what he wanted to hear.

"I thought you meant, ummm…y'know…anal."

He liked when she used naughty words. He liked when she asked explicitly for what she wanted. And he'd told her that one day, he wanted her ass, but she would have to ask for it.

"When you said everything wasn't quite true, that's what I thought you meant at first."

The hand on her hip dipped lower, then slid over her thigh and under her skirt. Amos pushed her legs apart and with his usual unerring accuracy, rested his thumb over her clit. Even through her thick tights, the warmth of his hand sent her body into shivers of pleasure.

"Is that what you want, Kitten?"

Katie sighed as he made lazy circles with his thumb.

"Yes." The word came out on a whisper that was nearly lost to the rustle of corn sheaves in the autumn breeze.

"How are you supposed to ask?"

Katie moaned. He wanted explicit. "We're in the corn maze. It's public."

"No one else is in here," he replied. "That's what Grace was telling me. They closed it off and we've got it to ourselves right now."

She could do this. It wasn't that she didn't like the words. She did. She loved it when Amos talked dirty to her. He wanted to hear those words from her lips? She could understand that desire. She just had to find it in her to do it.

"I want you to take my ass, please."

"Mmmm, I like that idea," he replied. "And you're getting closer. I think we can do better."

He shifted her off his lap, scooped up the flowers and stood. He held a hand out to her, but instead of taking her fingers in his, he dropped something warm and hard into her hand.

She opened her palm to see a silver band topped by a stunning black diamond surrounded by rubies. Amos plucked the ring from her palm and slipped it on her finger.

"You can show that off some other time," he said. "I think you and I have other things to do."

Katie reached up, wrapped her hands behind his neck and pulled until he bent closer to her. "I love you. Now, take me home and fuck me, please. And yes, I want you in my ass."

Amos lifted her, tucked her legs around his waist and kissed her. He didn't put her down until they got to the maze exit.

"I love you, Kitten. Trust me, you will get everything you want. Always."

Want to see more from this author? Here's a taster for you to enjoy!

Logan County Love: Arrested
Roxanne Blackhall

Excerpt

Glass shattered and bright blue liquid sprayed into the air. There was no time to duck or turn away. The blue arc landed, covering Grace Kimmel from her safety goggles to the bottom of her formerly white coat. She glared at her lab partner as the room went silent. The only sound was the slow dripping as the liquid ran off the table.

A few seconds stretched into an eternity.

"I am so sorry." That was her lab partner.

"Everyone freeze." That commanding voice was Special Agent David Ferris, the lab manager. Nervous chatter filled the room until he called for quiet.

"Kimmel! You okay?"

Afraid to open her mouth, Grace nodded — forget the broken glass. She was more worried about finding out what the gunk tasted like. Someone handed her a towel, and she blotted her face and goggles until she could see clearly again.

"Lacy, you wanna tell me what happened?" Ferris sounded calm, but he was practically vibrating with tension.

"I, uh…" Steve Lacy looked like a stout Clark Kent but had none of the charm. His head swiveled back and forth as if he was seeing the mess for the first time. "Not sure."

In any other circumstance, that would be Grace's cue to go off on the man. She knew what had happened — he'd opted for speed over safety and brought the whole mixing container to their workstation rather than decant the portion they needed into a smaller vessel. With a coveted internship on the line, she held her temper in check.

"Excuse me, I'm going to see how much of this I can wash off." Grace didn't wait for permission. Not blowing her top because her lab partner made a careless mistake was one thing, but standing around covered in viscous goo while the error was discussed was above and beyond.

The fluorescent lights in the bathroom made everything look worse than she'd imagined. Patches of blue streaked her face and the front of her hair. She grabbed a fistful of paper towels, saturated them in the sink and set to work scrubbing the worst of it off her face.

The door burst open, and Daniela Castillo hurried into the room, her arms overflowing with towels.

"Holy shit, that was intense!" Daniela tossed a bottle of liquid soap and a washcloth onto the edge of the sink. "Ferris pointed me to the staff bathroom and the clean-up station. You look like a Smurf. Or maybe some Celtic warrior, which is much cooler."

The soap helped, and Grace got most of the color off her face. She cursed herself for forgoing the optional hair cover. *Teach me to do that again.*

Multiple passes with a damp cloth left streaks that were now more green than blue. She scraped her hair back into a messy bun and secured it.

"The joys of being blonde, I guess. Yellow and blue make green. I hope this crap washes out, otherwise I don't want to think what it's going to cost to fix."

She stripped off the ruined lab coat then swiped a wet cloth over the spots on her legs. The gray pants would never be the same. At least her shoes wiped right off.

"Ferris called lunch, so you've got time. How bad are your clothes?"

Grace straightened up and surveyed her reflection in the mirror. *Not great, but not terrible.*

"I can survive the day with a few spots," she said. "Three cheers for lab coats. Let's eat. I'm starved."

Daniela led the way to the staff room, where they tossed the soiled linens into a hamper, then made their way to the lunchroom. They grabbed their box lunches and joined their fellow applicants at a long table on the far side of the room.

"Are you okay?"

"I thought Ferris was gonna blow a gasket."

"How the fuck does that happen?"

Yesterday, thirty-six college seniors had trouped into the Bureau of Alcohol, Tobacco, Firearms and Explosives' National Laboratory to start the final selection process for six fall internship positions. Over five thousand students had applied, and six of the finalists had already been cut.

Grace felt lucky to have made it this far, and now she was worried she'd be kicked out because of someone else's error. She looked around the table. Across from Grace, Daniela sat next to Eric Dietz. They had been flirting since they'd all arrived, and Grace would lay odds the two had hooked up when they got back to the hotel last night.

The rest of the applicants ringed the table, all talking about their morning. Steve Lacy was nowhere to be seen. All through lunch, Grace kept expecting to be called into the office and sent packing. Instead, back in the lab, Ferris handed her a clean lab coat.

"Good job not panicking. You're going to have to do the rest of today without a partner. Had Lacy owned his mistake, he might still be here."

She shrugged into the fresh coat. "What do you mean by that?"

None of what Ferris said gave her any confidence she wasn't next on the chopping block.

"He threw you under the bus. Or tried to. We have cameras in the lab."

"I should have caught it. Said something." While she knew there hadn't been time, she still felt responsible.

"You're at a disadvantage without a partner, so do your best."

That was a dismissal if she'd ever heard one. Grace buttoned her coat and took her seat. The station had been wiped clean, as if nothing had ever happened. Ferris moved to the front of the room and called everyone to silence.

"Accidents happen, but the mess this morning should not have." His gaze swept the room, pausing on each of the assembled students. "All of you here should be better than this. Lacy should have been better than this. You are experienced in lab protocols, and there is no excuse for carelessness."

The knot of tension in Grace's stomach doubled.

"For the next segment, you and your partner will collect and process samples from five sources, then follow the instructions provided and make your conclusions. Let's go to the chiller."

Grace fell into step next to Daniela and Eric.

"You wanna work with us?" Eric kept his voice low and raised his eyebrows.

"Yeah," Daniela added, "join our team."

It was tempting. Without a partner, Grace would have to do it all herself. She'd be slower than the two-person teams, plus she wouldn't have anyone to brainstorm with.

"Ferris said I was on my own. So, I'm guessing he'd frown on it."

Daniela looked stricken. Eric gave a muttered "fuck" and shook his head. Ferris pushed open the door into a large room with two rows of tables. Tall glass-front refrigerators and freezers lined one wall.

It's like a convenience store meets an autopsy room. Grace clenched her fingers and dug her nails into her palms to keep from giggling at the image. Then she spotted the tall man leaning casually against one of the tables at the front.

Like most men she'd seen at the ATF offices, his hair was short and tidy. His shoulders strained the seams of his lab coat and his legs seemed to go on forever. Or maybe that was the fact that he was parked with his butt resting against the table and his crossed ankles blocked the aisle that ran the center of the room.

What stopped Grace in her tracks was the lopsided grin that lit up his boyishly handsome face. So far, every staff member she'd met wore a near-constant Very Serious Expression. Grace imagined a little 'tm' following the term. This guy looked like he was ready to hang out with his friends.

I wouldn't mind hanging out with that. Damn.

She pulled her attention back to Ferris as he joined Mr. Smiley Face Holy Shit Hotness at the front.

"This is Special Agent Peter Adams," Ferris said. "He's here to supervise and get anything you need to complete your work. Your applicant numbers are already on the tables. Please find your places, and I'll leave you in Adams' capable hands."

Ferris left and Tall and Buff pushed himself to a standing position. Grace quickly found her spot—right next to where Agent Holy Smokes stood.

"Welcome. Each workstation has the basic equipment you'll need, as well as the list of tests you are to complete and questions." A hint of some accent tinted his voice—maybe a little southern, but the refined variety. "Please read everything before you come to the front to collect samples. If you need something, just ask. I'll be happy to provide."

Grace skimmed the sheet of instructions. Gunshot residue. Chemical analysis. Latent prints. All standard stuff with clear directions. Then she got to the last items. Blood and hair samples. *Good thing I'm not squeamish.*

She tuned out the excited chatter of the other teams discussing how they were going to divide the tasks. She was on her own, but she couldn't afford to rush. Rushing led to mistakes, and that would not happen here.

The moment she stepped up to collect her samples, the rest of the world faded out. She had one goal—landing one of the six internship slots. Then Agent Oh So Hot said something to her and Grace nearly dropped the swab in her hand.

"Sorry, sir, I was focused on getting this sample. What was that?"

She shouldn't have looked at him. Warm brown eyes gazed back at her and his lips curled into a smile that she was sure could make a stone statue turn its head.

"You can skip the 'sir'. It's never been my favorite honorific." His smile got even broader, making Grace wonder if there was some innuendo she was missing. "I asked how you were holding up after this morning. You good?"

She tore her gaze away from his. The last thing she wanted was special treatment because her lab partner had screwed up and people felt sorry for her. She tucked the swab into a baggie, then sealed and labeled it. Never mind that she was only carrying it three feet away and that no one else would touch it and there was no chain of custody to worry about. Protocol was protocol.

"Yeah, thanks. I'm okay. Just trying to get this done."

She hurried back to her workstation and away from his unsettling presence. Or at least as away as she could get, considering her spot was the next table over.

Get a grip. Yeah, he's hot. Since when does hot mean anything? Forget him and get to work.

She laid everything out, double checked the entire list, and outlined a plan of attack for maximum efficiency. First task, prepping samples for the centrifuge and spectrometer. That she could do in her sleep, thanks to several lab classes and two semesters spent as a lab assistant, including one at the medical examiner's.

All the more reason I should have said something when Lacy started cutting corners.

Grace tried not to think about the other teams bustling around. With the luxury of two people, they could afford to make multiple trips to request materials. She needed to get through the base tests first. Then she'd go to Agent Too Damn Cute… *His name is Peter Adams. Don't get distracted.*

She tucked her head and got to work. She had more vials to prep and slides to mount. Another task she could do without thinking. She kept her notebook handy and jotted observations, questions, and started a list of additional tests — *yay, more slides* — and supplies she'd need.

Grace labeled and packed the slides along with her notes, then headed to the front to consult with Agent Adams.

"You're efficient." He hooked his thumb toward the spinning machine on the other side of the room. "None of the other teams broke it down the same way. They're all doing one source at a time. How's your record keeping? Are you making sure you're not cross contaminating?"

"Wanna check my notes and review the pile of gloves in my trash bin?" She flipped open her notebook and tore out the page where she'd listed what she would need. "Can I get these, please?"

His fingers brushed hers as he took the page and the jolt she felt at that brief touch was unexpected, and very real.

Oh, hello. Stop. Not going there. Eyes on the prize, Gracie Lynn.

"I'll bring everything over." Had he smiled like that at everyone else? She didn't know. She'd had her head down trying to get through the work of two people.

"Thanks." Grace didn't see a reason to stand around and socialize. This was his job. She was trying to make it hers. Besides, she had test tubes to collect and more slides to mount.

She was on her last set of slides when a tray filled with everything she'd requested landed on her table with a soft thud and the chime of glass clinking together.

"You're doing a full tox screen on the blood sample." Agent Adams leaned against her workstation in a way she'd find annoying if he didn't look so hot while doing it. He didn't phrase it as a question, and Grace couldn't tell whether he thought the full screen was a good thing or not.

"Based on the information given, and my initial review of the materials, it seemed like a good call."

She knew better than to underestimate the value of going beyond the basics. Her brother had avoided a lot of trouble because someone had gone above and beyond when he'd been ordered to undergo a drug test.

Agent Adams nodded and returned to the front of the room.

"You've got an hour to finish." A collective groan rose from the students. "When your time is up, you'll label everything and store it appropriately, either in the evidence lockers or in the refrigerator. Leave nothing but equipment at your workstation—no notes, no samples, nothing."

Grace's fellow applicants exploded in a flurry of activity. She bent her head to the microscope and kept scribbling notes. She wouldn't think about the passing time. Wouldn't rush or get frantic. Smooth and methodical. Just keep going.

She labeled the last sample and put it in the tray for the refrigerator. Everything was done with seconds to spare, judging by the way Adams kept checking his watch.

"Good work!" He had his butt back on the front table and had unbuttoned his lab coat, revealing a slim-fitting dress shirt and pants so well-tailored they should be illegal.

"Clean up, then I'll escort you back to the main lab and turn you back over to Ferris."

Daniela grabbed her arm as they filed out the door.

"That was brutal. We didn't finish everything because Mr. Man kept second guessing my choices and insisting he had it right."

Grace clapped her hand over her mouth to stop the laughter. "I thought y'all were into each other."

She got an elbow in the ribs for that comment.

"That's the fun of being away from home," Daniela whispered. "Bonus, you know it's got an expiration date. This one may end a bit early."

Unexpected. Not like Grace hadn't been thinking similar things, just not about a fellow applicant. The idea of not seeing the handsome young agent again was mildly disappointing. Then again, as far as she was concerned, that was true of her interactions with men — fun to look at, even better to flirt with, but beyond that, she could take them or leave them.

Not like I'd fool around with a coworker, anyway. Or like he could date an intern.

She shoved those thoughts aside and followed his broad shoulders back down the hall.

About the Author

Roxanne Blackhall is a former magazine and newspaper editor from San Diego, California, now living in the heart of Baltimore, Maryland. When not at her desk coming up with new ways to torment her characters, she can often be found in the kitchen, glass of wine in hand, cooking a meal for friends.

Roxanne loves to hear from readers. You can find her contact information, website details and author profile page at https://www.firstforromance.com

Home of Erotic Romance

Sign up for our newsletter and find out about all our romance book releases, eBook sales and promotions, sneak peeks and FREE romance books!